W9-BSU-758

DONE TO DEATH

DONE TO DEATH

Charles Atkins

This first world edition published 2014
in Great Britain and in the USA by
SEVERN HOUSE PUBLISHERS LTD of
19 Cedar Road, Sutton, Surrey, England, SM2 5DA.

British Library Cataloguing in Publication Data

Atkins, Charles author.
  Done to death. – (The Lilian and Ada mystery series)
  1. Campbell, Lil (Fictitious character)–Fiction.
  2. Strauss, Ada (Fictitious character)–Fiction. 3. Older
  lesbians–Fiction. 4. Television programs–Fiction.
  5. Detective and mystery stories.
  I. Title II. Series
  813.6-dc23

ISBN-13: 978-0-7278-8374-2 (cased)

All Severn House titles are printed on acid-free paper.

Severn House Publishers support the Forest Stewardship Council™ [FSC™],
the leading international forest certification organisation. All our titles that
are printed on FSC certified paper carry the FSC logo.

MIX
Paper from
responsible sources
FSC
www.fsc.org   FSC® C013056

Typeset by Palimpsest Book Production Ltd.,
Falkirk, Stirlingshire, Scotland.
Printed and bound in Great Britain by
TJ International, Padstow, Cornwall.

ONE

*T*he worms crawl in and the worms crawl out, Ada Strauss mused as she stared at the flat screen, her fingers poised over the keys. She scanned the Medicare application. She'd filled them out for others in the retirement community of Pilgrim's Progress, now it was her turn. *Happy Birthday . . . another day older and closer to death.* Anxiety bubbled in the pit of her stomach as she clicked through the boxes: date of birth, marital status – widow . . . unless she and Lil formalized things, which was now legal in Connecticut. Aaron, her out-and-proud nineteen-year-old grandson, was on board for that. 'It would be awesome,' he'd said, rapidly followed by, 'It would kill Dad.'

Thoughts of Aaron were like a balm on her turmoil. And yes, she wouldn't miss his father Jack, her right-wing Nazi of a son-in-law, if he mysteriously vanished. Wishing someone dead seemed wrong. *Now if he dropped dead on his own – possibly choking on his small-minded bigotry – that would be fine*, she mused . . . *but you should never wish it on someone.*

She read the next question, which sent her tabbing to a separate screen. There she had the options for the various Medicare insurance plans. *Just fill this out*, she told herself. *Get it done.*

Caught in the complexity of tables designed to clarify the pros and cons of different health-care plans, but which in fact confused the issue, she didn't hear Lil. A teaspoon clinked against a mug and, like a Buddhist monk being called to prayer, she turned.

'How's it going?' Lil asked, placing Ada's tea on the coaster – an antique Minton tile, part of a Victorian fireplace surround they'd found suet-stained and caked with old grout at the local flea market.

'Fine,' Ada said, feeling Lil's strong fingers on her shoulders as they gently pressed and massaged. 'That feels good. And by fine, I mean someone is dancing on my grave.'

'You're not old,' Lil said.

'Yeah, filling out a Medicare application pretty much says . . . you're old. I'm sixty-five.'

'And I'm sixty-three,' Lil said. 'We're not old . . . we're just us.

Look at your mom, she's . . . ninety-five. The woman runs circles around people half her age.'

'Maybe not run, but she's still sharp.' Ada shook her head. 'I know it's just a number, you're as young as you feel . . .' Ada felt the warmth of the tea through the mug. She took a sip . . . good and strong, with two sugars and milk. 'I'm in a funk,' she admitted. 'It'll pass.'

'Well,' Lil said, and she leaned down and nuzzled a particularly sensitive spot behind Ada's right ear. 'Maybe I can help with that.'

Ada groaned, and putting down her tea leaned back into Lil. 'Maybe you can. I've always thought you'd have made an excellent therapist.' She swiveled her chair and came face to face with Lil. She stared into chestnut eyes, her hand on the side of Lil's cheek. Her fingertips brushing tendrils of wheat-blond mixed with gray. 'You are so beautiful,' she said.

'Back at you,' and Lil's lips found hers.

With Ada's tea and Medicare application forgotten, they headed to their bedroom for a bit of mid-morning therapy.

After, with cheeks flushed and a pleasant glow coursing through her veins, Ada pushed back in bed. She gazed out the sliders to the distant views of protected wetlands, with last year's cattails providing contrast to tender green shoots.

'So what's really wrong?' Lil asked, rolling on her side, her long hair loose around bare shoulders.

'It's a feeling,' Ada said, staring out at budding trees and clumps of marsh grass.

'The getting old thing?'

'I suppose, but more . . . with Aaron off to college, and you with your column. It sounds bad, but as I looked at that Medicare application, it's like this is it. I'm really old. Time to . . . what? Go on Elderhostel trips? We already play bridge and mah-jong. I don't like golf. I know I'm being ridiculous.' She met Lil's gaze. 'Stop smiling.'

'I get it,' Lil said. 'Why do you think I took that stupid job at the antique center a few years back?'

'To have a front row seat to the antique dealer murders,' said Ada. 'Admit it.'

'Well . . . that too.' Lil chuckled. 'But it was also about needing something to do. Obviously that wasn't it, but it was this feeling that I had to do something. We're so lucky, Ada, I try not to lose sight of that. We have each other, our health, and we're not hurting for money.'

'I know . . . and that's why I feel ridiculous. I should be content. I am.'

'And you're not,' Lil said, finishing her thought.

'Right.'

'You want more,' Lil said. 'I get it. There's nothing wrong with that. Any idea what?'

'No.' She wiggled her toes. 'Here's the thing . . . it's like all of my life I've been the one behind the scenes. With Harry' – referring to her deceased husband – 'I ran Strauss's, but he was the showman. I handled the books, payroll, dealt with the buyers, the designers, the properties, called the plumbers, oversaw store renovations, but it was his name that went out front. Which isn't to say I did it all, we were partners.' She looked at Lil, and felt for her hand beneath the sheets. 'I wish I knew what my problem was. I think having Aaron around helped . . . but he's at college now, and while looking after Mom is important . . . Rose is having a renaissance here and doesn't want me butting in. I really thought I was going to lose her after her second heart attack, but she's stronger than ever.'

'Yes, and a lot of that has to do with you and the decisions you made. She'd still be isolated in that apartment on the Lower East Side if you hadn't forced her hand. And yes,' Lil said, before Ada could interject. 'Clearly having the assisted care facility we moved her into burn down couldn't have been predicted, but it's turned out well in the end. She's happier than I've ever seen her. And so now you want something of your own. I get it. I've got my column, and am over the moon with this syndication thing. I love going out and doing the interviews, researching the antiques and the history behind them. Love it.'

'So what's this week's about?' Ada said, wanting to change the topic.

'Reality shows and the local antique dealers who've been featured on them. And . . .' Lil bit her bottom lip.

'What?'

'I'm on to a potentially juicy exclusive.'

'Really?' Ada squeezed Lil's hand. 'Care to share?'

'Of course. This morning I got an email from someone connected to Lenore Parks,' Lil said.

'As in *Lenore Says*? And "I can do everything better than you" Lenore?'

'Yes, *Lenore Says*, *Weeknights with Lenore*, *Living with Lenore*, bedding by Lenore and . . . you know she has a country home in Shiloh. So this producer person, Barry somebody,' Lil got out of bed and grabbed her blue fleece robe, 'wants to talk with me about the local antiques scene. Apparently he read my columns and thought I'd be a good resource on Grenville; they're planning on shooting something here, or at least thinking about it.'

'Like what?'

'Don't know.' She glanced at the clock. 'I was going to call this afternoon. Maybe get lucky and get a thirty-second interview with her highness, Lenore . . . although that's doubtful.'

'If you don't ask . . .'

'True,' Lil said, toeing into her slippers. 'I'll do it right now, we'll put him on speaker phone.'

'Tease.'

'You wanted something to do,' Lil said, grabbing an elastic off her side table and sweeping her hair back into a ponytail.

'Fine, Medicare can wait.' Ada threw on slacks and a silk tee and trailed Lil to her office.

It was hard shaking her Medicare funk. She thought about her mom, Rose Rimmelman, who'd pretty much taken over Ada's condo next door. Rose, who'd come kicking and screaming from lower Manhattan to an assisted living facility in Connecticut, which subsequently suffered a devastating fire, had become the poster child for the retirement community of Pilgrim's Progress. They'd had breakfast together – as they did every morning – and then Rose was off with a busload of her new friends for a day at the Indian casinos. On Saturday, she'd board another bus for a Broadway matinee. Three days a week she went for water aerobics at the health center, and recently she'd been getting chummy with a widowed firefighter named Stan.

She watched as Lil pulled up her browser and her emails. Glancing over her shoulder she scanned the message lines. Some referencing interviews Lil had done or was doing for her weekly 'Cash or Trash' column. She felt proud that Lil was finally pursuing her lifelong ambition to be a writer. Her column had been picked up by a syndicate and appeared in over forty papers, and her blog got thousands of weekly hits. But Ada could now put a name to at least some of her disquiet – *You're jealous. This won't do.*

'Here it is,' Lil said, and she clicked on the message from a Barry Stromstein.

Ada read the short message asking to talk to Lil about Grenville's antiques industry. It included his numbers and good times to call.

Lil dialed and pressed the button for speaker phone.

As it rang, Ada had another thought, which made her feel worse. For decades she'd been the brains behind the Strauss's department stores, and Harry got the credit. Yes, they'd been a team, and a successful one. But here she was again, literally standing behind Lil. *Face it*, she told herself, *you were the woman behind the man, and now you're the woman behind the woman.*

TWO

B arry Stromstein felt the migraine coming. His vision had wavy lines around the edges and it was hard to focus on Lenore's face. There was her trademark auburn bob and arresting green eyes; admittedly, her hair was wavering to the right and, at the moment, she had four eyes. He heard her words, but struggled to put them into sentences. *Just nod and smile*, he told himself, hoping he could make it through, knowing it was her perfume – Lenore's 'Possession' – that triggered what was blossoming into a headache that if he didn't take his Rizatriptan in the next ten minutes would leave him desperate for his bed and a dark room for the next three days. 'Right,' he parroted her last sentence, 'local color . . . petty jealousies, fun characters.'

'Are you even listening?' she asked. 'I don't think you're getting this, Barry, and to be honest, your first treatment I wouldn't use for toilet paper. *Bargain Bonanza*? What kind of crap project is that? We're not cable access. You either pull this together fast, or I'll give it to Carrie. And if that happens . . .'

He wanted to scream, and he knew she wasn't kidding. 'I've got it, Lenore,' and, struggling to find the words, he blurted, 'you want blood, guts, expensive tchotchkes and scenic New England. Kind of *Antiques Roadshow* meets *The Hunger Games* on the set of *Gilmore Girls*.'

There was a moment's pause. 'Hallelujah!' she said, closing the space between them.

Her perfume, like a wave of noxious gas, engulfed him. He had to get out of there. 'I'm on it.' He backed away. 'I'll have something on your desk by morning.'

'That's a good boy,' she said. 'And Barry, if you don't . . .'

He took that as his cue and, holding his breath, bolted from her inner office. Half-blinded by the oncoming migraine he raced out of Lenore's penthouse suite and down the hall. He bypassed the elevators and flew down eight flights of stairs, his thoughts fixed on the pill in his upper desk drawer. He sprinted to his offices and banged his knee on a glass top desk in the reception area.

Celia, his secretary, looked up. 'Oh crap,' she said. 'You've got migraine eyes.'

'Yeah,' he said without stopping, the words thick on his tongue. It was always the same. First the vision went, then his words, and then came the actual headache, like a vice squeezing his eyeballs while a steel pike pounded into his brain. He jerked the drawer open, grabbed the little blue box, pulled out the ridiculously expensive pills, fumbled at the packaging and finally popped the melty lozenge under his tongue. It tasted like chalk and like something trying to be a pastille mint, but bitter and metallic. He closed his eyes, and heard Celia as she quietly walked around his corner office closing the blinds and shutting out the spectacular views of Central Park and midtown.

'Do you want me to cancel your afternoon meetings?'

'Please.'

'You got it . . . you should go home.'

'Can't. Need to come up with a new concept. She hated *Bargain Bonanza*. Give me forty-five minutes. Wait!' Still tasting the pill's remnants on his tongue, he thought through Lenore's directive. 'Tell the team to toss everything on *Bargain Bonanza* but the locale . . . I think that's still OK – in fact, I know it is. Tell them blood lust and collectibles, and to be ready to pitch by one. And no one's leaving till we have a winner.'

'Will do. Anything I can do to help?'

'No . . . it's just got to run its course. Thank God for the magic melt-under the-tongue pills.'

'It was her perfume, wasn't it?'

'Yeah.'

'Why don't you tell her?'

Barry looked at his assistant through hooded eyes. 'Seriously?'

'Right,' Celia shrugged, as her phone rang. 'Hope you feel better,' and she shut the door.

Just breathe, he told himself, his head in his hands, his eyes shut tight. Let it pass. *What a bitch!* After three years with Lenore, Barry had no illusions. Either he came up with an acceptable pitch in the next twenty-four hours or he could take his résumé and try to find another producing job in an industry where thirty-five is over the hill and forty is washed up, and he was thirty-eight. To the outside world this was a great gig, a high six-figure salary, bonuses, a team of young and energetic wannabes snapping at his heels. His NYU Alma Mater, Tisch School of the Arts, wanting him to take interns, holding him up as an exemplar of someone making it in the entertainment industry. And in a single day it could all turn to ashes. Lenore was desperate to stay on top . . . of the ratings, of her celebrity, of everything and everyone. She was hunger personified, a gaping maw always wanting more. 'She's a monster.' He cracked his eyes open, and thought of his one point five million dollar apartment that was barely eleven hundred square feet, with a tiny patio, two modest bedrooms – one for him and Jeanine and the other for three-year-old Ashley. He pictured his gorgeous wife and their little girl, with blond ringlets that would darken with time, bright hazel eyes – they were his two treasures, his salvation. *You have to pull this together.*

He and Jeanine, a contestant on his last successful show, *Model Behavior*, had no more than a two month cushion in the bank and no family safety net. To Barry's blue collar Jersey parents and Jeanine's, who survived crop to crop on their Iowa farm, they were the affluent ones.

His phone buzzed; Celia's voice came through the speaker. 'Barry, it's Jeanine, do you want me to tell her you're out?'

'No, put her on.'

The line clicked.

'Hi sweetie,' Jeanine's husky voice even better than his magic pill.

Barry closed his eyes. 'Hey babe, what's up?'

'It's kind of stupid,' she said. 'But I felt like I should check before blowing twenty-five hundred bucks on a pocketbook.'

'What?'

'I know you'll tell me just to do it. But I'm looking at all the other high-end real estate agents and the ones who get the million dollar sales are all carrying Chanel or Birkin. It's part of the uniform – a Chanel suit, a pair of Louboutin pumps and a Birkin bag.'

'Then do it,' he said.

'You're sure?'

'Babe, if you need it, you need it.'

'What's wrong?' she asked.

'Migraine.'

'What triggered it?'

'Lenore's perfume.'

'That bitch! Are you going to be OK?'

'Yeah, actually just hearing your voice helps.'

'Why don't you take the rest of the day? Screw the purse, I'll pour you a bath, give you a massage . . .'

Barry let Jeanine's words fill his head. He imagined her soft hands kneading his tense shoulders, the tickle of her silky curls against his skin. 'That would be what the doctor ordered, but I can't.'

'Barry, tell me what's wrong, and I'm not just talking the headache. What's going on?'

He didn't want to tell her. He hated this crushing sense of failure, of letting her down. He also knew she wouldn't let up until he told her. 'She hated the pitch.'

'Barry, I'm so sorry. What's the backup plan?'

'Working on it now. I'll come up with something.'

'And if you don't? What did she say? Tell me, please.'

'Don't worry about it. It'll be fine. Everything's fine. Really. It's just the headache couldn't have come at a worse time. But I got to my pill in time, it's passing. You know me, it's all about pulling rabbits from hats. I want you to go out and buy that pocketbook. Because you know what they say?'

'What?'

Remembering advice from one of his first mentors in the industry. 'The more you spend, the more you make.'

'You're sure of that?'

'Absolutely. I'm going to want to see that purse when I get home. Although don't wait up, it's going to be a very long night.'

'I love you Barry,' Jeanine said. 'And that has nothing to do with a pocketbook.'

'I know. But I want you to have it. I want you and Ashley to have everything, and I'm going to make damn certain that this next pitch blows Lenore away.'

'OK then . . .'

He heard the concern in her voice. It was like a knife. 'I'm going to make this work.'

'I know you will.'

'Buy the pocketbook.'

'OK.'

'I love you.'

'I love you too,' she said, 'and I hope that bitch Lenore drops dead.'

'Please God no,' he said. 'Without Lenore there will be no Birkin bags.'

'Fine, then I guess she can live. And Barry . . .'

'Yeah?'

'I *am* going to wait up.'

After he hung up he felt a familiar tingle that pushed against the migraine. Eight years into their marriage and ten into their relationship, just her voice made everything right. If she wanted a Birkin bag, he'd make damn sure she'd get it. Lenore trashing *Bargain Bonanza* was not the end of the world . . . not yet. With his eyes closed he hung on to the sound of Jeanine's voice. *How did you get to be that lucky?* It was time to get to work.

He glanced at his monitor and braced for the stab of pain the light would send to his head. He squinted and focused on unread emails. His vision was clearing. The pill was doing its trick with the pain – holding it back. Sure, he'd have a headache, but he'd gotten to the med in time. *Just function*, he told himself. That was all that mattered – function, come up with something brilliant – *Antiques Roadshow* meets *The Hunger Games* on the set of *Gilmore Girls* – pitch it and get Lenore to love it. In spite of everything, he chuckled. 'That won't happen.' In his three years with Lenore she didn't love anything, and even when she did, she'd never let you know. 'I expect brilliance,' is what she'd say. 'It's what I pay you for.'

Celia, who pre-screened his emails, had divided them into files.

He started in with those related to the now tanked *Bargain Bonanza*. There was one from the field agent who'd been scouting locations – Grenville, CT being a front runner, as Lenore had a country place in Shiloh, the town immediately north. There were several from agents who represented prospective hosts they'd approached, and a small stack from assorted locals at the various sites. He flipped through a couple from freelance show runners and field producers, two of whom he knew well, one he'd gone to school with, Jim Cymbel.

He opened Jim's.

> *Hey B:*
>
> *Wanted to get back with some ideas for your killer new reality show –* Bargain Bonanza. *Where the market's saturated with these flea market contests, it's a tough sell getting a new boy to float to the top. I've got several ways we could do this. I'd love to talk it over and see if we could make a marriage.*
>
> *Love ya . . . and Jeanine.*
>
> *Jim*

He thought about calling, but only as a last resort. Sure, Jim wanted to help – help himself to Barry's job. Because that email – and several others in his queue – were a lot like the one he'd sent to Susan Grace, the woman whose offices he now occupied. Last he'd heard she'd fallen down the industry food chain to where she couldn't even get pitch meetings.

He looked back at the screen and shifted from prospective producers and their promises to deliver fresh ideas, scanning the ones from talent agents – *waste of time till you know what you're doing.* He scrolled past the smattering of locals at various sites. Those were a crap-shoot, everything from mayors and first selectmen, wanting Lenore's reflected glamour in their town, to B and Bs and prospective locations eager to sign lucrative deals.

His eye caught on one headed 'Cash or Trash – Lil Campbell'. 'That's as lame as *Bargain Bonanza*' – but he clicked it open anyway.

> *Dear Mr Stromstein:*
>
> *This is in response to the email I received about my syndicated antiques and collectibles column, 'Cash or Trash'. Yes, I'd love to set up a phone time to talk about one of my favorite things*

– my hometown Grenville, CT, the antiques capital of New
England (possibly the world). The thought of having a Lenore
Parks show feature our town is a thrill. Feel free to call any
time – the home number is the best, but I do carry my cell.
   Best,
   Lil Campbell

He replayed his Hail Mary pass that Lenore seemed to like – *Antiques*
Roadshow meets *The Hunger Games* on the set of *Gilmore Girls*.
Scenic Grenville, in the Litchfield Hills, fit a third of the equation.
Through hooded eyes he dialed Lil Campbell's number and pressed
the button for speaker. He leaned back and waited for an answering
machine.

'Hello?' A woman's voice answered.

'Hi, this is Barry Stromstein, of Lenore Parks Productions. I'm
trying to reach a Lil Campbell.'

'How strange is that? I had literally just dialed your number when
you popped up on call waiting.'

'Seriously?'

'Talk about synchronicity. Do you mind if I put you on speaker?
My partner Ada Strauss is with me and we don't often get calls
from TV producers.'

'That's fine,' he said. 'So what got you to dial?'

'You're kidding,' she said. 'The thought of having even a single
episode of a show shot in Grenville would be a big deal. I mean
several of our dealers have been experts on other shows, but nothing
in the town itself.'

'Right,' and Barry recoiled at the familiar scent of want. 'So,'
falling into his familiar role of gatekeeper to the brass ring, 'what
makes Grenville special?'

He listened as this Lil woman extolled the town's beauty. He'd
seen the pictures and knew she wasn't lying. It would be a dream
to film: the changing seasons, lovingly preserved Colonial and
Federal houses, the tidy greens with their romantic bronzes and
ancient cannons. Fine, it's pretty, he thought, lots of places are
pretty. And sure, it probably fulfills two out of three – *Antiques*
Roadshow and the set of *Gilmore Girls*. He imagined bringing
Jeanine and little Ashley out for the shoots; they'd love it. His
thoughts drifted, and he made polite noises as though he were paying

attention as Lil Campbell talked about the two hundred antique dealers, the weekly flea market and active council – *God save me from active councils.* He'd heard enough. He gently cleared his throat. 'It does sound like a place to consider,' he said, and prepared to launch into his kiss off.

'Lil, don't forget to tell him about the murder rate,' a new voice popped in.

'Excuse me?'

'The murder rate,' this other woman, with a slight New York accent, repeated. 'Grenville had the highest per capita murder rate in Connecticut for two years running. And if you think about it, all of the victims were in some way connected to the antiques industry, although in that horrible fire at the assisted living center it was mostly that doctor.'

'Which doctor? And I'm assuming you're Ada.'

'Ada Strauss. Long story short: it was a huge Medicaid fraud, we're talking millions, that centered on this doctor – who apparently was both an antique clock collector and a hoarder. We'd see him every week at the flea market. It wound up as an arson slash multiple murder at one of the biggest assisted care facilities in the state. And, considering the total population of Grenville is twelve thousand, it doesn't take much to bump our numbers up. That pushed us to the top for 2011, and in 2010 there was a serial killer who was taking out high-end antique dealers. Come to think of it, another doctor – what is with them? That one was a dentist. The freaky thing is he actually worked on a crown for me that came off when I was eating a crème brulée . . . sorry, too much information. Although both Lil and I barely made it out when he torched his place.'

'What? Wait a minute!' Barry was forward in his seat. 'Not too much at all.' His complacency and the throbbing in his head had suddenly been blown away like leaves in a storm . . . *meets* The Hunger Games. *Ding ding ding.* 'Tell me about the murders. It seems like you know a fair amount about them.'

'Please, we were there . . . I mean really there, as in almost got killed. You see Calvin Williams, the psychopathic dentist, had a lifelong crush on Lillian, and apparently his mother, who had Alzheimer's, had been selling off the family heirlooms to local dealers who'd essentially robbed her blind.'

Barry was mesmerized as plots and twists fell from this Ada

Strauss's lips. A town filled with competing dealers, a supply of merchandise that was hotly contested, corruption, bribes, small-town scandals, a child-molesting dentist . . . murder. *Too good to be true.* He tried to picture Ada Strauss. She sounded a bit older, knowledgeable and funny. At one point he interrupted her. 'Do I have your headshot?'

She laughed. 'Why would you?'

'Right . . . not an actress or on-screen personality, I'm assuming.'

'Hardly. I don't know if you're old enough to remember Strauss's department stores.'

'I remember them.' He laughed. 'I remember my mother putting us in matching caps so she wouldn't lose us during the back to school sales.' He felt a twinge of regret. *She might be too old for on-screen talent, or she could be a total dog.* 'You're that Strauss . . . and Mr Strauss?'

'Passed several years ago.'

'Sorry.'

'You didn't kill him. But it's kind of you to say.'

'You're quick.'

'You're surprised.'

His usual defenses were down. There was something here – at least he hoped there was. *You're desperate, Barry, this is a reach.* 'Is there any way I could get you – I mean the two of you – into the city for a pitch meeting this afternoon?'

'I have no idea what that is,' Ada Strauss said. 'I mean aside from what you read in Jackie Collins novels. Lil? What do you think?'

'We could be there in two hours. It's the middle of the day, and traffic shouldn't be bad.'

'Fantastic!' And he gave them the address.

After they hung up, he buzzed his assistant. 'Celia, we've got an Ada Strauss coming in from Connecticut. I want some test shots, and get Jason to get her on tape. Have her talk about anything: antiques, murder, whatever.'

He hung up and realized his headache was gone. *Please*, he thought, feeling the dangerous seed of hope take root. *Please, please, please.*

THREE

'What the hell was that?' Ada asked, after they'd disconnected with Barry Stromstein.

'Not quite certain, but he seemed rather taken with you.'

'Please, I was rambling.'

'Yeah, but you do it well.' Lil looked at Ada. 'Did we just say we'd be in midtown in two hours?'

Ada nodded. Lil was in her robe, hair mussed and in a messy ponytail after their morning's romp. 'We can do this. I say business casual in under fifteen minutes – ready, set, go.'

'It's funny,' Lil commented as they headed back to the master bedroom.

'What is?' Ada asked, as they moved with a practiced efficiency to their respective sides of the spacious walk-in closet.

'I'd swear that Barry was about to blow me off right before you piped in with the murders.'

'Why do you think I did that?'

Lil paused, her hand on a gray skirt suit. She looked at Ada, from her bright silver spiked hair to those amazing sapphire eyes. 'I sometimes forget.'

Ada, holding a cream silk blouse against a vintage blue Chanel suit, looked back and met Lil's gaze. 'It's OK.'

'You are amazing.' Struck by how beautiful she found Ada, and amused by their very different wardrobes – Ada's side filled with vibrant blues, greens and purples and hers a study in staid New England brown, gray and navy.

'We're a team, Lil.' She chuckled. 'You were striking out, so I decided to take a swing.'

'Baseball metaphors?'

'Sure, we're going to a . . . *pitch* meeting.'

Lil groaned, 'That was awful.'

'I can do worse,' and, grabbing a pair of pumps, Ada exited the closet and threw everything on the bed.

Twenty minutes later, and looking like Manhattan executives, the two women headed down the steep path toward Lil's white Lincoln Town Car. Knowing they were being observed, Ada waved and smiled at their across-the-walkway neighbor, Bernice Framm, the mayor's retired secretary. Out of perversity she also gave a wave to Clayton Spratt's living room window, assuming he was probably there as well, monitoring their every move.

'Such a vile man,' she said under her breath.

'I think he's jealous.'

'Because I wouldn't go out with him?' Ada asked.

'You hurt his feelings.'

'Please, the man's a sociopath. The way he tried to get the Association to tell me I couldn't have Aaron live with me.'

'Do you still think we should move out of here?'

'I used to,' Ada said, as Lil clicked open the locks on the car. 'I mean this is Twilight Town, but God knows it's convenient.'

'Houses are great,' Lil said, 'but the upkeep.' And she threw the car into reverse. 'You want to punch in the address and locate the nearest garage?'

'No problem,' Ada said, setting the GPS. 'In the abstract, I love the idea of owning a house, but let's face it, I lived in Manhattan my entire adult life, and you had the big house with Bradley. I think where we're at is fine; I wouldn't mind breaking through the wall between our two places, but you know the Owners' Association would never go for it.'

'They don't need to know,' Lil said.

'Really? Two problems – Bernice and Clayton.'

'Right. Although she's been much friendlier since our coming out party.'

'Is that what we're calling having pictures of us sleeping together posted on the Internet?' Ada asked.

'Hey,' Lil said, 'it was our fifteen minutes, not everyone gets that.'

'I'd be happy to return it. Two years later and I still have nightmares about that awful woman we let into our home.'

'I know,' Lil said. 'She had everyone fooled . . . including us. And considering the fact that she was responsible for five deaths, and for setting the fire at your mother's assisted care facility, having her shoot a few compromising, albeit chaste, candids of us in bed was getting off easy. When I think about what she was capable of . . . what she did.'

'Let's not dwell,' Ada offered. 'It was two years ago and Alice – may she rest in peace . . . or in hell – is gone. As to the fifteen minutes of fame – Miss Syndicated Reporter – you get yours every week.'

'You know I'm going to try to turn this thing today into a column.'

'Whatever this is,' Ada said. 'Why would that Barry person want to see us? And why did he want to know if we had headshots?'

'If *you* had a headshot,' Lil corrected. 'You were kind of fabulous on the phone.'

Ada blushed. 'Don't be ridiculous, I just didn't want him to hang up. So what's the deal with Lenore Parks? I can't see her actually being on some reality show.'

'I don't think she would be. It's like Oprah with all of her spin-offs. Lenore's a brand, so this would be something like that.'

'Right,' Ada said. 'Which considering all her other merchandise, she's practically taken over Martco. I bought a spatula with her name on it.' Ada stared out at the highway. 'So how does a reality show about antiques fit into knock-off made-in-China merchandise that pretends to be high quality?'

'It's a fantasy,' Lil said, 'a life people think they want: affluence, lovely things, grace.'

'What we have,' Ada commented.

'Yes, but we have something more.'

'Which is?'

'Contentment.'

'There is that,' Ada said, and she thought back through the morning. Her funk over the Medicare application, the joy of being with Lil . . . and now this. There was a tingly excitement in her gut. 'This feels like the start of something.'

'This meeting?'

'I don't know why, but there was something interesting about that Barry guy.'

'How so?'

'Hard to find the words, and it was just a phone call, but . . . he seemed desperate, hungry . . . searching.'

'Interesting assortment. And you're doing your weird clairvoyant thing, which if you weren't always right . . . You got that from the phone call?'

'Yeah, and it gets weirder,' Ada added, letting her thoughts drift. 'I think in some way he needs us.'

'You,' Lil said. 'I don't need a crystal ball for that. It's you.'

'Maybe . . . What I don't understand is why.'

FOUR

L enore Parks focused on the steady in-and-out of her breath as her nubile trainer, Jodi, corrected her kneeling pigeon pose. A bead of sweat trickled from her brow to the tip of her nose and dripped to the floor.

'Now take your left hand,' Jodi instructed, her voice soothingly accompanied by Japanese flute and harp music, 'and grip your left ankle. Sink your pelvis into the floor as you pull your leg into your buttocks. Feel the stretch in your quad, and hold for five breaths.'

Lenore's thoughts were anything but calm. She'd focus on the breath and then her mind was off running statistics and facts, such as that at the height of Lenore Parks Productions she'd had fifty-five full-time producers and now she had twenty-nine. Or the fact that her long-running talk and style show, *Lenore Says*, was on the network chopping block. Or that Martco was in conversation with that silly gay man from the Style Network. They'd assured her his brand wouldn't replace hers . . . but that was a lie, or at the very least a strategy to leverage her into a smaller cut. *Fine*, she thought, *they'll pay for that*.

'And one last breath on this side,' Jodi instructed, 'and push up into downward dog.'

Lenore felt the tug in her shoulders as she raised her ass skyward. It was all about staying hot and current. Truth was, *Lenore Says* had a great run, but the midday audience had shrunk. After all, who stays home in the middle of the day watching TV? The answer – and she'd done the research – was obvious: the retired, the unemployed and the unemployable. She snorted; these were her peeps, the legions of Lenore.

'Swing your right heel back, as high as you can go, and hold for three fluid breaths. In for five and out for five.'

She felt the blood rush to her head. She'd find her way through this slump. She knew what was needed – something new, something fresh. Creativity was a commodity; admittedly it was also a luxury item, something of which she was a connoisseur. She refused to listen to the bean counters, like her Chief Financial Officer, Patty Corcoran, with her constant worry over the day-to-day cost of keeping Lenore Parks Productions (LPP) afloat. What Patty, and even Lenore's son Richard, couldn't understand was that most basic truism of business – you have to spend money to make money.

'Now swing that leg through and let's repeat on the other side.'

She felt the pull in her hip as she pushed her torso straight. She felt a surge of pride: *not bad for a fifty-two-year-old*. She wouldn't worry about this temporary downturn in her empire. Another truth was that pruning was essential for new growth. It was time for some head rolling. She thought through her current roster of producers, those who still had it and those whose lights had dimmed or burned out entirely. Like Stromstein; his desperation was a kind of poison. He'd started so full of promise, with that successful *Model Behavior* that had brought him to her attention. But that was three years ago and since he'd come on board at LPP, he and his team had done a few mediocre episodes of *Lenore Says* and come up with two half-baked shows that barely made it through their pilots, each derivative of something else. He'd come to the end of his shelf life. It was familiar, and if Lenore were a sentimental person, she'd find it sad. But the Barrys of this world were like an expensive dish, a perfect Lobster Thermidor or exquisite Pinot Noir. You enjoyed them, savored the last morsel or drop. But when they were done it was time to toss the bottle and throw the carcass on to the compost.

'Let's finish the moving asanas,' Jodi instructed, 'with twelve sun salutations, one breath per movement, hands in prayer, and . . .'

Fifteen minutes later, Lenore thanked Jodi and chuckled as her trainer, with her severe blond haircut and warm brown eyes, chided her.

'I think you were with me maybe twenty percent?' Jodi said, handing Lenore a towel.

'At least that,' Lenore offered, openly admiring Jodi's flat abdomen and toned legs. If it wasn't that she was such an excellent trainer, she would have made a play for her. But lovely young bed-mates and eager-to-please producers were plentiful. A trainer that could keep her middle-aged body as a taut size two, however, was not to be messed with.

'We'll shoot for twenty-five tomorrow,' Jodi said as she pulled on sweats and a hoodie.

Lenore watched as Jodi returned their mats to the eighteenth-century armoire that housed a variety of exercise equipment. Yes, there was a fully equipped gym one floor down, but Lenore preferred these private before-airing office workouts. She felt invigorated, her blood pumping and her breath full. Even her pores tingled. She felt alive and vital, and ready to give her viewing public – however pathetic they might be – a glimmer of glamour.

Her reverie was interrupted by the phone. She glanced at the clock; it was too early for wardrobe and make-up. And her assistant, Justin, knew not to intrude on her quiet time unless it was a true emergency.

She picked up. 'Lenore,' her assistant sounded tenuous, 'it's Richard on three. He said it's important.' *Of course it is,* wondering once again why she'd ever thought having children was a good idea. 'Hello Richard.'

'Mother, we've got a problem.'

Her yoga glow dissipated as her son laid out the latest crisis. Before he'd said the words, she accurately predicted their content.

'It's Rachel,' he said.

She bit back the surge of annoyance. Richard was the good one, the one that stayed out of the tabloids, the one who'd get his MBA and take a meaningful role in the running of Lenore Parks Productions. Why she'd felt the need to have a second . . . *ratings* . . . 'I'm waiting.'

'She's in the emergency room. I'm with her now.'

She didn't flinch; *a hospital is better than jail.* 'Please Richard, I'm heading into wardrobe, so just the highlights.' She brought up her web browser and typed in 'Rachel Parks' and 'most recent'.

'She's stoned to the gills and not making any sense. They found her passed out in front of a club in Brooklyn and brought her in by ambulance.'

'I can see that,' Lenore said, scanning through a lurid piece with pictures of her nineteen-year-old daughter, legs akimbo, a black bar both concealing and underscoring that she wasn't wearing underwear, passed out on a sidewalk. She knew that while the paper had to put in the black box, there were probably dozens of others shooting explicit shots of Rachel's genitals, which would now be all over the Internet – and not for the first time.

'They were going to arrest her,' Richard said. 'And then she started talking about killing herself.'

'Can you get her out of there? Get her to say the right things and bring her to the country house. Call Doctor Ebert and see if he can do something.'

'Already done,' he said. 'What do you think about getting her into rehab?'

'If she'd sign in that would be great.'

'I'll see what I can do. Maybe if she thinks they're going to hospitalize her, she'll agree just to stay out of the nut ward . . . or jail. They threw some charges at her – interfering with an officer, resisting arrest . . . And Mom . . .'

'What?'

'She's cutting again. All over her upper arms, and I think on her legs. Like high up, I saw it in the emergency room. It's a mess. The psychiatrist in the emergency room asked me about it.'

'Shit!' At times like this Lenore could have killed her daughter. 'Why does she have to do this?'

'You really want to know?'

'Yeah, I'm a horrible mother . . . I get that. I didn't *validate* her enough. Somehow, this is all my fault. Richard, you know I love you.'

'I do. I'll take care of this, Mom. So what's the afternoon show?'

'Transgender chefs. We're making coq au vin.'

'Awesome.'

'Don't mock your mother.'

'Wouldn't dream of it. Pays the bills. And just for the record, Mom . . . you did OK. In fact, I think you're amazing. And Rachel is not your fault. It's more her than you. OK, the doctor's coming back, and Dr Ebert is trying to call. Do your show; I've got this.'

'Love you, son.'

'I know.' And he hung up.

Lenore let out a slow breath. 'Should have stopped at one.' But God, those two pregnancies had given *Lenore Says* its all-time highest ratings. She'd done reality TV before it existed, taking her audience step-by-step through the process of in-vitro fertilization. Up front and frank about the selection of the sperm donor, without revealing who it was – great TV. It was bold and flew in the face of every convention. She'd played it to the hilt – the successful talk show hostess who'd not made marriage work. Her audience could relate. They felt her pain as a woman unlucky in love who desperately wanted to know the joys and fulfillment of motherhood. She'd kept nothing back . . . well, almost nothing. She wasn't Ellen, after all, or even Rosie after she came out. Her love life was no one's business. And frankly, considering the wasteland of her romantic efforts, there wasn't much to speak about. Lenore didn't 'do' relationships, so why risk the L word? Instead, she'd dated the Hollywood hunks in her twenties and thirties, half of them gay. They'd provide mutual beards for the week or the month. Or A-list actor John Gregory, for a few years. Hell, she and John had even considered a marriage of convenience. She thought about Jodi and the other young women who orbited LPP. Young and vibrant, so many of them openly gay. They'd chat about their girlfriends in one breath and the nutritive value of quinoa in the next.

A rap at the door.

'Lenore.' Justin in the doorway. Like all of her assistants young, handsome, perfectly groomed. This one with skin the color of caramel, close-cropped black hair and amber eyes. 'Fifteen minutes till make up. Do you need anything?'

'No,' she said. She caught something in his expression; he was trying to read her. He'd probably been on the Internet and knew about the latest crisis with Rachel.

'Is everything OK?' he asked.

She suspected he'd eavesdropped on her conversation with Richard. 'Everything is fine.' She headed toward her richly appointed bathroom and dressing area. She stopped. 'Didn't you have an audition last week at The Public?'

'I did. I wasn't what they were looking for.'

She stood at the door and looked back at him. He was very good-looking, mixed-race . . . striking. She'd cast him as her assistant, but could easily see him in a T-shirt and tool belt on one of Lenore Parks Productions DIY shows. 'We should have you test,' she said. 'I think you're a natural.'

'You're kidding.'

'I'm not. You've been a good assistant, but we both know this isn't your dream.'

'I like working for you,' he said.

She weighed his words, and drew two cartoon bubbles over his head. One contained the words he said, and the other held the raw ambition that lay beneath them. 'Good.' They were all so transparent, these pretty young things. She saw her single word answer create castles in his head as she closed the door behind her.

'Damn Rachel,' she muttered as she tried to hang on to her yoga buzz. She turned on the shower, stripped off her workout gear and flung it into an open wicker hamper. She caught her reflection in the infinity mirrors that bounced off each other creating an illusion of endless Lenores, each one smaller than the one before. Mugging into the mirror with her trademark head bob and wink, she muttered 'Lenore says, age is a number.' She surveyed her toned body, her stomach still flat even after two natural child-births. She popped on a shower cap and, with a dozen jets blazing, stepped into the steaming spray. Her thoughts drifted to her daughter and her latest bout of drunken attention-seeking chaos. Sad thing was, the girl was too miserable to realize just how much she had . . . and was throwing away with both hands. A natural green-eyed blonde, Rachel had hit the genetic jackpot. Lenore's choice of sperm donor, a carefully guarded secret, was none other than sometime beard and long-time friend John Gregory, action hero, all round hunk and deeply closeted actor. Just like Lenore, his career was dependent upon the fantasy. Do twelve-year-old boys really want to pay twenty bucks to see gay super heroes? An unanswered question and one John, their mutual agent Max Titelbam, his publicity machine and his risk-avoidant backers were unwilling to answer.

But she's not grateful, Lenore realized. And according to Rachel's five-hundred-bucks-an-hour shrink, Dr Amos Ebert, she had Borderline Personality Disorder. Which, courtesy of *Lenore Says* and several episodes over the years on the topic, gave Lenore pause. *You weren't a horrible mother.* To which Rachel would reply – 'You were no mother at all.'

Unlike her brother, Rachel had been a hard child from day one. In constant need of nurturing, not sleeping more than thirty or forty minutes at a stretch – thank God for the nannies. But even there, too many of them; one that took pictures of her children and sold them to the tabloids, a couple more who viewed the job as a stepping stone to careers in entertainment. There'd been no stability and

Rachel had needed that. Lenore stepped out of the shower. *No use crying over spilled milk.* She chuckled . . . *and third time's a charm.* She felt a little thrill of excitement, knowing that, unlike the Barrys of this world, she still had it. Her pregnancies and unorthodox strategies to make a family had shot her to the top of the ratings, and she was poised to shock the hell out of them again.

She checked the misted dial on the clock over the vanity. In three minutes her hair and make-up people would knock. She stepped into her panties – no need for SPANX – and then into the underwire bra selected for the day's outfit. A knock at the door. *Two minutes early*, she noted. 'Come in.'

Without looking up she fastened the front of her bra. She felt a sharp pain in her back, at first thinking she'd pulled something in yoga, and then something wet and warm on her fingers. Confused, she saw red in the mirror, blossoming under the left cup of her lacy bra. An acrid smell, like something burning. *I've been shot.* She looked in the mirror; she was alone. She turned and her legs buckled; blood seeped from beneath her fingers. Her mind sped as her knees gave way. She slipped to the floor, clutching her chest, feeling the warm pulse of sticky blood over her fingers.

There was a knock at the door. She barely managed, 'Come . . .'

A smiling woman's familiar pudgy face: her dresser, Peggy. The smile vanished.

No, Lenore thought, missing that smile. Wishing she'd told Peggy how pretty she was, with her plump cheeks and lustrous brunet hair in a long French braid. *She'd been fun in bed, but clingy, and so long ago. How many years was that?* Her vision grew fuzzy and the pain in her chest and back seemed far away. *Just sleep. Just sleep.*

FIVE

'**W**hat's happened?' Ada asked, as she and Lil rounded the corner of Fifty-sixth and Fifth Avenue. In front of the towering glass and steel LPP Tower was a swirling lightshow of police cars and a single ambulance. On the street side of the building stood a bunched up line of mostly women – a few hundred – waiting to get into the afternoon taping of *Lenore Says*. Their attention not on the entrance, but on the gurney being rolled at a run out of the building by EMTs.

'It's Lenore,' Lil said, as she grabbed her camera from her bag.

'Come on,' Ada urged. 'We need to get closer so you can get a shot. Did she have a heart attack?'

Sirens blared as they jogged across the street. Lil's camera finger pressed record as she spoke over the video. 'It's April twenty-third 2013 and I'm outside the headquarters of Lenore Parks Productions.' Careless of the snarled traffic, she focused on Lenore's face. Her mouth and nose were covered by an oxygen mask. Her auburn bob was plastered to the side of her face, and – even without make-up – there was no mistaking that this was Lenore Parks.

Lil struggled to keep her in frame and pressed the zoom as the EMTs paused at the ambulance's rear doors. With efficiency of movement they collapsed the wheels of the stretcher, and on a quick count of three hoisted it into the back. One climbed in next to the stretcher accompanied by a uniformed officer, while the other ran to the front. With lights and siren it pulled away. The entire episode from start to finish lasted less than forty-five seconds.

Oblivious to a young officer trying to shoo her and Ada from the middle of the Avenue, Lil filmed the ambulance as it headed north and then west. 'What just happened?' she asked the officer.

'Ladies, I couldn't say, but if you don't get out of the middle of Fifth Avenue you'll be the only people in New York ever to have gotten a ticket for jay walking.'

'Sorry officer,' Ada said. She gently tugged at Lil's arm. 'Lil, come on. We've got a two o'clock with that Barry Stromstein. If nothing else, it gets us inside.'

Lil smiled. 'You're as curious as I am.'

'There was blood on the sheet,' Ada said. 'That was no heart attack. She was injured.'

Lil, who'd been a doctor's wife and frequently filled in for Bradley's nurse, shared her observations. 'I couldn't tell if she was breathing. They weren't bagging her, so you'd think she was breathing. There should have been condensation in the mask . . . but there wasn't.'

'You think she's dead?' Ada stopped as they came to the sidewalk. The waiting audience and gawkers had now swelled to where the sidewalks around LPP headquarters were an impassible mass of humanity. Cell phones were out, and a flatbed truck had pulled up, its back stacked high with wooden blue police barriers. 'We need to go in now,' Ada said, and she headed toward the building's revolving glass door.

Without hesitation, Lil followed, expecting to be stopped. They weren't. A heavyset guard sat in front of the elevators behind a U-shaped counter. To his left was a bank of monitors. He looked up as they approached.

Ada smiled. 'That was strange.'

The man looked at the two of them and nodded. 'Are you here on business?'

'Yes,' Ada said, 'we have a two o'clock meeting with a Mr Stromstein.'

'Thirty-second floor. I'll need to see some ID.'

As Lil retrieved her purse and driver's license, she fished for information. 'That was Lenore Parks. Do you know what happened?'

'Couldn't say.' He checked Lil's license and Ada's state of Connecticut ID. He picked up his phone. 'I have a Lillian Campbell and Ada Strauss for Mr Stromstein. Yeah, I know. Check to see if the meeting's still on. I'll hold.' He looked at Lil and then at Ada. 'Glad I'm not them,' he said.

Ada smiled at the man, who was close to their age. 'That's cryptic.'

With the phone to his ear, waiting to hear if Lil and Ada's meeting was still on, he explained. 'It's Tuesday; she tapes a ten o'clock and a three o'clock. She never misses . . . today will be a first.'

Ada held his gaze. 'You were a cop, weren't you?'

He nodded. 'Twenty years.'

'So what's with the circus?' She looked toward the bank of glass doors they'd just come through. The crowd was thick and spilled into the street. Officers had begun to pull barriers off the truck and were creating a blue wall around the entrance and perimeter.

His eyes narrowed. 'Kind of nosy, aren't you?'

'Curious,' Ada said and, knowing you have to give to get, she added, 'I saw blood on the sheets.'

'Good eyes,' he offered.

'Lasik.'

'Me too,' he said. 'You didn't hear it from me . . . she was shot.'

'Who did it?' Lil asked.

The guard's attention was pulled by a voice through the phone. 'It's still on?' He sounded surprised. 'Thanks.' He hung up. 'You're going up to thirty-two. Someone will meet you at the elevators.'

'Do they know who shot her?' Lil repeated.

'Couldn't say. But I bet you're the last two civilians coming through those doors today.'

'You miss being a cop?' Ada asked.

'Nah, too much bullshit. I'll tell you this: it's going to be fun watching from the sidelines.'

'Because?' Ada asked.

The guard chuckled. 'Twelve hundred thirty-six people work in this building. Half of them are scared by Lenore and the other half can't stand her. Fear and hate: that's a whole lot of motive.'

'Thanks, George,' Ada said, having checked out George Strand's photo ID.

'You're welcome, Ada.'

As they walked to the elevators Lil whispered, 'You were flirting with him.'

'Of course I was.' Ada smiled. 'You're just as curious as I am . . . if not more. You recorded that whole conversation, didn't you?'

'Maybe,' Lil said, as the door slid shut and they headed up.

'At least flirting isn't illegal, Lil. Audiotaping without consent is.'

'Details.'

'This is really interesting,' Ada said.

Lil's fingers ran down Ada's arm. She squeezed gently. 'How did we ever find each other?'

'Dumb luck . . . and lots of it.'

Lil let go as the elevator stopped and the doors opened.

A twenty-something blonde woman greeted them. Her face was drawn; she seemed dazed. 'Lil and Ada, hi, I'm Shana, Mr Stromstein's assistant. If you'd come with me. He was going to cancel, but . . .'

'It's fine,' Ada said. 'When bad things happen it's sometimes best to move forward with business.' She shot Lil a look as they followed Shana past a sea of mostly empty cubicles. Along the periphery of the large central space were offices. A few had their doors open to reveal long views of Central Park. Groups of people clustered in doorways and cubicles.

Lil and Ada caught snippets of their conversations. 'Horrible.' 'No surprise.' 'What's going to happen?' 'Without Lenore . . . I need this job.'

Shana directed them to an occupied conference room where six men and women sat around a gleaming mahogany table. The blinds were down, but through the slats was a dizzying view of Fifth Avenue. An attractive dark-haired man wearing rectangular frameless glasses and a beautifully draped charcoal suit rose from the head of the table as they entered. He looked first at Lil, and then his gaze settled on Ada. 'Mrs Strauss?'

'Ada, and you are?'

'Crazed, confused . . . or you can just call me Barry.'

'Barry,' Ada said. 'Should we reschedule, considering . . .'

'No. Trust me, if Lenore— Oh God, we don't even know if she's OK. We would have heard.' He shook his head. 'Times like this I don't know what to say. I suppose introductions would work.' He reached for Ada's hand. 'Here.' He named the three men and two women around the table: John, Ethan, David, Carrie and Melanie. None of them over forty, probably most of them closer to thirty, they were all white, all attractive. 'And of course my assistant, Shana, who you already met. Can we get you anything? A sandwich, bagel, something to drink?'

Ada was about to decline, her thoughts skimming over the surreal circumstances. 'Tea,' she said, feeling something frenetic pulse off of Barry. His hands were in constant motion, and she realized that under no circumstances would he have cancelled this meeting.

'And Lil?'

'Coffee would be nice.'

'Right back,' Shana said.

'So sit, please,' Barry said. His deep brown eyes never left Ada's face.

Unperturbed, she stared back, taking in his dark eyes, large nose and even features. *Good-looking and obviously successful*, she thought, *but is he always this wired?*

'You have exquisite eyes,' he said.

'I can't tell if that's a compliment or you're looking for donor parts.'

There was laughter around the table.

'Are we really doing this?' asked a short-haired brunet with a lily tattoo on her well-defined forearm.

'Melanie, we're here,' Barry said. 'You know this is what she wants.'

'"She" being Lenore?' Ada asked.

'Yes.' His eyes fixed on her as she and Lil took seats to his left.

'So what happened?' Ada asked.

'You mean who shot Lenore?' the striking brunet with the tattoo asked. 'I don't think anyone knows,' she said. 'And Barry's right – Ada, you have gorgeous eyes. And that haircut's right on trend. Are you wearing colored contacts?'

'No. And thank you . . . Melanie?'

'Yes. And is your suit vintage Chanel or is that a knock-off?'

Ada chuckled. 'Wasn't vintage when I bought it. And not to be rude,' Ada said, 'but what exactly are we doing here?'

'Trying to catch lightning in a bottle,' Barry said.

'And then package and sell it,' the sandy-haired man next to Melanie offered. 'There could be action figures.'

'Not for an antique show,' said the other woman, Carrie, who seemed closest to Barry in age. 'But certainly spin-offs.'

'Horse before cart,' Barry replied.

Shana returned with beverages.

Ada took a first sip of tea and sorted through the cryptic shorthand shooting around the table.

'So,' Barry said to Ada, 'Tell us about Grenville.'

'Lil's more the expert. She was born and raised there.'

'Never left,' Lil said. 'What do you want to know?'

'That's right,' Barry said, as though just seeing Lil. 'You do that column. What's it called?'

'"Cash or Trash".'

'Wasn't that a show?' asked the man with thinning red hair, David.

'No,' Melanie said. 'There was *Trash or Treasure*, *Cash in the Attic*, *Treasure Hunt*, *Treasure Wars* . . .' She paused, took a deep breath and, like some reality show savant, prattled off the names of a couple dozen more. '*Flea Market Wars*, *Bargain Wars*, *Bargain Hunters*, *Auction Kings*, *Storage Wars*. And then there's that whole sub-genre set in actual antique stores, like *Oddities* and *Oddities: San Francisco*.'

'And why are we doing this?' sandy-haired Ethan asked.

Barry said, 'Lenore thinks this vein has more gold in it, and I agree. Problem is, if we can't get something fresh, it's pointless. So here's the idea, but it has to be fleshed out.' He threw out his earlier Hail Mary pitch to Lenore. '*Antiques Roadshow* meets *The Hunger Games* on the set of *Gilmore Girls*.'

'So that's the connection,' Ada said.

'What is?' Melanie asked from across the table.

'Grenville – where Lil and I live – is the antique capital of New England. Basically, it *is* the set of *Gilmore Girls*, and as the result of recent and very horrible events, Grenville is no stranger to murder. So I think why . . . Barry' – inwardly shuddering at all of this unearned first name familiarity – 'has asked us here is he's wondering if maybe there's a show to be had in our sleepy – albeit murderous – little town.'

'Is there?' ginger David asked.

Ada sipped her tea and looked at Lil. 'Probably several.'

'Some kind of contest or game show?' Lil asked.

'Possibly,' Barry said. 'Those work well, as opposed to people just bringing in items for appraisal. But there's something to be said for developing a regular cast of characters.'

'That wouldn't be hard,' Ada said. 'You'd have a couple hundred antique dealers to choose from. Then you have the auctioneers, the flea market, but how do you tie in the—' she stopped herself.

'The blood?' Barry asked.

The door to the conference room banged open. A young man, his face flushed, looked around and then focused on Barry. 'She's dead,' he said. 'Lenore is dead.'

'Oh dear God!' Melanie gasped.

The ginger-haired man shook his head. 'Shit! Not good.'

The others were silent as they looked to Barry. He sighed as the man left to continue spreading the news.

'I think a moment of reflection is in order,' Barry said.

Heads nodded in agreement.

Ada thought of the stretcher and the barely glimpsed celebrity with her wet hair and bloody sheets. While she was not a fan of Lenore, the woman was ubiquitous, a style icon whose local appearances in and around Grenville were topics of frequent conversation. Lenore's children – especially her train wreck daughter – were frequently on the cover of checkout-line tabloids. She glanced at Lil, and wondered how she was taking this. Her chestnut eyes gave away little as she sipped her coffee. A moment's reflection . . . were there lessons to be learned from Lenore? A woman who gave a surface message of grace and perfection, she was fabulously successful, wealthy, famous, but there were cracks. And this group of people trying to make something out of thin air. Shouldn't they go home? Call it a day? For God's sake, their boss had just been murdered. Apparently the killer was still at large. And without Lenore, how could there still be a Lenore Parks Productions? *Why are they still here? And why are we here?*

'OK.' Barry broke the silence.

Melanie voiced what they all were thinking. 'Barry, do we still have jobs?'

'That's the question, isn't it? I don't have an answer. But right now let's do what Lenore would do . . . get the next new thing up and out there. So, the question we *can* answer is this.' He looked at Ada. 'How exactly do we turn antiquing into a blood sport?'

SIX

Richard Parks felt numb. He'd been escorted into the small family room adjacent to St Xavier's chaotic Midtown Emergency Room. The words out of this strange doctor's mouth were not making sense. *Impossible. I was just on the phone with her.*

'I'm sorry to tell you that your mother was dead on arrival. All attempts to resuscitate her were made. I'm very sorry.'

Richard swallowed; his mouth was dry. 'How?'

'There'll be an autopsy, but it looks like a single gunshot to the back. She lost too much blood. I suspect the bullet hit her aorta or one of the major vessels to the heart. She would have felt very little pain.'

'Can I see her?' He felt a tightness in his throat, and a welling behind his water-blue eyes.

'Sure.' The doctor sounded uncertain. 'But please, try not to touch anything. It's . . .'

'Right.' He tried to put words to the reality. 'She was murdered. Someone murdered my mother. Unless . . . no, she'd never kill herself . . . and you said she was shot in the back.' He looked at the doctor in his white coat over a polo shirt, the top button undone. 'It was murder?'

'Yes.'

Dressed in an Armani suit, he followed the doctor through a set of electronic doors into the emergency room. He moved as though wrapped in a cocoon, not registering the sounds and the smells. None of this felt real, he didn't feel real. Still trying to grasp what this doctor had just said. *How could she be dead?* They were just on the phone. He was doing what he'd always done, bailing out Rachel and minimizing the press. That was real, this . . . this could not be happening. *And who . . . murder? Who?* Faces from the past, angry producers escorted by security from their offices. Their belongings in a box, their hands clutching a multi-page termination document. Whole teams of LPP employees there one day and gone the next, generating anger, fury, often threats. 'It has to be done,' she'd say. 'It's not easy; it's not kind; but it's essential for the health of this organization.' She likened her frequent purges to pruning. 'It strengthens the tree. It creates shape out of chaos, it's the cruelty that allows beauty to exist.'

The doctor pushed open the door to a room with a sign 'Trauma 2'. 'Give me a second.' He paused and shook his head. 'On second thought, just come in.'

'Right.' He saw kindness in the man's eyes. Like Lenore, Richard had a talent for reading people. This doctor, who probably had fifteen years on him, was in a tight spot. He needed to be professional and compassionate, to allow a grieving son a last look at his mother. But he was aware too that he had a murdered celebrity in his ER and that these next few moments would be the last before the circus would begin.

Richard entered Trauma 2 – at least they'd covered her. Even so, *Mom would have hated this*. Her hair was disheveled and still wet, her face doughy under the fluorescents, her lips blue. There was blood on the sheets. He remembered how she'd never leave the house without full make-up. 'They're everywhere,' she'd instruct, referring to the paparazzi. But this . . . she looked ugly and naked; discarded gauze, IV tubing, needle cases and blue polypropylene gloves were scattered on the bed and the floor. Her eyes were closed. He took a deep breath. *She is dead.*

Random scenes from his childhood flashed to mind, late night room inspections. 'I don't like messes,' she'd say, going from his room down the hall to Rachel's. Those were tough nights. These weren't the memories he wanted right now. His room was always able to pass muster, while Rachel's was a nightmare. He'd wondered why his little sister couldn't pick up her things. Especially when she knew how it would set Mom off. It was years later that he realized – Rachel did it deliberately.

A pair of uniformed officers appeared in the doorway, escorted by a nurse supervisor. 'We're going to need you out of here,' one of them said. 'No one's to come in or out.'

The doctor looked at Richard. 'You OK?'

Richard heard the words, the man's professional, and genuine, concern. 'I've got to be,' he said. 'Is there a quiet room somewhere? I need to make some calls.'

'I'll take you back to the family room.'

Richard walked behind, his thoughts sluggish. He knew that a heavy weight had slipped from his mother's dead shoulders . . . on to his. 'You're the only one,' she'd told him. 'This will all be yours, and they will try to take it from you.'

The doctor asked if he needed anything.

'No, thank you.'

'I'm so sorry,' the doctor said.

'You're not the one who shot my mother.' He felt a surge of anger, his jaw clenched. 'There's no need to apologize.'

The doctor left and Richard was glad for the privacy. The room, with its dim lighting, stuffed chairs and quiet, was a sort of oasis.

Lenore's words: 'they will try to take it from you'. The 'they' was a moving target. Sometimes it was her executive team urging her to take LPP public so they could all cash out with seven and eight digit stock options. Sometimes *they* were her minions and underlings, all out to exact passive–aggressive revenges, from wardrobe mess-ups to on-air snafus. Often *they* were her producers who wouldn't or couldn't – perform up to her standards. As a child he'd listen to her rants: if people couldn't deliver they didn't belong at LPP. From day one, she'd confided in him. Not like a parent to a child, but like a mentor.

He pulled out his cell. So much to be done, but at that moment there was only one person he needed to call.

'Rachel?'

'She's dead, isn't she?'

'Yes.'

'They wouldn't tell me in the hospital. I pulled it up on the browser.'

'Where are you?'

'Half way to Shiloh.'

'Are you going to be OK?'

'You mean am I going to do some slicing and dicing?'

'Yeah, that. Or jump off a cliff, or do the suicide slushy.'

'I don't think so.'

'Did Dr Ebert show up?'

'Yeah, he got me out. He was pretty pissed . . . I can't blame him. Did she know?'

Richard paused, picturing his beautiful nineteen-year-old sister whose outsides had nothing to do with the pain and chaos she felt inside. Rachel was a twisted human puzzle. She could be explained, but the trouble was finding the key . . . 'She knew,' he said. 'I called her from the hospital . . . and right after—'

'So she knew?'

'Yeah.'

'Good. You know she really loved you, Richard?'

'I do.'

'You're lucky. 'Cause she couldn't stand me.'

'That's not true, Rachel.'

'Yeah, it is. But it's OK, maybe I'll be better with her dead. Course she's still in my head. I was asking Ebert about electric shock. Maybe they could just zap her out.'

'I don't think it works that way.'

'Probably right. You seem to know these things. I doubt they'd let me have it now, anyway.'

Richard felt a familiar twinge; he and Rachel and Mom all knew how to trip each other's strings. She was holding something back and wanted him to go for it. 'Just tell me.'

'You mean they didn't say anything? They didn't tell you?'

Great, he thought, *another 'they'*. He said nothing, knowing she'd blurt whatever it was.

There was a long silence. 'I'm pregnant. And I'm keeping this one.'

There was a knock at the family room door. He looked up. Rachel's pronouncement rang in his ear, and sent a rush of terror down his spine. *Mom dead, teenage sister knocked up, what now?*

The door opened and a woman in a dark suit entered. 'Mr Parks?' she asked.

'Yes.'

'I'm Detective Murphy.' She held out her shield. 'I'm very sorry about your mother. I was hoping to ask you some questions.'

'Sure,' he said. Still holding the phone to his ear: 'Rachel, we'll talk later.'

'You'll come to Shiloh?'

'As soon as I can.' Richard knew his sister well. Although how she'd process Mom's death was a wild card. She was probably upset about not being able to drop her pregnancy bombshell. Fear clutched his throat, as he suspected there was more. Knowing Rachel, the father would turn out to be a doozy, someone especially selected to enrage Mom.

'So what do you think?' Rachel asked.

'About what you just told me?' He felt the detective's eyes on him and wanted to end this call. Of course, hanging up on his sister was not something he'd ever do lightly.

'Yeah.'

'Congratulations, if it's what you want.'

'It is. It really is. I'll give this baby everything she never gave me.'

'I got to go, Rachel.'

'Be careful, Richard. You're the heir. They're going to think you did it.'

He looked across at the detective with her sensible shoulder length haircut, minimal make-up and gold stud earrings. 'Bye . . . I love you.'

'Love you too.'

He hung up the phone as the detective sank into the chair across from him. She pulled a form from a briefcase. 'I'd like to record this,' she said, sliding the document toward him with her pen.

Richard thought of his mom and her famous tag line: *'Lenore says . . .'* He looked at the form and the detective's dark eyes that were fixed on him. *Lenore says . . . be careful. Be very very careful.*

SEVEN

Barry could not believe his luck. He stared at the duo from Connecticut. This was like hitting the reality show lotto. Even Lenore, who was stingy with praise, would have been thrilled. 'Say that again.' Barry stared at Ada. The woman was gorgeous – yes, older and adorably short, which wouldn't matter on TV, but those eyes, her pointed chin and pixie hair . . . and the things that popped unscripted from her mouth. People would trust her, confide in her. She seemed fit, quick, had a wicked sense of humor, and something else. The 'it' factor that could only be assessed with a test.

'I don't think it's been done before,' Ada said. 'It's gruesome, but let's face it: the entire antiques industry is predicated on things passing from owner to owner. You could call it *Final Reckoning*. Or . . . *At the End of the Day* . . . *Final Tally. Cashing Out*.'

'OMG,' Melanie whispered. '*Final Reckoning*. That could really work.'

'So a few years back,' Ada continued, 'our friend Evie died and named me her executrix. Just for general information, if you want to make someone's life a living hell, make them your executor. Anyway, she had good things, lots of antiques worth from a few hundred to several thousand dollars and, as it turned out, an American Impressionist painting by Childe Hassam that sold at auction for nearly two million.'

'I can so see this,' Barry said, as he studied the subtle movements in Ada's face. How she used her eyes, the charming way her brow arched when she was amused, the sly curve of her lips. He knew he wasn't alone, as his team of young and talented writers – all of whom, with the exception of Carrie, had followed him from California – hung on Ada's every word. She was that rarest of people, unaffected, at home in her skin, a natural storyteller. 'Heirs hungry to get what's coming to them.'

'Fights over the good stuff,' ginger-haired David added.

'Sibling rivalries,' Melanie said. '"Mom wanted me to have that. No she didn't. Yes she did."'

'Tell them about the dealers,' Lil prompted.

'This is where I think you could have a winner,' Ada said. 'In order to keep everything on the up and up, we had a series of antique dealers come in to appraise Evie's estate and give us quotes. The numbers were all over the place. As it turned out, two of the three dealers ended up murdered, and the third deliberately undervalued the two million dollar painting . . . by one and a half million dollars.'

'I remember this,' Melanie said. 'It was this bizarre series of murders in small-town Connecticut. The guy responsible ended up killing himself.'

'Yup,' Ada said. 'He wanted revenge against the antique dealers and an auctioneer who'd ripped off his mother. She had Alzheimer's and a house full of priceless eighteenth-century antiques. The whole thing was sad and sordid. Lil and I were there – I mean literally – as he burned his house and everything in it to the ground. I'm surprised it's not been made into a movie.'

'This is too perfect,' Barry said. 'I can't believe it's not been done before. So like this, every week a fresh estate and a cast of dealers who come in, appraise it and try to get the heirs to have them liquidate. We can focus on the family, highlight a few prized possessions and, at the end, give the final total and who got what. And the Final Reckoning is . . . drum roll. It's fucking brilliant!' He stopped and stared at Ada. 'Forgive my language. But you . . . Where have you been all my life?'

'We have to test her,' Melanie said. 'She's even dressed for it. I mean really, vintage Chanel. That couldn't be more perfect. That could be her thing.'

'Absolutely,' Barry said. 'It's what I thought even over the phone. Ada Strauss, I think you could be a star.'

Ada looked around the room. All eyes on her. Lil twined their fingers together under the table. 'You people are deluded,' Ada said.

'So true,' Barry said. 'Melanie, set up a test . . . like now. Just have her talk about liquidating Evie's estate. Then get back up here. It's going to be an all-nighter.'

Melanie gave Barry an excited smile, and then paused.

'I know,' he said, and turned toward the rest of his team. 'But what else can we do? If it turns out that this is all for nothing and LPP ends with Lenore, then at least we went down fighting. Right?'

Heads nodded in agreement.

'Good,' Barry said. 'Honestly . . . worst case scenario, we keep this under our hats, but if LPP doesn't green-light this, we'll shop it around. Because this is fucking gold.'

An hour later, Lil stood back as Ada was fussed over by a hairdresser, James, and make-up woman, Gretchen. 'Not too much,' Melanie cautioned. 'I like the crow's feet.'

'That makes one of us,' Ada quipped.

'You're gorgeous the way you are,' Melanie gushed. 'People are going to want you in their home.'

Ada caught Lil's eye and gave a questioning nod.

Lil shrugged. 'I'd have to agree.'

'Fuller on the lip,' Melanie instructed.

'Melanie,' Ada said, as Gretchen, the make-up artist, ran a sable brush over her cheeks. 'This all seems strange.'

'Does it? How so?'

Ada looked at the pretty young woman with her sparkling eyes, glossy short hair and flower-and-vine tattoos on her toned arms and, she suspected, in other places as well. 'Your boss, the head of this corporation, was murdered a few hours ago, and we're down here doing . . .'

'A screen test,' Melanie said. 'I know what you're saying. But this is show business. Lenore would be the first to say – the show goes on. Let's face it, you stop and you're history. You're only one good idea from the unemployment line. The pressure is unreal. And then, people steal your ideas, or you find out someone beat you to it. Just saying *Final Reckoning* in that meeting and coming up with this idea . . .' She lowered her voice, as though scared they'd be overheard. 'It's gruesome and it's gold, and Barry is smart enough to know it. While we're down here he's checking with legal to see if we're the first to stake this claim. I'm sure he's also . . .'

'Also what?' Ada prompted.

Melanie looked at Ada and then to Lil, who was standing back in the shadows. 'I shouldn't say . . . I mean I don't know.'

Ada chuckled. 'It's OK dear, I've been around the block. Not this particular block, but I have the sense – and I couldn't say why – that Mr Stromstein wants to make sure I don't turn around and steal the idea . . . that I came up with.'

'It's not that,' Melanie stammered.

Ada fixed her with a look in the mirror.

'Not just that. He's getting legal to draw up a contract for you.'

'Based on a phone call and a meeting, and a contract for what?'

Melanie smiled. 'I don't think he knows for certain. He'll cover his bases.' She glanced at Gretchen and then at James, who was deftly teasing and spraying Ada's bright silver locks into artful curls and spikes.

'It all sounds a bit desperate,' Ada said.

Melanie stood back and looked at her, the blue Chanel protected from the make-up and hair products by a black polyvinyl cape. 'It is,' she admitted. 'But . . . it's not all that. I mean sure, that's the downside, but—'

Lil spoke, completing the woman's sentence, 'But what if you hit the jackpot? What if you're responsible for the next big thing?'

Melanie beamed. 'Yes. This could be huge.'

Ada stared into the mirror as the hairdresser stepped back and the make-up artist pulled off the plastic cape. Ada, who knew her way around the make-up aisle, was speechless. Lil was at her side and the two of them stared into the glass. 'Who is that woman?' Ada asked, looking at her reflection. Her short silver hair artfully spiked and curled, her skin flawless, her eyes lightly framed with smoky gray shadow that made them even more luminous.

Lil looked from the mirror to Ada. 'No offense – and you know I love you – could you always do this?'

'What did you do?' Ada asked.

Gretchen smiled. 'TV magic. The key is the foundation. And don't worry, it won't mess up your skin. It's my own mix and it's loaded with jojoba oil – won't clog the pores.'

'I have no pores,' Ada remarked. She tilted her face, checking the artist's subtle efforts. Her firm jaw and pointed chin given extra contour, her cheekbones accentuated. Her only jewelry a pair of creamy pearl earrings.

Melanie beamed. 'You look awesome! From here we'd head to wardrobe, but that suit . . . it's perfect. This could be your thing, high-end vintage. The only thing it needs—'

'I know,' Ada said. 'Pearls. I was going to wear them, but figured we didn't know where we were going and I'd been a New Yorker for enough years not to want to risk it.'

Melanie looked at Gretchen. 'Any chance Peggy's still here?'

Gretchen looked down.

'Shit,' Melanie said. 'I keep forgetting.'

'Who's Peggy?' Lil asked.

'Head of wardrobe . . . and Lenore's dresser for more years than any of us have been here.' Melanie looked at Gretchen. 'How bad is she taking it?'

'I think she's in shock.' Gretchen looked at Ada. 'She's the one who found her. Lenore was apparently still alive, but just. Peggy's the one who called nine one one.' She turned to Melanie. 'And we all know how Peggy felt about Lenore.'

'The poor thing,' Melanie said. She shook her head. 'Well, so much for pearls. Ada, it's time to get you in front of the camera.' She pulled out her cell. 'Jason, is Studio C set? Yeah, at least two, preferably three cameras. Great. Like we're doing it for real.'

EIGHT

Barry looked around the LPP penthouse conference room. They'd all gotten the memo signed by the executive team and Richard Parks. The line under Lenore's son's name – 'acting director and CEO, LPP' – answered one question, and raised more.

They were seated three to a table and there was not an empty place; extra tables and chairs had been added. He nodded at fellow producers, putting names to faces and taking note of which ones currently had shows, and of those, which were hits and which were headed toward the chopping block. Of course the biggest question was: *come tomorrow, do any of us still have jobs?* Lenore's death was a game changer. The central premise of this corporation was Lenore, her style, her personality, which on video was warm, engaging and gave her audience the absolute assurance that they too could master whatever it was they set out to do.

It was nine p.m., barely nine hours since Lenore was shot. They were all there, even the west coast producers and show runners for the scripted dramas LPP had developed over the past few years. The memo had been brief and carefully crafted.

To all LPP management:
Topic: Interim Planning
In this time of grief and transition, we will be holding the first
of a series of meetings to review changes to the LPP structure.
While attendance is not mandatory, your presence, and input
as we move forward, are greatly appreciated.

It had been signed by the three people seated on the raised platform at the front. In the center – Lenore's seat – was Richard Parks, every dark hair in place, his navy suit making him look a decade older than his actual twenty-two. To his right was Patricia (Patty) Corcoran, LPP's Chief Financial Officer, her hair bright blond and cropped above the collar of her white button-down blouse, her black suit as stiff as armor. On Richard's left sat Garston Green, the Chief Operating Officer, also in black with a tie the color of fresh blood and recent hair plugs made obvious in the harsh glare of the overheads. They were Lenore's inner circle.

Richard tapped his microphone. 'Thank you for coming. And thank you for the outpouring of condolences. My mother' – he gripped the edge of the table – 'was a great lady, and if it seems callous to do this so soon after her death . . . anyone who truly knew her would know this is what she would want. We . . . LPP . . . all of us, we are her legacy. The future and health of this corporation now rests in our hands.

'As most in this room are aware, the ongoing and unprecedented transformation of the entertainment industry has created tremendous opportunities, as well as a contraction in traditional media that shows little sign of stopping. At this time—' his throat constricted. Patty Corcoran poured a glass of water and passed it to him. 'At this sad time, we are faced with harsh realities. As LPP's executive team, we must move forward with an aggressive corporate restructuring. While plans for this have been under way for some time, my mother's . . . death, necessitates advancing the time frame.'

Barry's anxiety spiked. He wasn't alone. 'Restructuring' was a euphemism for 'heads will roll'. Lenore's death was no reprieve and, as he'd feared, loss of the company's major asset – the bitch herself – could cost him his job. Listening to her son Richard, it seemed things had gone from bad to worse. Barry knew that without a show – a hit show – his fifteen thousand a week salary and those of his team were a three million dollar annual drain on the corporate coffers. Lenore couldn't have been clearer: produce . . . or get out. The ax would fall swift and certain. Barry tried not to panic, but what was he supposed to do at thirty-eight? Pack up his family and head back to LA? Back to the shark tank of the younger and more desperate? Or try to stick it out in New York, going from pitch meeting to pitch meeting, where he'd get warm smiles and vague promises and nothing that would pay the rent. Or worse, see ideas he'd thrown on the table worked into someone else's show. His pulse raced, and glancing about he knew that every producer in that room – his competition – was thinking the same thing.

His only hope, as Richard Parks went on about his mother's plans to increase the use of 'outside contractors', was the incredible footage of Ada Strauss in vintage Chanel making antiques and murder in the Connecticut countryside sound charming and funny. Even the title she'd thrown out – *Final Reckoning*. *It has legs*, he thought.

As Patty Corcoran laid out the grim financials, Barry was left with little illusion. If he didn't get something green-lit fast, he'd be out of a job. It wasn't just a question of *Final Reckoning* having legs, but of legs that could hit the ground running.

And then the meeting turned. Lost in his anxiety, Barry didn't notice the dark-suited man and woman until they were at the podium. At first he thought they were consultants brought in to chop heads. But a cursory look at their suits – off the rack, the man's a bit shiny around the collar, the woman's boxy and out of style – said no, definitely not consultants, or even anyone associated with entertainment.

He listened as Richard introduced them as a pair of NYPD detectives, in charge of investigating Lenore's murder. The cops had been around all day, Lenore's entire penthouse suite now a crime scene. He wondered who'd get tapped to do the made-for-TV movie. Worst case scenario, maybe it was something he could pitch. After all, he was here the day it happened.

The woman detective took the microphone. 'Thank you Mr Parks.' She looked over the conference room. Her dark gaze moved slowly over those assembled. It reminded Barry of old-school mysteries . . . *someone in this room is the murderer*. But no, she was all business.

'My name is Detective Jean Murphy. As I'm sure you're aware,'

she started, 'Lenore Parks was shot and killed today. I'd ask anyone
in this room who believes they have information that can help the
investigation to please come forward. If you saw something unusual,
it doesn't matter how small or seemingly unimportant. If you're
aware of anyone who might have had a grudge or some resentment
against Ms Parks.' She paused. 'A disgruntled employee, someone
terminated, or in fear of termination. We want to know about it.'

Several people coughed, and Barry heard a woman choke on her
water.

Good luck, he mused. Because similar sentiments would be
running through the heads of everyone in that room. Lenore ruled
through fear. And from the sounds of things, her death wasn't about
to change that. It gave him pause. How many people hated her?
Feared her? Wished her dead? He thought of his corner office and
the woman who'd occupied it before him. She'd had a semi-
successful show. It ran four years, got cancelled and within three
months of it getting pulled, she was out of a job. And as he knew
through the grapevine, she was borderline unemployable.

He replayed his last meeting with Lenore. The way she'd toyed
with his fears. It was cat-and-mouse stuff, her claws raking over
his insecurity. Her message was clear – produce or get out. He
meant nothing to her. It hadn't always been like that. Not when
he'd had a hit with the Home and Style Network and been recruited
by LPP and one of the major networks. It had been 'the sky's the
limit', a corner office in midtown. 'We want you to bring your whole
team – hell, they'll all get a twenty percent bump.' The offer was
too good to resist, and for a while he let himself believe he was
home free. He'd uprooted his pregnant wife from the San Bernardino
Valley – no more LA traffic – to the excitement of Manhattan. It
had started well, a spot producing episodes of *Lenore Says*, and
then on to a weekly model competition that attempted to recapture
his success with *Model Behavior*. It didn't, and tanked in its first
season. He knew that everyone has shows go under, that wasn't the
issue. It came down to what he currently had on the air, which was
zip. One day he'd been the golden-haired boy, the next . . . He
looked up at the detective, who was fielding questions. *Good luck,
lady*, he thought.

Anyone in this room, and quite a few outside, had motive to want
Lenore dead. In the end her murder didn't help him, it just made

things worse. He wished this detective would get off the stage. He knew there was more bad news coming from the trio on the podium. *Just get this over with.*

He studied Richard Parks' somber face. *He's just a kid, and now he's my boss.* They'd been introduced, but he had no sense of the intense young man. Objectively, he had the most to gain from Lenore's death. Although supposedly he was one of the few people who genuinely cared for her, unlike his sister, who'd also inherit untold millions and who delighted in publicly humiliating Lenore. He looked at Patty Corcoran and Garston Green; they'd been with Lenore from the first episode of *Lenore Says.* Would they profit from her death? Or were they like everyone else in this room, wondering if there'd still be an LPP if the L no longer existed?

And then it came, as he knew it would. The detective left with her partner and Patty Corcoran stood. He pictured the ax in her hand. 'In light of today's tragic events all scheduled tapings of *Lenore Says* will be cancelled. All employees may take the rest of the week off with pay. We'll have made decisions about how to move forward by Monday.'

Barry, as if reading a teleprompter or subtitles for a foreign movie, translated Patty's caring tone and vague words into something closer to the truth: *everyone connected to* Lenore Says *is getting canned.* You can't really do a show called *Lenore Says* without Lenore. Four hundred people were about to get their pink slips.

And the bad-news buffet continued. Patty cleared her throat, no longer making eye contact as she read from a prepared statement. 'All employees of LPP are to present on Monday. These are the exceptions: shows currently in production with scheduled tapings are expected to move forward.'

Shit! He had to get out of there. He had work to do, and the more he thought about it the more he knew the window of opportunity, if there even was one, would slam fast. He had no illusion as to what was going to happen on Monday. Anyone without a current show in production would get fired. He, and his team, would show up for work and find their belongings in boxes and security guards with checklists wanting their badges and their keys.

His time with LPP was up. The only sliver which might save his ass, his apartment and his career was to get *Final Reckoning* green-lit and in production – and do it now. It was a long shot – *Antiques*

Roadshow meets *The Hunger Games* on the set of *Gilmore Girls*. It was what Lenore wanted, but with her dead, would anyone else? He knew he'd been stupid, he'd believed what he'd wanted to be true, that a producer position with LPP meant job security. That illusion was gone, replaced by a sucking pit of despair. He was so screwed. He thought of Jeanine, and that fucking Birkin bag. No, he could do this. It wouldn't be the first time he'd pulled a rabbit out of his hat. But if he couldn't . . . he had no Plan B.

NINE

A da and Lil awoke to a ringing phone. It was five a.m. It had been after midnight by the time they'd made it back home.

'It's got to be for me,' Lil muttered, assuming it was someone from the paper.

'Calls this early are never good,' Ada said, bracing for news of some relative's death.

Lil focused on the caller ID. 'I don't recognize the number. Should I pick up?'

'Let the machine get it,' Ada said. 'Maybe it's a wrong number . . . my head . . . how much Scotch did we drink last night?'

'We,' Lil said, 'not so much. You? You were pretty wired.'

'Remind me not to do that again.'

The ringing stopped and their outgoing message clicked on. They listened as Lil's voice ended and a chipper young woman spoke. 'Hi Ada, sorry to call so early. This is Melanie Taft, I was hoping to—'

Lil picked up the phone and held it toward Ada. 'Hollywood calling.'

Ada pushed back in bed, took the phone and clicked the green button. 'Hello Melanie.'

'I'm so sorry if I woke you; it's just that none of us have been to sleep and we're driving out to Grenville.'

Ada stared at Lil as Melanie blurted out Barry Stromstein's and the company's ambitious plans for the morning. 'Dear,' Ada said, trying to break into Melanie's excited rant, 'exactly how much coffee have you had?'

'Pots of it. This is so exciting. Barry thinks we can get a pilot shot by the end of next week. It's crazy, but I think we can do it.'

'How is that possible?' Ada asked, and immediately regretted it. She turned to Lil, who'd left the room. She heard her in the kitchen, and hoped she was getting her a cup of tea. She was going to need it.

'There's so much to do. I'll be coming down with David and a crew to start scoping locations. The big thing is how to get that first estate. I mean really it's a fabulous idea, but the details. Ugh! Although you'd be surprised what people will do to get on a reality show. I don't think we'll have trouble. Neither does Barry, it's just the time. Like there's none of it. So your friend Lil works for the local paper; I was hoping she could help us place an ad, probably a few, one putting out a call for a fresh estate . . . is that gruesome? I mean I know the whole *Antiques Roadshow*, *Hunger Games*, *Gilmore Girls* thing is kind of morbid. I mean someone will bite, won't they? What am I saying? They always do.'

She spoke without pause. Ada wondered when the girl managed to catch her breath.

'And then we'll need a casting call for the talent . . . you know, the dealers. We'll want some real characters. But also eye candy 'cause, let's face it, the demographics for these shows are women and gay guys. We need someone who's going to look hot with their shirt off. You must know some of them. And Lil, I bet she knows loads of them. Maybe she could start chatting people up, letting them know we're coming to town. Just think of the publicity for their businesses. They should both be full page. Is there a specialty paper, like something just for antique dealers we should target?'

'There's the *Auction and Antiques Weekly Trader*,' Ada said, and she heard the clicking of a keyboard over the line.

'Fabulous! I'm on their website. Crap, their offices don't open till nine. What about the paper where Lil works? That's a daily, right? They should be open. How quickly can I get our ads in there?'

Ada looked up as Lil came in with her mug of tea. 'Lil, Melanie needs to ask you a few things.' She took the tea and passed the phone. She mouthed 'thank you' and savored that first delicious sip.

Fifteen minutes later, Lil hung up. 'Oh my, is she on something?'

Ada leaned back against her pillows, set the tea on the nightstand and grabbed her iPad. She opened her browser; the top item was Lenore's murder. 'It all feels so strange,' she said, as she scrolled down.

Lil perched on Ada's side of the bed and looked on. 'Do they have anyone in custody?'

'No, not that they're saying.' She tapped on a slide show of Lenore through the years. 'I can't get that image out of my head, seeing her on that stretcher. So raw . . .' Ada looked at Lil and then leaned her head against her shoulder. 'It's all so short.'

'It is,' Lil said, 'one day you're here and the next . . .'

'There's a Poe poem called *Lenore*.'

'Lenore nevermore,' Lil added.

'No, I think that was *The Raven* . . . still. So what exactly did Melanie want?'

'She's bringing the circus to town,' Lil said. 'Are you sure you want to do this, Ada?'

'Honestly I don't know what *this* is. All of that craziness yesterday – *this* could be a big thing, or nothing at all. And I've the sense it could go from one to the other in a heartbeat.'

'I got that too. The way that girl talked. Like she was planning a wedding overnight. It could all happen . . . or someone could get stood up at the altar.'

'They're all so high-strung,' Ada added. 'I don't think it's just the shock of their boss being murdered. And what I don't understand is how do they expect Lenore Park Productions to exist without Lenore at the helm? Isn't she the de facto reason they have jobs?'

'Let's look at their website,' Lil suggested.

Ada punched in the URL for her favorite search engine, tapped in 'LPP' and clicked on their hyperlink. The home page had a moving banner that switched from upcoming episodes of *Lenore Says* to the dozen or so shows the production company had running on major networks, plus several more on style and DIY channels. There was a tab for Lenore's magazine – *L* – and links to pages and articles on everything from wine pairing, through buying foreclosed real estate, to 'The Seven Secrets of Mind-blowing Oral Sex'.

Lil clicked on that one.

'What are you doing?' Ada asked, pulling her tablet away.

'Maybe there's something I don't know.'

'Hmmm. I don't want you loading my browser with smut.'

'Fine,' Lil said, snuggling next to her.

'What time did Melanie say they were coming here?' Ada asked.

'She didn't,' and Lil turned in to Ada. She ran a finger down Ada's side.

'Stop that!' Ada said, 'you know I'm ticklish.'

'I do,' and Lil squeezed closer, loving the feel of Ada against her, the smell of her hair conditioner, the warmth of her body. Their eyes connected and then their lips. And then the phone rang again.

'You have got to be kidding.' Ada didn't move. Her lips brushed Lil's. 'Let's ignore it.' They listened as the recording came on.

Melanie's voice came over the speaker. 'I forgot to say that we grabbed a Scooby bus and are . . . five minutes away. I was hoping to get some locations scouted and shot this morning. It's going to be a gorgeous day and I know we can fake our way through some opening banter. But don't worry . . . we've got breakfast. See you soon. And Ada, if you can do the Chanel thing again, it would be awesome.'

'You're sure about this?' Lil whispered, her breath tickling Ada's ear.

'Uhuh.' Ada felt a tingle down her spine as Lil nipped her lobe. 'I've got to get dressed.'

'Yes, you do.'

'Maybe if we ignore them, they'll give us an hour.'

The phone rang again, followed by a knock at the door. Then the doorbell.

The machine picked up. 'Guess it wasn't five minutes,' Melanie gushed. 'I think we're at the right address. These condos all kind of look alike. We're at the front door. I'm not sure which one is yours and which one is Lil's. I'll walk around back.'

Ada stared at the sliders and the breaking dawn over the wetlands. They'd not drawn the curtains last night. Her arm shot across Lil and she grabbed the phone. 'Melanie, stay where you are! We'll be right out.'

The morning was a blur, and awkward. As Ada explained why she was in Lil's condo . . . and bed . . . at five a.m.

'So you two, are like together together?' Melanie asked, as she, the film crew and the hair and make-up artists she'd met the day before filed into Lil's condo with cartons of coffee, juice and bags of bagels.

'Yes,' Ada said, 'for the last three years. Although we were friends for much longer. Best friends.'

'But you were married, you and your husband ran Strauss's.'

'We owned Strauss's and were married, yes, and I have a daughter and Lil has two. We're both grandmothers. Our relationship,' she looked across at Lil in her matching blue robe and smiled, 'it just happened.'

'I am so in love with you,' Melanie said, and then, to Lil, 'As in total admiration, not as in, steal your girlfriend. Those are the best kind of relationships, you know, the ones that start with friendship.' Melanie poured a mug of coffee. 'You take it black, right?' She handed it to Lil.

'You're observant.'

'It saves time,' Melanie said. 'Speaking of which, we need to get Ada dolled up. My goal is to get at least three locations shot, so Barry can get a feel for the visuals. In the meantime the ads will have done their thing and we can start winnowing through the talent.'

'By talent you mean?'

'Dealers who want to get cast . . . possibly as regulars. But the make-or-break for this show is someone willing to let us turn the liquidation of a loved one's estate into compelling TV. There's a timing element there that's never been done. People don't die every day – I mean they do, but . . . it's the logistics of the thing . . .'

'You think there'll be takers?' Ada asked.

'Pretty sure. If we're lucky, we'll get a few. Because if – when – this takes off, we're going to need to move fast. The goal right now is to figure out the process and film a pilot. We'll hash through the rough spots later. So, I say Chanel. Yesterday's outfit still good to go? Every wrinkle gets magnified on screen.'

'I was thinking of the green,' Ada said.

Melanie's head tilted. 'You have more than one?'

Lil snorted.

'Don't do it,' Ada warned.

'You should be filming *Hoarders*.'

'Lillian, that is not fair.'

'Doesn't matter if it's true.'

'Ignore her,' Ada said. 'We need to go next door. Lil has no appreciation for my wardrobe.'

With coffee in hand, she led Melanie, David, James the hair guy and Gretchen the magical make-up artist out Lil's front door and around the trimmed yew hedge to her mirror-image condo.

'Will my relationship with Lil be an issue?' Ada asked, with her key in the door.

'I don't think so.' Melanie glanced at David.

'You just get more interesting,' he said. 'The viewership for this show – if we do it right – will be women and a whole lot of gay men. This could be a plus. It's a bit cart-before-the-horse, but I think there's marketing gold here. Cover of *The Advocate*. Are the two of you out?' he asked.

Ada caught movement in Bernice Framm's kitchen curtains. *Does that woman ever sleep?* She waved and shrugged. She wondered if her neighborhood nemesis and vocal homophobe, Clayton Spratt, was also up and about. She imagined what he'd make of this band of young and enthusiastic Manhattanites – probably call the cops and say she was having an orgy. She chuckled and turned the key. 'Yes, we're out.' She led them down the hall. 'It wasn't our choice. We were outed on a local blog, as though anyone should care about such things.'

As they passed her living room with its dark wood furniture and glass-fronted cabinets filled with late nineteenth- and early twentieth-century art glass, her mother Rose – shy of five feet and with light-blue eyes – emerged from what used to be Ada's bedroom. Her fine white hair mussed in bedhead wisps. 'What's going on? Who are these people?'

Ada filled her mother in on yesterday's activities.

'I always thought you should be on TV,' Rose said. Her eyes, since recent double cataract and lasik surgery, no longer magnified behind Coke-bottle lenses.

'Since when?' Ada asked as she headed back to the smallest of the three bedrooms.

'Your home is lovely,' Melanie said, looking between Rose and Ada. 'What was Lil talking about with that *Hoarders* crack?'

Rose snickered. 'And behind door number three . . .'

'Mother!' Ada opened the door, needing to give it an extra push since there was a free-standing steel clothes rack blocking it.

Ada barreled in; she rarely let strangers see the extent of her years of collecting. If she were being honest, Lil wasn't entirely off the mark with her *Hoarders* comment. It had been less than a year ago that Lil had discovered that Ada had been paying for a storage unit in Manhattan. 'Why?' she'd asked. 'We have so much space.'

'Holy mother of God.' David whispered.

Ada braced for their responses. She knew her 'collecting' had crossed a line, and when she'd reluctantly brought Lil to see what was in her 'Lock and Walk' Storage unit she hadn't known what to expect.

'Is this heaven?' Melanie asked, her voice reverential as she scanned the rows of garment racks and carefully stacked boxes labeled YSL, Givenchy, Chanel, Dior. The only furniture in the room was a row of steel drawers that filled an entire wall. 'OMG!' Melanie exclaimed. 'Tell me that's not Dior.' Her gaze glued to a black-and-white pencil dress.

'Lil and my mother don't get my love of clothes.' Ada stood in the middle of her fashion hoard, enjoying the smells and letting her fingers play over the silks and satins. 'I spent over thirty years in the garment industry. Yes, it was work, but I've always loved fashion. That's what made Strauss's a success. I wanted the people wearing our clothes to look and feel good. So, yes, I got some custom-made samples along the way. Harry and I spent big money, and the designers wanted me in their clothes. It was win win.'

'This is so not hoarding. Will you adopt me?' Melanie asked.

'My granddaughter Mona gets it all, and trust me, she'll be stopping by with a pickup truck the day I go. At least she has the height for fashion. With me, it was always finding things that would work on a dwarf.'

'You're not that short,' Melanie said. 'And the beautiful thing about TV is that height is not an issue. Weight, on the other hand, can be. And on your test you looked perfect. Maybe we should pick more than one outfit. I was hoping to start at the cemetery.'

'Something black and cocktail length?' Ada suggested. She pulled out a full-skirted black dress from the fifties, with lace across the bust and three-quarter length sleeves.

'Perfect . . . a little Morticia Addams, but not too much, and you said you had a green Chanel.'

Ada chuckled. She grabbed Melanie's hand and led her back toward the walk-in closet.

She turned on the light. Mclanie was stunned into silence.

Ada turned. 'Which green do you like the best?'

Armed with three outfit changes, Ada, Melanie, David, Gretchen and James piled into the tall black RV they'd dubbed the Scooby van. The interior included a dressing and make-up area, with a bathroom in the back and a central lounge area with comfortable couches. The film crew followed in a white van with the LPP logo on the door.

Lil had begged off, needing to work on her column and also offering to help Melanie and company get their ads placed ASAP into both the *Brattlebury Register* and the *Grenville Sentinel*. Her parting words to Ada: 'You are going to be amazing.'

Their first stop was the cemetery. For downtown Grenville this was big news. Cars stopped and morning joggers and walkers drifted toward the unusual activities.

'We have to move fast,' Melanie said as the crew set up. 'I didn't have time to pull permits.'

'Do you need to?' Ada asked, as Gretchen applied the finishing touches to her make-up and whipped off the apron. 'This is essentially public land.'

'Yes and no, and in my experience once you start to ask for permission people say no, or at the very least want some money. We'll come back later and make nice. Right now, let's just get something filmed.'

Initially, Melanie had Ada read from a teleprompter.

Ada did as instructed. 'Melanie, I know this is your business, and I don't want to insult anyone, but I sound forced. Can I maybe do what we did yesterday?'

'Sorry. I know, it's total crap. We wrote this intro at like three a.m. You want to go off script?'

'I didn't think reality TV used scripts.'

The entire crew broke out laughing.

'What?' Ada asked.

'It's all scripted,' Melanie said. 'Just don't tell the Writers Guild. All reality shows have some kind of script. Kev,' she called to the man running the teleprompter. 'You can take a break.'

'Do you know what to say?' Melanie asked.

Ada smiled. 'You want me to introduce the show and explain the rules, correct?'

'That's about it.'

'And if I screw up you can edit, correct?'

'Absolutely.'

'Great, so this is my spot,' she said, standing in front of a row of eighteenth-century graves, the center one with a weathered carving of a winged angel.

'When I say "action",' Melanie instructed, 'just start talking.'

Ada nodded. She looked past the film crew at the gathering crowd, most of them hanging back behind the cemetery's outer stone wall. Some ventured closer, one woman striking up a conversation with James the hairdresser.

'Quiet please,' Melanie shouted.

Ada took a couple breaths; she felt a surge of excitement. A moment's doubt; *what if I freeze up?*

'And . . . action.'

Ada smiled, looked into the camera and, just as she'd done for decades when running Strauss's, welcomed her audience as she'd welcomed shoppers to her stores. 'Thank you so much for joining us and welcome to *Final Reckoning*. I'm Ada Strauss and we're in lovely Grenville, Connecticut, the antiques capital of New England . . .' she lowered her voice to a whisper '. . . if not the world. Today we're going on a trip that, sadly, everyone takes. The final trip.'

Transfixed by the unusual activity, the crowd surged closer to hear Ada. She spotted familiar faces, and found it actually became easier if she spoke directly to them. 'We're here today to see what happens at the end of life, when all of our worldly possessions pass on to the people we love, or get sold at estate sales and auctions.

'The rules for *Final Reckoning* are easy. Three antique dealers will have the opportunity to appraise and bid on an estate. This can be an outright sale, or the heirs may choose to have the winning dealer earn a percentage at a three-day estate sale. Along the way we'll explore the history of fabulous – and sometimes not so fabulous – antiques, works of art and collectibles. Our goals are for the heirs and loved ones of the recently deceased to get a bit of closure . . . and as much cash as possible.'

Ada caught smiles and looks of concern. She nodded. 'Ghoulish? Perhaps. But something we all have to face. So, I'm Ada Strauss and welcome to . . . *Final Reckoning*'

'And cut!' Melanie shouted. She stared at Ada, poised and elegant in vintage black, in the scenic cemetery, where clumps of purple crocus and yellow daffodils sprouted among the graves. She looked at the camera and sound guys. 'We got all that?' she asked.

'You bet. Want to get a second?'

'No, we're good. Really good.'

TEN

'You're not sending me away, Richard. You need me.' Rachel, with red-rimmed eyes, glared up at her brother from her bathroom floor; her arms and legs were smeared with blood. 'I'll be fine, and what do you care if I'm not? It's just more pie for you.'

'You're not OK.' He fought to keep the anger from his voice. 'Look at you.' He bit back all the things that would turn a bad situation into a nuclear meltdown. People who are OK don't curl up in their bathroom and slice at their arms and thighs with a box cutter.

'You don't give a shit! You're like Mom two point zero. Second verse as shitty as the first.'

'I do care, Rachel,' and that was the truth, one of several.

'You should.' She sniffed and batted at her eyes.

He saw the fresh cuts on her upper arm, not deep, none more than an inch, none requiring stitches and a trip to the emergency room. It would be a call to her psychiatrist, Dr Ebert. 'Rachel, please give me the box cutter.'

She thrust it toward him, displaying the fresh cuts and a meshwork of scars dating back to puberty. 'I'm sorry I'm such a fuck up. I'm sorry Mommy couldn't pop out two perfect children. God,' she hiccoughed, and put her fist in her mouth. Like a baby with a pacifier, she sucked her knuckles. 'She's dead. Oh God.' Tears popped through thickly smeared mascara.

'Yes,' Richard said. He clicked the box cutter closed and shoved it into a pocket. He sank to the cool tile floor and wrapped an arm around her. He never knew what Rachel needed. And unlike his mother, who couldn't tolerate her volatile mood swings, he wanted to help. Growing up had been a war zone, where he was the peace-keeper and his mother and sister the combatants. The fights would start from nothing and go from zero to nightmare in seconds. It was like neither one could stop herself. His sister's rages and crushing depression set off by the trip wires of Mom's coldness, her disdain, her cruelty. He couldn't argue when Rachel accused Mom of not loving her; it was probably true. Certainly, Lenore never showed Rachel the affection she showered on him. He hugged Rachel tight, feeling the fragility of her frame, her shoulders just bones. *She's too thin again.* In the laundry list of psychiatric disorders Rachel had been diagnosed with, an eating disorder with both bulimic and anorectic symptoms was included. 'We'll get through this,' he said, his thoughts pulled by calls from lawyers, the detectives who wanted to interview both him and Rachel, anxious producers, the CFO and COO wanting to bring in consultants to handle the post-Lenore restructuring. But as he thought about it, with Mom dead, Rachel and he were it. And she was pregnant, and threatening to keep the baby. Which, considering who the father was, was a decidedly bad idea.

Rachel gazed at the base of the toilet. 'I wanted her dead,' she said.

'I know, and you shouldn't say that around anyone but me. Not even Ebert; I'm sure his records will get subpoenaed.'

'They're going to think we did it, but we have an alibi,' she said. 'I was in the hospital and you were with me when Mom was shot.'

'We could have hired someone,' he said, having already wandered down this road.

'So I would have faked my tantrum at Murielle's, gotten hauled to the hospital . . . or to jail if those bastard cops had had their way. Really? Seems far-fetched.'

'Why not?' he said. 'Either one of us has more than enough money to hire someone, although how does someone find a hit man?'

'Craigslist?' she offered.

'Or Angie's . . . it's kind of like a workman. Wouldn't you want references?'

'Like stars,' she pressed in against Richard. '"John was an excel-lent assassin and I couldn't have been happier with the clean-up. A five star professional."'

Richard looked down, his chin tickled by the soft strands of her hair. Something relaxed as he caught the hint of her smile. His sister was beautiful – or could be – with Lenore's green eyes and ash blond hair that was currently platinum.

'I didn't do it,' he said, knowing she'd believe him.

'I know that. I didn't either, although,' she turned her face up to his, 'I'd thought about it. I never would have, though. Or not like this – I mean this was planned. Someone who knew Mom, her schedule . . . it's probably someone we know. Someone who worked for her.'

He held his tongue, as years of skirmishes between Mom and Rachel played in his head. Some had gotten physical. Once, Rachel had pushed Mom down the stairs, leaving her with massive bruises. She'd retaliated by sending Rachel – then fourteen – to a residential psychiatric hospital. There'd been plenty of slaps, but it was the things they'd said to one another, hateful and unforgivable. Rachel twisted in his arms. He looked into her eyes, so like their mother's. He felt her tremble.

'You've got to stop doing this stuff,' he said. 'I'm not Mom. I don't want to hurt you.'

'I know.' She bit her bottom lip and her leg curled in, her thigh grazing his, her knee nudging his groin. 'You just want to love me,' she said.

'We shouldn't,' he answered, those words having long ago lost their meaning.

'I need it.' Her lips parted and she pushed up and locked her mouth to his. Her left hand clutched the back of his head to pull him in. Her arm, still wet with blood, held him fast as her fingers twisted in his hair.

He groaned and opened to the kiss. Her tears wet against his cheek, her tongue lashing against his. Her hands pulled his shirt free from his pants, her fingers kneaded his bare flesh. His mind skittered over how wrong this was, and how good it felt. It always had, and he suspected it always would. Rachel was the spark to his fire. He scooped and lifted his little sister in his arms, his pregnant sister.

Carrying her out of the bathroom, he headed toward her four-poster bed. 'No,' she said.

'OK,' feeling a mix of relief and regret; if she didn't want this anymore he'd be fine with that.

'No, silly.' She brushed a finger down the side of his face. Her tongue flicked between her lips. 'Not here; let's do it in *her* bed.'

After, as his heart returned to its normal rhythm and the orgasmic glow dissipated, he tried to reorient himself.

'Let's spend the day in bed,' Rachel said. 'Keep the doors locked, tell the staff to take the day off. Pretend we're normal people. I'll make lunch.'

'You can't cook.'

'I can so.' She twirled a length of hair between her fingers and ran it through her lips. 'You take the box of mac and cheese, a stick of butter and a little milk. It's not hard.'

'Would you eat it?' he asked, knowing he was treading on shaky ground.

'I might.' She arched her back and posed for him. She used his eyes as mirrors. She leaned toward him, her face close to his. Her hand snaked up his thigh. 'What would be the harm of a day in bed? It's not the sex, Richard . . .' There was an openness and vulnerability in her eyes. 'Although we do it really well. It's you. Can I please just spend some time with you?'

His chest tightened. What's the harm? he thought. Right, spend the day in bed . . . with your sister. He breathed out a sigh. 'I have to take care of business, Rachel.'

He braced for her fury.

It didn't come. She pulled back, her hand grazed the crumpled sheets. 'I suppose you do; after all our dear old mother was just shot dead.' She mimed a gun with her hand. 'I'm dying to know who did it. At the very least I could send them a thank you card. Sorry,' catching something in Richard's expression. 'You loved her. That was really insensitive. You'd think with all of this therapy, I'd be better at this. Are you really sad?'

'Numb,' he said, trying to identify the emotions attached to yesterday's events. 'Like it's not real yet.'

'It's denial,' she said. 'One of the five stages of grief. Let me see; there's denial, bargaining, depression, acceptance and . . . what's the fifth? Sneezy?'

Richard met his sister's smile. 'Dopey.'

'No,' she said with a lopsided leer, 'Horny.'

*   *   *

It was after ten when the maid tried to get into Lenore's locked suite.

'Jenelle, it's OK,' Richard shouted from the bed. 'We're going through Mom's things. Why don't you do the other rooms? In fact, maybe leave this alone for a week till we know what we're doing.'

He crept naked out of bed and placed his ear to the double doors in the outer room. He looked back at Rachel.

She smiled. 'Do you think Mom knew?'

His ears strained for the sound of the maid's cart going down the hall. Rachel's question was one he'd often asked. 'I don't know.'

'I bet she did.' Rachel got out of bed and wandered back toward Lenore's dressing room.

Richard grabbed his boxers from the floor and followed her, his eyes tracing the lines and shadows of his sister's body. 'What makes you say that?'

'She wasn't stupid, and we weren't always careful. I mean *I* wasn't always careful. You, brother, are the epitome of cover your ass.' She turned back and openly admired his mostly naked physique. 'And such a fine ass at that.'

'Thanks. Then don't you think she would have said something? Shipped one of us off?' He regretted the words as they left his mouth.

'She did.' Rachel pushed open the door into one of Lenore's walk-ins. 'More than once, unless you've forgotten. There was Trinity Hills, Silver Brook, Silver Glen.'

Back on dangerous ground, Richard knew to hold his tongue.

'She knew. I think she was jealous. Wanted her precious son all to herself.' Rachel unzipped a garment bag and then another. 'But I always knew how to get out of those places.' She selected a long black knit bandage dress, unzipped it and stepped in. Holding up her hair she turned her back to Richard. 'Do me up.'

'Did those places help?' he asked.

She turned in to him. 'I'd like to say no. But I did learn some things. Like whenever I wanted to come home, I'd let Mommy know that I was going to blab all her secrets to the most indiscreet people I could find. It was the one thing about her I kind of liked – she was a dyke. Or the time I got knocked up by the grounds-keeper at Silver Brook. That was fun. And Richard, to be clear, I am keeping our baby.' She smoothed her hand down her still concave belly.

His throat caught. 'Rachel . . . it's such a bad idea.'

'No it isn't. Egyptian royalty did it all the time.'

'Yeah, check your history and look at some of the shapes of their heads. This is crazy.'

She pushed past him and into Lenore's shoe closet. She turned on the light and tapped the button for the black shoe display, all still in their boxes with a color photo of the contents on the outside. She pressed a second time and then a third, the boxes shifting from back to front. She picked a pair of low-heeled pumps. 'This is not a discussion. I want this baby, and you should too. We're going to be awesome parents. All we have to do is ask, "What would Lenore do?" and then do the opposite.'

'Rachel, you can't.'

And like a spark to gasoline, she turned on him. 'Really? But I can, Richard, and I will. In case you try to stop me, let's discuss the new world order, shall we? You've been fucking me since I was twelve and you were fifteen. Yes, I know I started the whole thing, but you weren't exactly a lamb to slaughter. Now, I've checked some fun facts. You want to hear them?'

'Rachel—'

'Here they are: the age of consent in both Connecticut and New York is sixteen. At some point you crossed that line and for three years were having sex with a minor. While, yes, there is a one year statute of limitations in New York and two years in Connecticut. None of that matters, and aren't you thrilled that you let Mommy bully me into pre-law? So let's forget all that and move on to the federal Mann Act. Where basically transporting anyone across state lines for illegal sexual activity is criminal, and sex with a minor most certainly counts. There we've got a five year statute, which started to tick on my eighteenth birthday. Which leaves you with four years to wonder when, or if, I'll drop that dime. And once convicted, you'd be a registered sex offender – that is, after you got out of jail. Now let's think of what this exciting news – rape, incest and Lenore the lesbian – would have on your precious LPP. I'm thinking you would lose all sponsors, no network would run any of your programming, the magazine would tank . . . maybe get a last issue for the freak value. So, any ideas you have to look me away, or get me to abort our child, you need to shut them down right fast. Do you understand?'

Stunned, he said nothing. He felt a rage and the strong urge to hit her. To wrap his hands around her throat.

'Oh dear.' She stared back at him. 'You know I can actually tell what you're thinking. You want to hit me? Do it.' Holding the shoes in one hand she stood still, barely a foot separating them.

He caught the trace of her smile. *And I can read your mind too*, he thought. And he did the one thing he knew would hurt her. He turned and, without saying anything, walked out.

'Get dressed,' she shouted after him.

He stopped. 'Why?'

'I want to go into town. Wear something somber.'

ELEVEN

I t felt odd and, if Lil were honest, not great. She stood behind the stone wall of Grenville's picturesque cemetery and watched Ada, who looked like a chic fifties hostess who'd just left a cocktail party to hang out among the graves. All she needed was a Martini and a cigarette.

Earlier, they'd asked Lil if she'd wanted to join them in the RV. She'd declined. Ada had given her a look, as though she knew something was off. She'd asked, 'Your column?'

Lil had nodded, as though it were true. *Face it*, she thought, *you're jealous. You're feeling like a third wheel. And you know what? Get over it.* Unobserved, she felt another emotion, pride at how lovely Ada looked and at how natural she seemed in front of the camera. Not just here, but since that first phone conversation with Barry. As though Ada could speak this other language and pitch TV shows, albeit gruesome ones, off the top off her head. *Why didn't I know this about her? Don't take her for granted.* As she watched Ada, she realized this would be her next column. She'd have to be careful not to have it come off as self-serving. But the Grenville antiques industry could get a needed shot in the arm from having a hit reality show filmed in its midst. While the dealers she interviewed on a weekly basis downplayed the soft economy, the fallout had been severe. Sales had tanked across the board, with the notable exception of the very high end. The Grenville Chamber of Commerce had rallied – to the extent possible – around the two hundred plus dealers. But up and down High Street, where most of the eighteenth- and nineteenth-century homes had long ago been turned into antique shops, stores had closed and the town's once bustling center was dotted with for-sale signs. Single dealer businesses, to survive the hard times, had merged into multi-dealer shops and co-ops in efforts to lessen the crushing weight of their overheads.

Aware of the effect her weekly syndicated column could have on her hometown, Lil did what she could. Like the stock market, it too wasn't all bad news, and that provided some of her more thought-provoking pieces on the up-and-down nature of antiques. What was hot ten years ago – like Victorian furniture – now gathered dust in the shops. And the Danish modern teak chairs and tables she and Bradley had purchased brand new in the seventies for his office were fetching exorbitant prices.

As she thought of how she'd work this show into a column, she pulled out her camera. Zooming in on Ada, her breath caught. After all those emotions, jealousy, guilt, came the biggest of all. *I love her.*

Searching for an interesting shot, she framed the cameraman and Melanie calling out directions from behind him. Her attention was suddenly pulled by a woman's voice.

'What the hell is going on? That's an LPP truck.'

Lil turned and faced a rail thin blonde girl in a clingy black dress, followed by a broad-shouldered young man in a charcoal gray suit. Her immediate thought was there must be a funeral. This was a cemetery after all.

'What's a film crew doing in Grenville?' The woman grabbed the man's arm. 'Did you know about this?'

Lil couldn't hear his response. She recognized the girl as Rachel Parks. The man she wasn't so sure of, either her boyfriend or her brother. Based on how she was hanging on his arm, she suspected the former. In general, spotting celebrities around Grenville was not a big deal. Quite a few movie stars, writers and Hollywood producers kept homes in this part of Connecticut. Often it was an attempt to give their children a normal childhood. The schools were top notch, and by and large people didn't bother them.

Rachel Parks looked at Lil. 'Do you know what's going on here?'

'Yes. I'm Lil Campbell,' she said. 'I am so sorry to hear about your mother.'

To her surprise the man answered. 'Thank you.'

'So what's going on?' Rachel asked.

Despite the girl's black dress and severe ponytail, Lil got no sense of grief. Not from the girl. The man on the other hand looked green. 'You're Richard Parks?' she asked.

'Yes.' He turned to his sister, who seemed fused to his side. 'I have no idea, it's something that must already have been in production. Maybe Mom wanted to do another piece about country living.'

Lil was pulled by the hollow sound of his voice. 'I can tell you what I know,' she offered.

'Please,' Rachel said, her green eyes wide.

Lil wondered what a more seasoned reporter would do, and was also struck by how much Rachel's eyes were like those of her famous mother. *A real reporter would start snapping pictures*, she thought. *I can't do that.* 'They're filming the pilot for a reality show.'

Richard Parks stared across the cemetery. His gaze fell on Ada and the crew members. He looked at Melanie and squinted. 'Who's the producer?' he asked.

'Barry Stromstein.'

'Where is he? I don't see him.' Richard said. His jaw was tight.

He sounded pissed, and Lil wondered what kind of hornet's nest was being kicked. 'I think he's meeting with the mayor to try and push through some permits for the filming.'

'My goodness, Lil Campbell,' Rachel said, 'you really do know a lot about this. And that would be because?'

'You see the hostess?' Lil asked.

'You mean the old lady in the black dress? She's sweet.'

'I think so,' Lil said, and something about hearing Ada called old made her blurt, 'She's my girlfriend.'

'Really?' Rachel's eyes widened. She looked at her brother, who clearly wanted to get out of there. 'Girlfriend as in . . . I love you, you love me?'

Lil found herself fascinated by this thin – almost to the point of cadaverous – young woman. Something about her was simultaneously engaging and off-putting. Then again, she was the one who had offered the information. And, as her curmudgeon of an editor had correctly stated, *you have to give to get.* 'We've been together for three years, but friends for a lot longer than that.'

'Fascinating . . . and right here in butt fuck Connecticut. I wonder if Mother knew.'

Lil recoiled at the vulgarity. Rachel was beautiful, but the angles of her face were a bit too sharp and her smile seemed brittle, as though applied like a layer of make-up.

Richard stared straight ahead. 'Don't.'

'Things have a way of coming out.' Rachel pressed in against her brother.

Richard looked at Lil, as though just seeing her. 'What's the show about?'

'It's a twist on the antique appraiser shows.' She sensed he wasn't really listening but wanted her to talk as a way of keeping his sister quiet. 'It's a little morbid.'

'I love morbid,' Rachel said. 'That's why they're filming in the cemetery?'

'I think so, trying to set the tone. Each week the focus will be on the estate of someone who's just died. A group of appraisers will come in and compete to settle the estate. At the end they tally it all up – that's the name of the show.'

'*Tally it all up?*' Richard asked, as though he'd tasted something sour.

'No, it's called *Final Reckoning*,' Lil said.

'Huh. It's not bad,' he admitted. 'Certainly better than a lot of the other crap out there.'

'Oh my!' Rachel gushed. She gently kicked Richard. 'This is the pilot. Oh my God, oh my God!'

Richard stared at his sister, who was pulling at his arm like a child demanding cotton candy at the fair.

'Richard.' She was staring up at him, her eyes wide, her smile luminous.

'No,' he said without hesitation.

'It's perfect. Oh my God! This is fate. I mean what are the chances?'

'Absolutely not.'

Rachel turned to Lil. 'So if this is the pilot, whose estate are they using?'

Lil felt their focus. Blue eyes and green eyes. She tried to recall from those long ago tabloids whether Lenore had used the same father for her two children. She couldn't remember. 'To be honest, I don't think they've gotten that far.'

'So they need the estate of someone who just died.' Rachel's hands flew to her lips. 'Richard, think about it.'

'Rachel, please. Don't. No, absolutely not!'

'No.' Her teasing and flirtation were replaced by something hard. 'Listen to me. And if you can't listen to me, think about our beloved mother. Everything she did was for the camera. Everything. She filmed our inseminations, brother.'

Lil shuddered at the memory. It had been groundbreaking and the kind of thing discussed in Bradley's waiting room. Lenore Parks, the modern woman, taking things into her own hands. And here, some twenty years later, were the products. She looked at them, realizing she'd not a clue as to what kinds of lives these two must have lived, like another species. She couldn't help but stare, and wonder what was passing between them.

Rachel was determined. 'You think she would object to a few of her prized possessions being hauled out for the viewing public? Really? If she were here right now, you know she'd tell you to go ahead and do it.'

'It's a bad idea.' His tone was less certain.

'The hell it is. Hear me out,' Rachel said and then, to Lil, 'I'm not supposed to know about these things, but it doesn't take a brain surgeon to realize that having our murdered mother's items come up for sale on a show like this could be a huge ratings grab.'

Richard stared at her. 'You're serious.' His gaze narrowed. 'Why?'

'Call it a whim . . .' Her voice trailed, and the corner of her lip turned up. 'Or maybe a craving. But no, the more I think about it . . . This isn't a coincidence, this is happening for a reason. And I'll tell you something else.'

Lil felt like an interloper. Yes, any reporter would give their eye teeth for this opportunity. She couldn't do that, and felt the decent thing would be to leave these two to hash out their differences. But neither had given any sense that her presence was unwanted, as though having strangers view their personal conflicts was to be expected. So she stood there, trying to piece it together.

'It's our house now, Richard.' Rachel turned to her brother. Their gazes locked.

Lil stood frozen as Rachel rested her head against Richard's chest. *This isn't how brothers and sisters normally act. Is this grief? Or . . .*

'It's our house,' she repeated. 'I want all her things gone. All those old dead people's things.' She looked up, her voice little more than a whisper. 'I want everything to be new. Everything. Please, do this for me.'

And the part said for his ears only, that Lil clearly caught.

'. . . do this for the baby.'

The part Lil agonized over and knew she must have misheard was . . . did she say 'the baby' . . . or 'our baby'? Rachel's whispered words played in her head and her gut churned – yes, these two were mourning the loss of their mother, but she'd never seen a grown brother and sister so physically close. *She couldn't have meant . . .* Her confused reverie was interrupted by Barry Stromstein's voice calling from the curb. 'Richard?'

TWELVE

B arry, no stranger to big-stakes risks in his career, could not have predicted the shit-storm waiting for him at the cemetery. What the hell were Richard and Rachel Parks doing at his location shoot? There'd been no warning. Everything he was doing was on his own say so. If pressed, he'd say that it was agreed to in his last meeting with Lenore which, while a lie, was at least plausible. He braced for the worst: getting the plug pulled and having to tell his staff that they – and he himself – were unemployed. And what would he tell Jeanine? How could he break it to her?

But this? He stood dumbfounded outside the black RV and listened to the outrageous crap spewing from Rachel Parks' mouth. Ever fast on his feet, he knew two things – if he wanted to keep his job and have *Final Reckoning* make it off the blocks he'd need not only to accept this insanity, but to make it work. The second realization, as he looked from the manically excited blonde to her stoic brother, was *she's the one with the power. How the hell did that happen?*

'Don't you think it's an amazing idea?' Rachel asked.

Barry, whose career was based on a series of fortuitous events combined with an ability to read people, was faced with a choice. Attempt to talk sense into this deranged – possibly grieving, but it sure didn't look, smell or feel like that – young woman, or nod his head and agree. 'Amazing,' he said, pumping as much enthusiasm into that single word as possible.

Rachel grabbed her brother's hand. 'We can film at the house . . . and have a tag sale. Can't you see it? All of Mom's stuff on the lawn, people pawing through her clothes, haggling over the price.' She giggled. 'Welcome to Lenore's final reckoning. She won't just roll in her grave . . .' – she nearly choked on her laughter – '. . . she'll be spinning.'

'I should get a producing credit,' she said to Barry. 'And that old woman you had in the cemetery. You sure she's right for this? I think she's too old.'

Barry winced as his fun and quirky show got shredded by this out-of-control brat. 'I don't know,' he said. 'You might want to meet her – she's different.' And was Rachel serious? Using Lenore's estate? Yes, there was supposed to be a bit of creep factor, but . . .

'We met her girlfriend,' she said. 'She explained the concept. It's brilliant. I can't believe it's not been done before.'

'Lil Campbell, I saw you talking to her. She writes a syndicated column on antiques.'

'So you knew?' Rachel asked.

'Knew what?'

'You know.' She shrugged her shoulders and spread her thumb and forefinger into an L and mouthed 'lesbians'.

Barry didn't know, having spent the morning away from his team in a series of rapidly arranged handshake-and-promise meetings with Grenville's mayor, police chief and head of the Chamber of Commerce. In light of the insanity Rachel had just proposed, having a gay hostess barely registered.

Rachel turned to her brother. 'That's kind of cute, older lesbians.'

Barry watched as she stared at Richard, who seemed unnaturally quiet. His jaw was tight, his gaze fixed on his sister. Something was going on. On Rachel's part he saw a playful edge, but the way a cat toys with a mouse, where someone's having fun and someone else is about to get their belly ripped open. He stared across at the film crew, surrounded by a circle of curious townspeople. They'd wrapped the shoot. Melanie was looking in his direction; it was easy to put words to the questions on her face.

'Rachel . . . Richard, I don't mean to interrupt,' Barry said. 'But we've got a tight schedule and we need to get to our next location.'

'Where were you going next?' Rachel asked.

'I want to film the town center and get footage of the antique shops. I've got a bunch of potential locations lined up. If we can get through two or three that would be great.'

'And the castings?' Richard asked, his first words to Barry.

'We have ads in today's paper and the mayor and Chamber of Commerce people felt they could spread the word. I'm not too worried about that; it's more a question of sorting through and finding the three or four dealers that will work on camera.'

Richard glared at Barry. He ran his hands through his hair. 'Rachel, think about this. Strangers in the house going through Mom's things. Selling them on TV.'

'It's fucking brilliant! And don't try to talk me out of this . . . and we're both going on camera.'

'Not a good idea,' he said.

'But that's the show. You heard . . . and because it's going to be Mom's stuff. I cannot believe how fucking brilliant this is! *Final Reckoning*. We'll keep it classy. This is so what Mom would want. Considering how she filmed everything else, we might want to see about taping the funeral. It could be like a Kardashian wedding.' Not waiting for her brother's response, she turned to Barry. 'I'm still not sure about that old lady. Why don't you introduce me? I mean, if this is going to be my first producing credit, I want to make sure I feel good about it. You know what I mean?'

'I do,' Barry said, wondering if it would be possible to bash Rachel's head on to a tombstone and have it look like an accident. 'I'll introduce you.' And, leaving Richard by the RV, he trailed after Rachel.

Ada sat on a weathered stone bench as the crew packed up their cables and equipment. The sun had pushed away the early morning chill and warmed her skin through the fabric of her dress. She'd spotted Lil off talking to a young couple she didn't recognize, and then lost track of her.

From the few times Ada had been involved in filming ads for Strauss's she was used to this waiting around. It gave her time to think about the past couple days, from dealing with her sixty-fifth birthday and the Medicare application to seeing Lenore's body rolled out of the building. Then there had been that manic pitch meeting and now here she was, not twenty-four hours later, dressed for a cemetery cocktail party.

Near the sleek RV she spotted Barry with the same couple who'd been talking with Lil. The young woman in her form-hugging black dress was pointing in her direction. Something about her seemed familiar as she made eye contact with Ada and headed toward her. She watched the blonde, her head high, as she passed with a smile through the hundred or so curiosity seekers. She stopped and signed a piece of paper a woman pulled from her pocketbook, which triggered a flurry of other articles for her to sign, including a girl's arm.

As one thing flowed to the next in this crazy day, Ada realized that this was Lenore's daughter, Rachel. Who, after she'd finished her impromptu signing, headed straight for her.

'You're Ada,' she said.

'I am,' Ada replied, taking in the girl who for some reason struck her as younger than nineteen. Almost like a little girl playing dress up in her mother's clothes. 'I am so sorry about your mother.'

'No need,' Rachel said. 'Unless *you* shot Lenore.'

Her joking tone threw Ada. 'Didn't know her that well.'

'I did,' Rachel said. 'Can I sit with you?'

'Of course,' and she slid to one end of the small bench. 'Are you feeling OK?' she asked.

Rachel stared back at the RV and at Barry, who'd been following her and now stood about fifteen feet away. 'I've got this,' Rachel shouted back to him. 'Go talk to my brother. Try to calm him down.'

Barry looked at Ada. His face was flushed.

There was something he was trying to communicate. As prescient as Ada was, she'd no clue what he wanted to say, though it was clear that Rachel had upset him. 'What exactly have you got?' Ada asked.

'You're direct.' Rachel said.

'It cuts down on wasted time.'

'That's true. The shortest distance between two points.'

'And you'll be coming to yours . . .' Ada's words trailed.

'Oh my God.' And Rachel shifted to face Ada. 'I thought you were just some old lady. Are those colored contacts?'

'No. They're real, how about your breasts?' Ada shot back.

'I paid real money for them, or my mother did.'

'Then they're real. So are you always this rude?' Ada asked, trying to get a feel for this young girl whose face rested in a smile, but whose words and posture spoke to deeper layers.

'I don't know what I am most of the time. It's nice here.'

'It is,' Ada said. 'I always go by this cemetery and think how peaceful it would be just to spend some time, look at the headstones. But I never do.'

'My mother was a lesbian,' Rachel blurted.

'OK,' Ada said, realizing this was not general information about Lenore. And also not the kind of thing people typically share in the first few moments of an acquaintance. She felt Rachel watching her. 'You're telling me this because?'

'I met your girlfriend . . .' Rachel's poise faltered. 'I was wrong about you. Do you have children?'

'A daughter,' Ada said, trying to piece this odd conversation together.

'I bet she's perfect.'

'We have issues.'

'Do you love her?' Rachel asked.

'Of course.' Ada sensed some powerful need inside Rachel. She tried to find a word, but there wasn't one that fit – 'hunger' perhaps, but vast. 'I don't care for her husband, and that's made things difficult.'

'Do you still talk to her?'

'All the time, and I've got two grandchildren that I adore. My grandson Aaron is probably your age.'

Rachel's smile faltered. 'I never knew my grandparents. Lenore's parents were both dead before we were born and . . . crap.'

'I don't know what to say, sweetheart.' Ada felt something tug. 'It seems wrong that I know so much about you from TV. You don't know who your father is, do you?'

Rachel bit her bottom lip. Tears spilled from her eyes, but her smiled stayed.

'I'm sorry.' Ada instinctively pressed up next to Rachel and placed her arm around her shoulder. She was shocked at how bony she felt. 'It's going to be OK.'

'It's not,' Rachel said, as tears fell. 'Nothing's OK. And I make things worse. It's what I do.'

'It is OK,' Ada said. 'You're here, it's a beautiful day. Yes, some awful things have happened. We get through those, and it's not always happy, and sometimes we mess up. Lord knows I do.'

Rachel stiffened. 'Maybe it's like that for you . . . for other people. My mother hated me. She told me, more than once, that if she'd known how I was going to turn out, she would never have had me. And even if she'd never told me, I would have known from how she treated me. It's just a fucked up fact of my life, and now that she's dead I can't do a damn thing about it.'

Ada felt the girl's sorrow and her rage. There seemed no good response. 'I'm so sorry.'

Rachel batted away her tears. 'This is why I get waterproof mascara. God, you must think I'm a total nut job.'

'I think,' Ada said, 'you're going through one of the biggest losses anyone can go through. And I think . . .' she hesitated, fearing the answer to her next question. 'Is there anyone in your life who cares for you?'

Rachel stared at the ground. 'I don't know. Maybe Richard, but I make him nervous. My shrink, but he gets paid for that. I guess Richard's the closest, and right now we're fighting.'

'About your mom's death?'

'About everything. And I can't seem to stop myself from pissing him off.'

'How's he handling your mother's death?'

She shook her head. 'I don't know. I'm such a shitty sister.' She stared at her brother, who was in a heated conversation with Barry by the black RV. 'As much as Lenore hated me, she loved him. And I love him. So he gets two helpings. Only now she's gone and I'm being a total bitch. I should go see what's happening. See if I can – as Dr Ebert puts it – take a bad situation and make it worse.'

Rachel shrugged and Ada pulled back her arm. As Rachel pushed up from the bench she swayed. 'I don't feel so good.'

Ada came to her side. 'What is it?'

Rachel doubled over. She started to dry heave.

Ada put her hand on the girl's back and rubbed gentle circles.

'It's OK.' She turned to see if maybe Richard Parks wanted to
come help his sister. As she spotted him at the RV she also noticed
several cameras and cell phones pointed in their direction. She felt
a surge of rage. How could people be so thoughtless? 'Rachel, is
it passing?'

'Yeah.'

'Why don't I take you to your brother?'

'Trying to get rid of me?'

'No, I just think you should be with whatever family you have.'

'I'm good,' she said, standing up. She caught Ada's expression,
and then looked at the onlookers who were blatantly filming them.
'I don't even notice any more.' She pasted on a smile and turned
to the cameras. 'This is nothing. These are just some locals who'll
Instagram pictures on Facebook and Twitter of Rachel Parks puking
in the cemetery. Try getting chased down the highway at three in
the morning by real paparazzi. You know,' she said, 'as I think about
it, they didn't come out here so much when we were growing up.
Like Connecticut is off limits. It's what I want. A whole different
life. A place where kids can grow up and know their mother loves
them, where someone's not always shoving a camera in their face.
You have to think about that, Ada.'

'About what?' Surprised to hear the girl use her name.

'You're going to be on TV, and this show is going to catch a lot
of buzz. People will want to know about you, about your girlfriend.
If you get famous enough, it goes further. Nothing is private, just
what's inside your head.'

'So that's it,' Ada said softly, as they headed toward the RV.
'That's why you smile.'

The side of Rachel's mouth twisted up. 'You're quick. I bet you
could give Dr Ebert a run for it. So let me ask you this. My smile
is my armor; do you know what I'm protecting?'

'Rachel,' Ada said, as Richard left a flustered-looking Barry by
the RV to join them. 'We've just met, so I don't want to pretend to
be something I'm not. So take what I say with many grains of salt.
But what I sense beneath your smile is suffering, and I'm very sorry
that you have to go through that.'

'What's going on?' Richard asked. He looked from Rachel to Ada.

Ada couldn't help but stare at the handsome young man, his
emotions hot and on the surface. The two of them like polar opposites,

her with a smiling facade and him flushed, angry and possibly scared. *That's odd*, she thought. *Scared of what?*

Rachel's smile for her brother seemed a bit bigger than the one for the camera-toting locals.

'Are you OK?' he asked. 'Were you sick?'

'I'm fine. You look like your head's about to explode. What just happened?'

'I was having a talk with that producer.'

'You mean Barry,' Rachel said. 'And considering I'm going to insist on a producing credit for this myself, you should let me know what your concerns are.'

Richard's mouth opened and then shut. He reminded Ada of a fish gasping for air.

'Just spit it out,' Rachel said.

'He had no right to do this!' Richard said. 'None of this was approved. This Barry Stromstein decided to take advantage of . . . the situation and green-light his own show.'

'So,' she said. 'You and I both know it's a weird enough idea to catch on. And if we're talking about Mom and the situation . . . for God's sake just say it. A day after our mother is shot dead, we're in a cemetery filming a new reality show. The media is going to scoop this up. Now stop, Richard, and think about Mom. Just ask yourself: what would Lenore do? And you know the answer.'

He stared at her.

'You really loved her and she really loved you. Now, I'll tell you something she loved more.'

He nodded. 'I know . . . this.'

Ada was fascinated by the rapid shift in his demeanor. Like his sister had stuck a pin in his anger, it all ran out and was replaced by grief.

'I don't want to do this here.' He sank to the stone bench.

Rachel rested her hands on her brother's shoulders. 'You see,' she said to Ada. 'This is what's coming.' She looked at their camera-phone-toting audience, who were maintaining the seventy-five foot perimeter the film crew had set. 'Mom thrived on this. She didn't exist if she wasn't being filmed.'

'But this?' he said. 'Rachel, it's in bad taste.'

'So? Our mother was the queen of bad taste. That was Lenore's shtick. And I know you don't like to hear this . . . she taped our inseminations. Our mother was a pioneer in tasteless TV. Her talent was that she made it all look elegant.' Rachel looked at Ada. '"On today's show"' – her impression of Lenore was chilling, from how she held her head to her carefully clipped syllables – '"we'll examine how to get knocked up using common items found in your kitchen, and then later we'll practice the art of ikebana, Japanese flower arrangement."'

Richard snorted.

'You know I'm right.'

'Maybe.'

'No maybe about it. So stop ripping that Barry a new one and wrap your head around this, because no matter what you think, Mom would fucking love this.'

Richard Parks' tirade played in Barry's head. Intellectually, he knew the man was right and that his mother had just been murdered. Still, having to stand there and take it as the twenty-two-year-old chastised him, and within earshot of the crew: *'You had no approval, no authorization. What the fuck were you thinking?'* And, twenty-two years old or not, the man lasered in to his deepest fears: *'You think this will save your job when over twenty producers and their staff will get their marching orders on Monday?'*

He climbed into the RV, grateful to find it empty. Through darkly tinted windows he watched Rachel and Richard. They'd probably already told Ada she was too old and off the show, essentially what they were telling him. The crew were packed and waiting for directions from either him or Melanie. They knew something was going down and no one wanted to make a move. Not like him. He'd taken his shot . . . it had been a long one, and now it looked like it would fall short of the hoop.

His cell buzzed. He saw Jeanine's number. He'd gotten home late and left before she was up. His last image her gorgeous profile and flaming hair fanned against white linen. He'd peeked in on Ashley in her thousand-shades-of-pink bedroom. His beautiful girls safe and snug, having no clue as to how tenuous their lives really were. 'Hi babe.'

'What's wrong?'

'That bad?'

'Barry, the day you can hide how you feel from me is the day we're done. The shooting's not going well?'

Ever since he'd met Jeanine on the set of *Model Behavior*, a show that played with people's expectations of beauty, he'd struggled to feel worthy of her. From the moment he first saw her at the contestant auditions, he knew this farm girl from Iowa was different. Her head-turning beauty reflected a strong and loving woman. Throughout the taping of *Model Behavior* he'd waited and watched. No one could be that perfect. She'd never stooped to the back-stabbing shenanigans that were fueled by his team to boost ratings. On screen, she moved with the grace of a ballerina. When people naturally asked how much dance training she'd had, she'd reply 'None, unless you count mucking stalls, riding horses and hunting down stray cattle.'

As the season had progressed, he'd fallen in love. He remembered the moment that he knew. It was during a challenge where the models had to do a photo shoot with Arabian stallions. The stable they had used had assured him that the selected animals were docile and that the models/contestants had nothing to fear. The day had been a farce of high-strung young women pitching fits about the smells and the oppressive heat. But not Jeanine. Unbidden, she had attached herself to the trainers and coached the other contestants in how to work with the animals. When it was her turn, she was the only one to put a horse through its paces, her long hair unbound, her impractical gown billowing across the animal's flank. As she'd passed him at a full gallop on the black stallion she'd turned, smiled and blown him a kiss. In that moment he'd known.

Since then, everything he did was for her, and then for her and Ashley. How could he admit that it was falling into the crapper?

'Where are you?' she asked.

'Connecticut.'

'OK. Were you planning on coming home tonight?'

'I don't know.'

'Barry, you're scaring me. What's going on?'

Perched on the edge, his career about to tank, he knew this moment had to come. The moment where it all turned to dust and Jeanine would realize she'd married a loser. This was like the contrived situations they ran the models through on *Model Behavior* to see if their outward beauty matched their inner morals or if it was all just on the surface. 'I think Richard Parks is going to pull the plug; I made some decisions, and . . . Jeanine, it's not going well and we need to brace for the worst.' He waited, hearing only silence.

'Then I need to be there,' she said.

It was not what he expected.

'I don't see what—'

She interrupted, 'I'm grabbing Ashley. Just give me an address. I need to be with you, Barry. Please.'

With a numbness in his belly he looked toward the cemetery. Richard, Rachel and Ada were heading back toward the RV. Everything felt wrong. How did he wind up, at thirty-eight, in a cemetery in Connecticut with his future, and that of his family, in the hands of a pair of spoiled socialites? 'It's a town called Grenville, just south of Lenore's place in Shiloh. There's really no reason to come. Whatever's going to happen—'

'Barry, listen to me. Don't let them get to you. You are an extraordinarily talented man. They are lucky to have you. You are a wonderful father and the man I love. Do not let them get to you. I'll be there as fast as I can.'

Her words helped, but in his head he heard the theme music for *Model Behavior* that got played when a contestant was eliminated. He knew the score. Women like Jeanine didn't stick with men like Barry when their careers flew apart. That was just the way it was.

THIRTEEN

'We're going to the Parks' mansion in the morning,' Ada said from the dining room table. It was eight o'clock and they were only now sitting down to dinner. She was still in the skirt and blouse from her last outfit of the day, a 1970s green Chanel suit. The pumps which had caused her ankles to burn for the last three hours were now replaced with L.L. Bean Wicked Good slippers. Across from her sat Rose. And on the end was Ada's grandson, Aaron, who'd arrived unexpectedly.

'Can I come?' Aaron asked.

'You have classes,' Ada said, feeling a mix of emotions as she took stock of Aaron. He was tall, the only good thing her vile son-in-law had contributed to the gene pool. His hair was dark blond with floppy bangs she wished he'd cut, and he had hazel eyes like his mother's.

'Everyone cuts,' he said, with the authority of a second semester University of Connecticut freshman. 'Please, this is going to be more educational than sitting in the auditorium with a hundred grade-grubbing pre-meds watching a PowerPoint about shark cartilage.'

'He has a point,' Rose said, 'and besides, he could take me too. I wouldn't mind seeing my daughter in all her glory.'

'You're not kidding,' Lil added from inside the galley kitchen, which had a pass-through window and counter into the dining room. 'It's as if Ada was born for this.'

'It's just like having a conversation, only I think of the cameras as people,' Ada said.

'And you used to do those ads for Strauss's,' her mother added.

'You liked it?' Lil asked.

'Of course she did,' Rose said. 'Ada's always been a ham.'

'Thanks, Mom.'

'Just being honest,' Rose said. 'It's so sad about Lenore. It was all over the news today. I even saw the two of you.'

'Really?' Lil asked, as she pushed just-from-the-oven sweet potatoes and roasted vegetables across the granite pass-through.

Aaron got up to serve. 'It was the number one item on the Internet,' he said. 'Lots of YouTube videos. Everyone must have had their camera phone out. So, you actually saw her getting wheeled away. You realize the two of you are like murder magnets.'

'Aaron, that's a terrible thing to say.' Ada pushed a trivet in his direction.

'Not if it's true,' Rose commented. 'Regardless, let's accept the fact that you and your girlfriend are modern angels of death. I'd say it's just Grenville, but apparently your killer touches extend to Manhattan. Who do you think did it?'

Lil, while plating the roast chicken (dark meat for Ada and Aaron and white for her and Rose), commented, 'People didn't like her.'

'Speaking of which,' Ada said, 'I met her children.'

Rose stared at her. 'Oh my goodness, you didn't.'

'No way!' Aaron added. 'I leave the two of you alone for a few months and just look what happens. Maybe I should transfer to

West Conn and commute. Who'd have thought life in a retirement community was more exciting than living on campus?'

'I met them both.' Ada got up and grabbed the plates as Lil passed them through. 'And so did Lil.'

'Briefly,' Lil commented. 'It was odd.'

'Agreed,' Ada said. 'Even taking into account the fact that their mother had just been murdered.'

'They stand to gain the most,' Rose said, taking a sip of her evening sherry, which she insisted her cardiologist had told her was medicinal. 'Financially, at any rate. Fortunately for me it's my daughter who's loaded.'

'Yes, Mother, that's the only reason you're still breathing.'

Rose raised an eyebrow. 'It's not to say you haven't tried, dear.'

'Rose,' Lil said, putting a skinless breast in front of Ada's mother. 'Your daughter did not set that fire.'

'So you say. And?' She looked at Ada.

'What?'

'Rachel and Richard,' Aaron prompted. 'What were they like? What did you talk about? Details.'

As Lil spooned out the sides, Ada filled them in about her day. 'You going to do a column on this?' she asked.

'Of course. It's a no-brainer. The Lenore angle, while admittedly gruesome, might get me some additional papers. It's a great topic and, with you as the show's hostess, I'm assuming I'll get any good scoops. Even Barry came straight out and asked me to do it.'

'Who's Barry?' Aaron asked.

'The producer,' Ada said. 'I'm not sure my agent would approve.'

'Agent?' Lil asked.

'Apparently I need one,' Ada said. 'Rachel Parks gave me the name and number of Lenore's. I called him this afternoon, because it seems that doing what I did today is almost illegal.'

'How's that?' Rose asked.

'Working without a contract. The crew kept asking me stuff I couldn't answer, and so I referred them to Melanie or Barry. It's just everything has happened so fast, which is odd. I got the distinct sense from Richard Parks that this show didn't go through the right channels. He was pretty upset about it. And that's not even the weirdest.'

'Which was?' Lil prompted.

'Rachel wants to use Lenore's estate for the first show.'

The others stopped eating. 'You're kidding?' Lil asked.

'Oh no. She was serious, and one thing's quite clear. The girl is not stable.'

'I think she's pregnant,' Lil added.

'What?' Aaron said. 'That's a scoop. Some tabloid would give big bucks for that.'

'Interesting,' Ada said. 'That explains her throwing up in the cemetery. So about my new agent, Max Titelbaum. At first he said he wasn't taking new clients and was going to pass me along to an associate. Then Rachel got on the phone. I wouldn't say she blackmailed him . . .' Ada paused. 'No, that *is* what she did. Talked about her mother's residuals, and handling her royalties posthumously. The girl may be mad, but she's sharp. By the time she got off the phone, he was my agent. He told me not to worry about anything but to refer all the business to him and he'd vet the contracts and handle the negotiations. I told him that I didn't really need the money. His response was,' she paused again, '"Don't say that. Don't ever say that." As though I'd somehow voiced something forbidden.'

'Of course,' Rose said. 'You're talking about his fifteen percent. The more you get, the more he gets. It's a perfect arrangement. It's why you always gave your sales help commissions. The more they sold the more you made.'

'True, money is a great motivator. But he said something else . . . that while *I* may not need the money, how much he's able to get sets my worth. That's not exactly how he said it, but it's as if there's a hierarchy based on how much you're able to command.'

Rose sucked the last drops of her sherry. She looked at Aaron, who got up to get her a refill. 'So how much are you worth?'

'I don't know yet,' Ada admitted. 'He told me to go ahead with filming the pilot, but anything related to money or contracts, I'm to refer back to him.' She looked at Lil. 'I did ask about Lenore.'

'And?'

'He started with a canned response, how sad he was, what a great lady, good friend, but what I really wanted to know was why a star as big as Lenore would still need an agent. Apparently, Max was with Lenore back in the beginning. He was her one and only agent for thirty-something years; that says something.'

'On both ends,' Lil added. 'Because I think you're right, at some point Lenore didn't need an agent. I'm sure LPP has more than enough entertainment lawyers to handle any kind of contract.'

Aaron topped up Rose's sherry glass.

'Mother,' Ada said, 'will we need to send you to rehab?'

'Your mother is old, dear,' Rose said. 'If I want to be a ninety-five-year-old lush, it's my prerogative. So about your agent and his fifteen percent of Lenore. That's a lot of money, millions. Why would she keep him? He's got to be doing something.'

'True,' Ada said, 'and I don't have a good grasp on what any of these people do. Though it is fascinating.'

'See,' Aaron said, 'this is much better than the life cycle of some jellyfish.'

Before Ada could respond, the phone rang.

'Let the machine get it,' Lil said. They ate and listened as the phone rang four times and then Lil's familiar outgoing message came on. A man with the hint of a British accent started to speak. 'Hi Lil, Ada, it's Tolliver Jacobs, I was hoping to get in touch with you. I understand you have something to do with the taping of the show they're doing in town . . .' He left his number. 'I hope to hear from you, thanks.'

'Not in this lifetime!' Ada said.

'He's not that bad,' Aaron said.

'He's a thief!' Ada shot back.

'Aren't they all?' Lil replied.

'Who's Tolliver Jacobs?' Rose asked.

'One of the local antique dealers, and it's a long story,' Ada said.

'You know,' Lil added, as she listened to the machine and realized Tolliver hadn't hung up, as though he knew they were screening calls, 'if it weren't for him' – she looked at Ada – 'we might still be just friends.'

'Do you want to talk to him?' Ada asked.

Lil glanced at the phone. 'I'm hoping to get a series of articles out of this show. I might as well.' She got out of her chair and grabbed the phone.

'Put it on speaker,' Rose said. 'I want to hear.'

'Hello?'

'Lil?'

'Hi Tolliver.' She looked at Ada, who was making faces.

'Lil, I'm glad I caught you, although I'm wondering if maybe I need to speak to Ada.'

'About?'

'The ad in the evening edition of *The Register*.'

'I've no clue what you're talking about.'

'For the TV show they're filming,' he added.

The line clicked. 'Tolliver, hold on, I've got someone on the other line.' Before he could respond, she pressed to get the incoming call.

'Mrs Strauss?' A woman's voice.

'No, this is Lillian Campbell. Who am I speaking to?'

'Lil, it's Belle. How are you?'

'Good,' wondering why her one-time employer at the Grenville Antique Center, a sprawling multi-dealer shop, would be calling. She grabbed a pen and paper from next to the phone. 'Belle, I've got Tolliver Jacobs on the other line. Can I call you back?'

'That sneaky bastard.'

'Excuse me?'

'He's calling for the same thing.'

'The ad in *The Register*?' Lil asked, noticing Ada had left the table.

'Yes; please call me right back. And I'd be much better than Tolliver. So what that he's handsome and has that stupid British accent. He's from Grenville for God's sake! It's all a put on.'

'I'll call you right back,' Lil promised, as Ada reappeared with the evening paper. Lil clicked back to Tolliver. 'Sorry, it was one of your colleagues.'

'Not surprised. Could I speak to Ada?'

Ada shook her head in the negative.

'She's not available right now,' and Lil read over the full-page ad that Ada was holding up.

Open Casting
Lenore Parks Productions
– Final Reckoning –

We are actively scheduling auditions for FINAL RECKONING, *a new competition-based reality show to be filmed in and around Grenville. We are looking for experienced, articulate and established antique dealers interested in being on-screen experts for a new show.*

Applicants should be familiar with estate liquidations and come prepared with a headshot and résumé. We are seeking experts who are comfortable on camera and who have broad-based knowledge of antiques and collectibles, as well as specialty areas of in-depth expertise.

'Do you know when she will be available?' Tolliver asked.

Lil read the last paragraph where it gave a number for people to call and another for faxing headshots and résumés. 'Tolliver, Ada doesn't have anything to do with casting the show.'

'It's just . . .'

'What?'

'Everyone knows that she's involved. We all saw her with that film crew. I'd really like to get on this show, and with how things got left—'

'You mean when you deliberately undervalued a two-million dollar painting that belonged to a friend of ours?'

'I didn't know it was worth that much. And in the end the heirs got the correct amount.'

Ada rolled her eyes.

'I'll tell her you called.'

'Lil, it was a horrible time for me,' the accent now pure New England. 'If I made a mistake I'm sorry. Business has not been good, not for any of us. I need this.'

'Tolliver, I don't think Ada will have anything to do with who gets picked for the show.'

'But she might,' he said, 'and I think if my name were in the mix—'

Lil's focus was pulled by the ringing of a phone from the living room.

Ada mouthed, 'It's my cell.'

And then a knock at the door.

'It's like Grand Central,' Rose remarked from the table, her sherry glass once again full.

'Tolliver,' Lil said, 'I've got to go. I'll let Ada know you called.' And she hung up.

The knock at the door was followed by three rings on the bell, and a woman's voice. 'Hello! Lil? Ada?'

'Do you want me to get that?' Aaron asked, getting up from the table.

Lil followed him down the hall as Ada retrieved her cell from the living room.

Through the small windows on the side of the door Lil saw their across-the-walk neighbor Bernice Framm holding a tray of cookies. *What now?* she wondered. She opened the door. 'Hi Bernice.'

'Lil.' Bernice held out the cookies. 'I saw the light on and thought I'd bring these over.'

'Thanks, Bernice.' Lil accepted the tray, noting at least four types of home-made treats through the cellophane wrap. On the best of days, Bernice was barely civil to Lil, but baked goods? This was unprecedented.

'My pleasure,' Bernice said, giving Aaron a tight smile and looking expectantly down the hall.

Lil felt trapped. The cookies were clearly a ploy to get the two things Bernice lived for – information and power. As the secretary to Grenville's mayors for over three decades, Bernice had reveled in her role as gatekeeper. It was well known that, if she didn't like you, applications, building permits, variances and various other bits of small-town commerce could become lost. As one of the seven members of the Pilgrim's Progress Owners' Association, Bernice had again worked her way into a position of local power.

'These look delicious,' Lil said, weighing the pros and cons. 'Would you like to come in for some coffee?'

Bernice hesitated, her attention pulled by unfamiliar voices coming from over the crest of the steep walk that led to their cluster of condos. 'It's getting busy around here,' she remarked. 'Are you really going to be on TV?' she asked, keeping her voice low.

'Ada is,' Lil said, realizing that Bernice's curiosity was at war with her fear of being associated with her and Ada.

'It's very exciting. Can you talk about it?'

Lil glanced behind Bernice as Melanie Taft appeared, one hand holding her cell and her other pulling a wheeled legal-style briefcase. 'I'm right outside your condo,' she said into the phone. 'Hi Lil.' She glanced at Bernice. 'Hi, I'm Melanie Taft.'

'Bernice Framm, I'm Lil and Ada's neighbor.'

'Fantastic! This whole town.'

Lil stared at the perky assistant producer. It was getting on to ten p.m. and the young woman's eyes were wide and bright.

'We like it,' Bernice said, her body positioned between the door and Melanie.

'Lil,' Melanie said, 'I've got a stack of headshots, I was hoping you and Ada could talk me through them. You know who's for real and who we maybe shouldn't waste our time on.'

'You're with the TV show,' Bernice said. 'I saw that ad in the paper. You mean people have already responded?'

Melanie laughed. 'Cookies! I love cookies.'

'I made them,' Bernice said, taking the plate from Lil and pulling off the wrap. 'Here, help yourself.'

Melanie shoved her cell into a pocket and snatched one of Bernice's oatmeal raisin cookies. 'Love these! So good. And yeah, I grabbed a stack off the fax. Would you mind, Lil? I know it's late, but if we can go through this batch it'll give us a jump in the morning. I was hoping maybe to pick a few and do some tests.'

'Sure,' Lil said.

Oblivious to tension or any past history between Lil and Bernice, Melanie grabbed a brownie and a shortbread and wheeled her case into Lil's condo.

Bernice's curiosity won the day and she followed, as though popping into Lil and Ada's home was something she did all the time. 'I might be able to help,' she added. 'I was the mayor's secretary forever.'

'Awesome,' Melanie said. 'Hi Ada, sorry to do this, and I want you to get as much rest as possible. And I have to say,' she glanced at Rose, Aaron and their half-eaten dinner, 'the scenes we shot this morning were awesome.'

Like some overwound toy, she jogged to the table. 'Hi, I'm Melanie,' and she introduced herself to Ada's mother and grandson. 'So, where can we work?' She opened the oversized briefcase and pulled out stacks of faxed headshots and résumés.

Aaron cleared away the dishes.

'What are we doing?' Rose asked, buzzed on sherry and ready for the evening's entertainment.

'Looking for talent,' Melanie said, dropping a stack on to the dining room table. 'I figured you'd know who some of these were.'

The phone rang. Lil scanned the caller ID. 'This is crazy.'

'Who is it?' Ada asked.

'The Greenery,' she said.

'Makes sense,' Ada replied. 'The Auchinstrasses.'

Bernice rolled her eyes. 'I bet it's Frieda trying to get the inside track.' She turned to Melanie. 'They're not real Grenville. But they want everyone to think they go back to the Pilgrims.'

'You might want to turn off the ringer,' Melanie suggested. 'And I'd recommend keeping your cell number just for family, and for me and Barry, of course. And trust me, after this week we'll be like family. So, let's look at some pictures.'

Lil, whose family did go back generations, and Bernice, who had intimate knowledge of most of the antique dealers, helped whittle Melanie's pile down.

Bernice was in her element as she picked up picture after picture, dropping tantalizing bits of small-town gossip. 'Ugh. You don't want this one,' she said, holding the résumé of one of the higher end dealers in town.

'Why?' Lil asked, having known the man for decades.

'I don't like to speak bad about people . . . big lush.'

'Don't need that,' Melanie said. 'How about this one?' holding up a photo of a handsome man with thick blond hair and an angular face. She read the name off the résumé she'd clipped to the back. 'Harrison Baker.'

'He must be new,' Bernice said. 'Does it say where his shop is?'

'Four two two Main Street.'

'The Brixton Building,' Bernice said. 'There's three shops in there, and one's a multi-dealer. He's probably in that.'

'He's cute,' Aaron said.

Bernice looked at Ada's grandson. She shook her head.

Ada chuckled. 'Yes, Bernice, everyone is gay.'

'I'm not,' Rose said.

'I am,' offered Melanie.

Bernice looked at the attractive young woman with her short hair and tattooed arms. 'I didn't say a thing.'

'No,' Ada said, 'but you thought it.'

'So how many of these do you think you're going to get?' Aaron asked, trying to step in between his grandmother and Bernice.

'Thousands,' Melanie said, putting the photo and résumé of Harrison Baker into the small stack of possibles. 'And normally it's not something the producers, or assistant producers, get into. LPP has on-staff casting agents for this. But since we're moving at warp speed to get something taped, today I am a casting agent. I do have the credential, so if anyone wants to make a stink, we're covered.'

'But there aren't nearly that many dealers in town,' Ada said.

'Doesn't matter,' Melanie said. 'I can tell you that back at the hotel there's probably three hundred more of these on the fax. It'll be over a thousand by the morning. Half of them from people who don't even come close to what we're looking for. They'll all think that we're going to make an exception because they're so special, and we just need to give them a shot. The reality . . . they go straight into the trash.'

'That's harsh,' Aaron said.

'It's a harsh business, Aaron.' Melanie said. 'It still amazes me how brutal it gets. End of the day, it's a waste of precious time returning their calls.'

'You OK?' Ada asked her. 'You must be ready to drop.'

'I'm fine,' Melanie said, pulling photo after photo and dropping them into the discard pile as she kept a running commentary. 'Too old; too weird-looking; who the hell thought this was a good picture?'

By midnight Melanie's stack was down to less than two dozen, all Grenville dealers. 'Ladies,' and, looking across at Aaron, 'and gentleman, I think we're done.'

'And we'll get to the other few hundred in the morning?' Aaron asked.

'Goddess, no,' she said.

'What happens to them?' Lil asked.

'We hold on to them until we're sure we've got what we need, and then we dump 'em.'

'But what if there's someone better in that stack?' Bernice asked.

Before Melanie could answer, her cell buzzed. 'It's Barry.' She took the call.

'You sitting down?' he asked.

'Uh crap,' she said. 'They pulled the plug. What are we going to do?'

'Melanie. Listen. Richard Parks is dead. They've taken Rachel into custody.'

'Oh, God! What? How?' She stared at Ada and then at the others. 'This is horrible! So, we're done then.'

Barry paused. 'No. Go ahead with the auditions. We've come this far. If someone wants to pull the plug, they're going to have to come down here and do it themselves.'

FOURTEEN

R achel stared at her hands, and then at the clock sunk into the cinderblock wall of her cell. It was two a.m. 'This is a police station,' she said aloud, the reality of her voice the only thing keeping her from completely losing it. 'This is not a hospital.' *Because if this were a hospital,* she reasoned, *I'd be in a gown and not an orange jumpsuit.* She looked at the dome camera overhead. *Maybe it is a hospital.* It was impossible to focus. 'Someone needs to call my brother,' she shouted, knowing that was the thing to do. She screamed, 'Call my brother!' She rattled off his cell from memory. They had to call Richard; he'd figure this out. *'How much did you drink?' But you didn't . . . you're not drinking. Why is that? You like to drink . . . maybe that's what happened. But pregnant women don't drink, don't smoke. Where's Richard?*

'I want my brother!' she screamed at the tiny wire-laced window in the steel door. 'I want Richard!'

She heard a door open. Richard would come, and he'd take care of this. It was what he did. Maybe because she'd been such a bitch to him he'd keep her waiting. She deserved that. Her thoughts touched something dangerous. She stared at her hands. *Why are my nails clipped so short?* The edges of her fingers felt raw; someone had clipped her nails, and the pads were sticky.

Voices were coming closer.

'Richard?'

She heard a woman on the other side, and a man. She couldn't make out their words. 'Please,' she cried out, 'get Richard!'

The door opened.

Rachel looked up to see a short woman with tightly curled salt-and-pepper hair; *like a poodle*, she thought. Behind her stood a tall woman, her reddish-gold hair in a ponytail, and next to her a pudgy man with sparse blond hair and a shiny pink scalp. They were staring at her.

'Where's Richard? Have you called him?' She smiled. 'Whatever I did, he'll fix it.' *Why are they staring?*

The woman with the poodle hair came in. She settled next to Rachel on the edge of the platform bed. 'Ms Parks, my name is Detective Perez. I'm with the state's major crime division. That's my partner, Detective Jamie Plank. You don't have to say anything, Rachel. Your lawyer will be here soon.'

She remembered someone reciting the Miranda Warning. It wasn't the first time she'd heard it.

'Why did they cut my nails?' she asked, looking into poodle woman's dark eyes. 'What's happening? Why can't I remember?'

The woman looked skeptical. She shook her head and turned back to the two standing in the door. 'Chief Simpson, I'd strongly recommend placing someone outside her door.'

'We've got her on video,' the heavyset man replied.

'Don't risk it.'

'You think she'll hurt herself?' he asked.

'I'm not suicidal,' Rachel said. 'Not right now.' *Maybe that's what this was about. It looks like a jail but maybe it is a hospital and they just want me to say that I won't hurt myself, and they'll let me go. And why isn't Richard here? Is he that mad at me? I'll make it up to him. I shouldn't have told him like that. What is wrong with me? Why do I always fuck things up?* 'Have you called my brother?' she asked. 'Do you need his number?'

'Rachel.' The poodle-haired woman was speaking.

Why is she looking at me that way? She's going to say something bad. I won't listen. I can't hear this.

'Rachel,' she repeated. 'Your brother is dead. You called nine one one a little after eleven p.m. Do you remember that? Do you remember calling? On the phone you told the operator it was your fault. Do you remember?'

I can't hear this. I won't listen. I'll go away. Like a turtle into its shell, she drew a wall around herself. Richard called it her armor;

no one and nothing could get through. Dr Ebert said it was a dissociative state. He said she was good at it, the best he'd ever seen.
Not her mother's criticism, or the paralyzing fear that now surrounded
her, could pierce her shell. The poodle lady was gone and there was
only fuzz. She closed her eyes. *Richard will come*, she told herself.
He always does.

Detective Mattie Perez stared at Rachel Parks. The girl was shutting
down in a way she'd seen before with rape victims and others who'd
been through severe trauma. And Mattie hadn't missed the scars on
the undersides of Rachel's wrists.

Yet facts were facts: the girl had been found with her brother
Richard, his blood on her hands, and there was a small caliber pistol,
quite possibly the same one used to kill Lenore Parks, in the dead
man's bedroom. As with Lenore, it had been a single bullet, but
this time at close range from the front. He'd been shot in the heart.

There was ample motive and means. It could be a slam dunk.
Not to mention the possible nine one one confession: *'My brother's
been shot! It's my fault. It's all my fault.'* Unless . . . she stared at
the blonde, her hair like a curtain over her face, her body curled
tight. Was this the opening salvo in a not-guilty-by-reason-of-mental-
defect defense? From what little she knew of Rachel Parks – wealthy,
privileged, disturbed and a first year pre-law student – she didn't
want to jump to conclusions. The girl had brains, and if you want
to off your mother and brother and do a minimum of time . . . *Is
she that good an actress?* Maybe not a slam dunk.

She'd been paged at home, the Middletown dispatcher unaware
of Detective Perez's history with Grenville. 'Kevin.' She looked at
Chief Simpson, remembering how she'd first met him. It was something
of a surprise to find he'd replaced the prior police chief, Hank
Morgan, who was eminently qualified and unfortunately corrupt,
in that small-town 'it's just how we do business' kind of way.
She thought of something Hank once said about Kevin: *In the
valley of the blind man, the one-eyed man is king.* 'Kevin, you need
someone to sit with her. She's very high risk.'

'OK,' he said, not offended by the reminder. 'I'll make sure of
it. You going to the house?'

'Yeah.' She got off the bed and, away from Rachel, whispered,
'I need to see the body before they move it.'

'I'll meet you there,' he said and, before she could say it again, 'and don't worry, I'll get a sitter.'

The ride north of Grenville to the Parks' estate in Shiloh took eight minutes. It was a clear night with a half moon and a country sky bright with stars. Jamie drove while Mattie accessed the case file for Lenore's murder. 'No weapon was recovered,' she said.

'So what does that mean for jurisdiction if the one used on Richard Parks turns out to be the same gun?'

'Good question. Answer is, it depends.'

'On?' the young detective asked.

'Whether Rachel confesses. That would be easiest. Just take our time, make sure all the proper psych evaluations take place and see if she tries for an insanity plea.'

'It's a tough standard,' Jamie said.

'Yes and no, but she's doing a good job so far. No attempt to conceal anything. Acting nuttier than a fruitcake. If she keeps it up . . .'

'Interesting,' Jamie said, as she turned down the private road to the Parks Mansion. 'So on the surface it's text book. She schizophrenic or something?' She slowed as they approached a quaint two story red-brick building close to the road and next to an open security gate. The lights were on. 'This can't be it . . .'

'No,' Mattie said. 'It's some sort of guest house, maybe for the help. And no to Rachel being schizo, at least not likely. It's something else. At the very least, she's a cutter.'

'You got to wonder what's wrong with these people. With that kind of money, you'd think they'd be happy.'

'You never know,' Mattie said as they rounded a curve and got their first look at Lenore's imposing weathered-brick mansion, four stories high with white-mullioned windows and copper gutters. Shaped like a U with two large wings, it reminded the detective of something out of Masterpiece Theatre. This wasn't a house for real people . . . at least not for any she knew. The surrounding trees were artfully illuminated and edged by walls of pruned azaleas, their peach and purple blooms muddied like bruises in the artificial light.

The road ended in a circular drive where two of the state's crime scene vans were parked by a tiered marble fountain. Behind them was the Medical Examiner's Bronco and three Grenville cruisers.

'What do you think a place like this goes for?' Jamie asked.

'Millions, no idea how many.'

'And this is just one of her houses.'

'Yeah.'

'In *The Post* they said Lenore's estate is close to a billion dollars. So if the son is dead and the daughter goes to jail, or gets locked up in Whiting Forensic, who gets the money?' Jamie asked.

'Excellent question,' Mattie said. 'Always keep your eye on the cash.'

Jamie pulled in behind a Grenville cruiser and the two got out.

Mattie cringed as a familiar male voice called to her. 'Detective Perez, we really must stop meeting like this.'

'Hello Arvin,' Mattie said.

The short, fat and balding Medical Examiner stamped out his cigarette and headed toward them. 'If it isn't the two loveliest detectives in the state of Connecticut.'

'You know that could be considered sexual harassment,' Jamie said.

'Only if you object and tell me to stop,' he said.

'I object, please stop,' Mattie said.

'Naah.' He waggled his eyebrows. 'You want to look at a dead body?'

Mattie chuckled. Arvin was a lech, but over the years he'd been helpful and never crossed the line into being truly creepy. 'It's why we're here.'

'We have so much in common.' He led them up the broad stone steps. 'If only you could see beyond my ageing exterior to my inner beauty.'

Mattie ignored his prattle as she took in her surroundings. The house, she realized, was something of a fraud. Her prior outings to Grenville, where the antiques industry was king, had educated her. The built-to-impress Georgian-style mansion was a reproduction, likely built by some wealthy Manhattanite at the turn of the twentieth century.

The front door was wide open. Mattie, Jamie and Arvin paused on the threshold and put paper booties over their shoes.

'Holy crap!' Jamie said, as they took in the grand hall with its sweeping double staircase and thirty foot coffered ceilings. In front of the stairs was a massive marble table, its surface a Pompeian mosaic of semi-precious stones.

'He's upstairs,' Arvin said, unfazed by the extravagant house. At the second floor landing he led them past a photographer who was documenting blood spatter in the carpet. 'This way,' and he brought them into a sitting room that could have been featured in *L* magazine if it hadn't been for the dead man lying curled on the floor in nothing but a pair of baby blue boxers. 'He was shot a single time.' Arvin knelt beside Richard Parks' muscular body and pulled a pair of blue polypropylene gloves from his back pocket. 'This,' pointing to an area of dried blood between the man's shoulder blades, 'is your exit wound. And this . . .' he pulled out a small LED flashlight and handed it to Jamie. 'Hold that,' and he repositioned himself on the front side of the body. 'See, right there? Just right of the sternum is a powder burn, so very close range. I'd say no more than three feet.'

'But the blood in the hall?' Mattie asked, letting her senses drink in the scene. She wondered how much had already been altered by the crime scene team. She inhaled deeply. She'd smelled this before. *Right, Rachel's perfume.* She looked toward an open door at the back of the room. It led to a bedroom. Without touching anything she peered through. The four poster bed was unmade, the bedding rumpled and pillows mashed. *Someone was having fun.* 'He wasn't shot here.'

'No, he took a long walk.' Arvin said.

'Show me.'

Arvin got up and led them back through the house. Mattie's gaze took in the lavish surroundings, like walking through an antique store where everything was well beyond her detective's salary. She noted the work that the crime scene team had already done. The trail of blood droplets protected by small white cones. They led from the suite where Richard was found to a second, almost identical set of rooms in the opposite wing.

Arvin led them back, through a sitting room with leather chairs and couches, to the bedroom. 'There,' he said, indicating a ragged circle of blood on the white linen. It was roughly half a foot in diameter; the center was still moist and there was a pucker where the bullet had pierced the bedding.

'He was shot in bed,' Mattie said, picturing it. 'Kind of early. You'd think a guy his age would still be up.' She looked over the surface of the mattress, past the blood. 'No obvious indentation on the other side. I'd say he was alone.' There was a tablet computer on the bedside table, a phone in a charger, a set of keys and a black alligator wallet. 'Was the light on or off?' she asked.

'Off,' Arvin said.

'This has all been photographed?'

'Yes, but not dusted.'

Mattie nodded, and let the tips of her gloved fingers peek into Richard's wallet. Credit cards and several crisp hundred dollar bills. The bedroom windows were closed, the curtains open. She looked out on to the backyard. Like the front, several of the taller trees were illuminated, and she caught the glitter of moonlight on a body of water in the distance. There was a French door with a lever handle. She noted two sets of contact sensors, one for the security system and the other needed by building code for any door that opened into an area with a swimming pool. She stood and watched for the red light on the latter; it didn't come on. No surprise, as most people disconnected the battery to avoid the jarring siren.

She pressed down on the door handle. 'Has this been unlocked?' she asked.

'They know to leave things as they are,' Arvin said.

Mattie grunted, 'Yeah, right,' and she stepped out into the cool spring night. She felt Jamie behind her. Even in the dark, the view was spectacular. Manicured lawns and gardens, the sounds of frogs, crickets and a swollen spring river in the background. Off to the right was a pool with a cabana. She walked the perimeter of Richard's second floor deck; there was a staircase that led down. Her thoughts ticked through the shoddy security and easy access into and out of Richard Parks' bedroom. Chances were good the security system had been entirely off.

'So why didn't he just pick up the phone and call for an ambulance?' Jamie asked. 'Why go to his sister's room?'

'Could have been running from the shooter,' Mattie said, not happy with that hypothesis.

'Or maybe he wanted to make sure his sister was safe,' Jamie offered.

Mattie thought of the shell-shocked girl in custody. What if that wasn't an act? This was feeling less and less like a slam dunk. 'So alone and either asleep or on the computer. The property has surveillance cameras?'

'Yes, but not as much as you'd think.' Kevin Simpson appeared on the deck. 'And don't worry, I got a sitter in with Rachel.'

'Good,' Mattie said. 'I'll want all the tapes and files. Jamie, you

could start in on those. And check to see if the alarms were armed
or not. I'd be willing to bet they weren't.' She looked around. 'So
where's the staff?'

'They come in the daytime,' Kevin said. 'Clarence is the only
one who lives here. He's got the caretaker's house. Been here for
years.'

'Where is he now?'

'I saw him outside. You want me to bring him in?'

'You sound like you know him,' Mattie said.

'We went to school together.'

'Right,' Mattie said, remembering this was Kevin's strong suit.
'Why don't you introduce me?'

'Cool.'

'Let's go this way,' Mattie said, heading down the outside stairs.

There was a chill in the air, and a soothing blanket of rushing water.
Someone creeping in the backyard, even with the moon and the
ornamental lighting, would have had little trouble finding cover. She
noted the pool area off to the right; the two-story brick cabana would
have a clear view of the back of the house. She stepped off the bottom
landing and her rubber-soled shoes sank into the grass. She froze and
stared at the ground. 'Maybe not a good idea,' she said.

'Why?' Kevin asked.

'Who else has been down here?'

'Hard to say.' He glanced at his watch. 'Crime scene team's been
here a couple hours. Before them you had the responding officers.
They would have done a perimeter search.'

'You're thinking it might not be Rachel,' Jamie said. 'She pretty
much confessed when she called nine one one.'

'It's tempting to go with that . . . but why did he go to her room?'

'And,' Jamie added, 'what sort of moron leaves an outer door to
his bedroom unlocked?'

'We do,' Kevin said. 'At least we used to. Hell, this is the country.
We leave our doors unlocked.'

Mattie nodded. 'And this is a private road, with a gate. So anyone
coming here would either have to get through the gate and drive
in, or just walk around. Then it's a few hundred yards to the house
up the back way, shoot Richard, retrieve your car . . . or just go
back through the woods.' She pulled out her LED flashlight and
trained its beam on the lawn that led to the stairs. She ran it off to

the right and swept it back. She turned in place, ever conscious of how subtle evidence could be altered and destroyed. She examined the treads on the synthetic wood steps, the grass stains and dirt. Access to Richard would have been easy, but would also have required inside knowledge of his bedroom and the layout of the property. And Rachel hadn't actually confessed. *'My brother's been shot! It's my fault. It's all my fault.'* 'Let's meet this Clarence guy,' she said.

Mattie, Jamie and Kevin sat around the square oak table in the caretaker's cottage as Clarence Braithwaite poured coffee and passed them each a heavy white mug.

'So the sirens coming down the road was the first you knew something was wrong?' Mattie asked. Her gaze stayed fixed on the deeply tanned man in black sweats, a *Lenore Says* T-shirt and running shoes. If Kevin hadn't said they'd been classmates she'd have figured the fit dark-haired man to be in his early thirties as opposed to forty or forty-one.

'Yeah. I was still up and heard them coming. When they turned down I knew something was up. Just didn't think . . . you know, I thought it was the usual.'

'The cops have been here before?' she asked.

He glanced at Kevin. 'This feels . . .' He shook his head. 'She had us all sign non-disclosure forms. She was serious about those. I guess it doesn't matter any more.'

'I'm not following,' Mattie said.

'With Lenore, if you wanted to keep your job you kept your mouth shut about anything you saw. And trust me, I did not want to lose this gig.'

'So that's a yes to the cops coming out here?'

'Cops, ambulances. It was always the same thing. Big fight between Rachel and Lenore, and then Rachel would do some stupid shit.'

'Define stupid shit.' Jamie prompted.

'You name it. Swallow pills, cut herself. Once we found her in the car with a hose hooked to the exhaust – that one was bad. Sometimes she'd just talk about it, sometimes she'd do it. And, to be honest, for someone who's so famous for being the perfect homemaker, Lenore treated Rachel like crap.'

'Give me an example,' Mattie said.

Clarence took the fourth place at the table. He sipped his coffee. 'There's so many to choose from. OK, here's one. It was a couple years back and I was supervising a team of arborists. It was before Memorial Day and we were prepping the grounds for a party where they were going to shoot an episode of *Lenore Says*. I didn't hear what started them going, but I remembered thinking how fucked up this was to hear them over the chain saws. Although you mostly didn't hear Lenore, but Rachel was screaming at her. Awful stuff, like "you just want me dead . . . you should never have had me."' He paused. 'That's the one thing I did hear Lenore say, and I wasn't the only one who heard it . . . she said, "I should have stopped with Richard." I mean, what kind of mother says that to her kid?'

'Apparently the kind who gets a TV show,' Jamie said. 'So how did you get this job?'

'Right place at the right time,' he said. 'I'd just gotten my degree in landscape architecture and forestry and was hoping to get a job as a park ranger. In the meantime I was working for the landscape company Lenore hired when she bought this place. She wanted to redo all the gardens, a huge project, and she was already thinking of this as a set for her show. Anyway, something went south between her and my boss.'

'What do you mean?' Mattie asked.

'Stupid shit,' Clarence said. 'My boss drank, and half the work crew was stoned at least half the time. Lenore is a sharp lady. She saw what was going on, fired my boss and asked me if I thought I could do the job and subcontract the labor. I guess she liked the way I handled things, and a few months later she asked me to be her caretaker. That was almost eighteen years ago.'

'She trusted you,' said Mattie.

'She does . . . did.' He shook his head. 'And Richard's dead. Man. Rachel's got to be bugging.'

'So you know them all pretty well.'

'I guess, as much as anyone. Poor kids. God,' tears swelled. 'This is so messed up. It's terrible to say, but you can kind of see why someone could get pissed off at Lenore, but Richard was cool. He was the peacemaker.'

Mattie studied him: nothing about him seemed forced or false.

She looked around his kitchen, normal and cozy. 'You live here by yourself?' she asked.

'Yeah.'

'Kind of my job to pry, so I've got to ask . . . good-looking man like you. You've been here for eighteen years, with no wife? Girlfriend? Boyfriend?'

He shook his head. 'Got a girlfriend in town, no kids; kind of the trade-off for living here.'

'I don't understand,' Mattie said.

'Lenore said I could have the job as long as I wanted, and it is a very good job. I don't pay rent, pretty much bank everything I make. I get full LPP benefits. But, just me. She didn't want anyone else living on the estate. She knew how fucked up some of the stuff was that went on in that house. She wanted to keep her exposure down.'

'There's no live-in help?' Jamie asked. 'That place is massive.'

'There's plenty of help,' Clarence said. 'Just none of them live in. I'm in charge of everything on the outside, and Lenore's assistant oversees the household staff. Her cook and trainer stay in New York and just came out when she was here. Which was never much; this was pretty much the place for the kids.'

'What about when they were young?' Mattie asked.

'They had nannies, but they never lasted, which was really messed up.'

'Why?' Jamie asked.

Clarence stared at the young detective. 'Think about it. Two little kids, their mom is a celebrity who's mostly not around, so you've got the nanny and me. But the nannies never lasted, they'd always do something that Lenore didn't like. She didn't give second chances. Screw up and you were out of here. I remember when one of the nannies left – Rachel was probably four – she wouldn't stop crying. Richard held her and the poor thing just wailed.'

'What did Lenore do?' Mattie asked.

'She wasn't there. She'd have me collect the keys and later the pass cards for the gate.'

'That's harsh,' Jamie said. 'Kind of got you to do her dirty work.'

'Sometimes. Lenore was constantly on the move. She used this place like a movie set. The kids lived here, but Lenore stayed in the city, or was off on location. I'd say on average she'd be here no more than a week in any month.'

'So how did you survive?' Mattie asked.

Clarence looked at her. 'I don't get your question.'

'If Lenore was constantly letting people go, how is it you've been here so long?'

Clarence looked at Mattie dead on. 'I never disagreed with her. I'd offer my opinion only if asked and, if she didn't want to take it, we'd go her way. Her money, her way, it's fine with me.'

Mattie nodded. 'So let's go through what happened tonight.' Since he was one of three – possibly four – people on the estate at the time of Richard's murder, Mattie wanted a clear accounting of Mr Clarence Braithwaite's whereabouts. She observed his posture, his ease in the telling, his lapses into emotional states when he realized that Lenore was dead, and now Richard too. 'Would you say that you were friends with Rachel and Richard?' she asked.

'Friendly,' he replied without pause. 'I was the help. Lenore told me early on to be careful not to cross the line. Her family was her business and no one else's.'

'You think that's why she wouldn't keep the nannies?' Jamie asked.

'Something like that . . .' He hesitated.

'What were you about to say?' Mattie asked.

'It's speculation, so I don't want to say.'

'I'll take that into account,' Mattie said, 'but I'd appreciate hearing it anyway.'

'Lenore didn't want people knowing her business.'

'That was vague,' Mattie said. 'You're saying what? She had secrets?'

'Yeah.' Clarence stared at his now empty coffee mug.

'Clarence,' Kevin said. He glanced at Mattie, who always made him nervous. He knew what she thought of him. Hell, it was what most people thought – the Simpson boy, good guy, but not the brightest bulb in the box. 'In these investigations everything comes out. It makes everything run smoother if you just give it up now.'

'Kevin' – his expression was panicked – 'I didn't kill Richard.'

'Whoa! Not what I'm saying. No one's accusing you of anything. But let's face it, you've had a front row seat to the real Lenore show for eighteen years. Detective Perez needs to know what you've seen, even the stuff you're not sure of. It's her job to sort it out, but she needs everything.'

Clarence looked at Kevin. His shoulders sagged. 'I guess the non-disclosure agreement doesn't matter any more. This is so many types of fucked up.' He looked around his kitchen. 'And this is real petty, but with Richard gone, I don't know if I have a job or a place to live . . . and Rachel . . .'

'What about her?' Mattie asked.

Clarence shook his head. 'I don't think she'll be able to handle this. When I heard the sirens, like I said, I thought it was for her. Course without Lenore to egg her on, I was a little surprised. For the most part she and Richard got along. In some ways he and I were alike. You know, just agree and things go smooth.'

'And if you didn't agree?' Mattie prompted.

'I'd keep it to myself, 'cause I was the help. Rachel never agreed with her mother, so it was a foregone conclusion the two of them would go at it. Lenore was never wrong, and in her world view her daughter always was. Richard was in the middle and, for the most part, he could make it work. Tell both Lenore and Rachel they were right, even when they were saying totally opposite things. I used to think you could send Richard to the Middle East and he'd be able to solve the thing with the Israelis and the Palestinians.'

'When you said Lenore had secrets, what did you mean?' Mattie asked.

'It's why she didn't like people knowing her business. Like who the sperm donor was for the kids, or why she never married.'

'Why was that?' Jamie asked.

'Lenore was gay,' he said.

'What?' Kevin asked.

'Yeah, a lesbian, and I don't . . . no, I know that's not something she wanted known. It may be part of the reason she kept me around.'

'I don't follow,' Mattie said.

Clarence nodded and got up from the table. He refilled his mug and then went around topping off theirs without being asked. 'It had to have been a year, maybe not even, after I first came here. I'd see Lenore, and I was very eager to please. I had school loans, she was paying me a decent salary, I had free housing, and let's face it a degree in landscape architecture isn't much more than saying you're a gardener with a bachelor's. No way was I going to screw this up, so like it said in the agreement, anything I saw or heard here – especially something she didn't want her adoring public to know – I kept my mouth shut.'

'What did you see?' Mattie asked.

'Right.' He shook his head and sat back down. 'I can't wrap my head around her being gone . . . and Richard. Shit. I'm sorry. Old habits. It feels wrong talking about this stuff, and it's all so clear, like it just happened.'

'Clarence,' Kevin said, 'you're killing me with the suspense.'

'I know. I saw Lenore making out with her cute little wardrobe lady, Peggy. They'd done a filming at the house and the rest of the crew had left. I had the tractor and was trying to get a jump on the clean-up and as I came around the corner I saw them. They were in the hot tub, naked, and going at it. It was the end of the day and I'd wanted to clean up the mess the crew had left. I must have been going so fast they didn't have time to separate, or maybe the noise of the tub blocked out the tractor. But I saw them and Lenore definitely saw me. I was sure my ride on the gravy train had just come to an end. I figured, what the hell, and kept going. It wasn't my business who she was with.

'The next morning I got a call at six a.m. She wanted to see me. I was sure the ax was going to fall. I met her at the house. She asked me if I was happy with my job. I told her I was.' He stared across the room. 'She said "good, it's yours for as long as you want it", and that was it.'

'She didn't bring up what you'd seen?' Jamie asked.

'She didn't have to. We both knew what was going on. I'd seen. I knew, and I really liked my job. But more than that, whose business is it anyway? If she wants to screw around with Peggy the wardrobe lady, or Krista her Pilates teacher, or that pastry chef she has on her show, or . . . Although I think that woman has her own show now.'

'Seriously?' Mattie asked.

'Oh yeah. I didn't keep track, and because the secret was important to Lenore it became important to me. I built a pergola over the hot tub, always made certain there was no day staff here after six. I looked on it as part of my job.'

'Who else knew?' Mattie asked.

'Other than her girlfriends . . . the kids, a couple of her friends. Oh, man . . .'

'What?'

'Just thinking how at least one person must be real nervous that their own gay secret's about to pop out.'

'Who? The girlfriend?' Jamie asked.

'No. And I wouldn't use the singular when talking about Lenore's gal pals.'

Jamie stared at Clarence. 'No way.'

'Oh yeah.'

'But . . . really? No. He's so . . .'

'What are you talking about?' Mattie asked.

Jamie shook her head. 'Really . . . John Gregory is gay?'

'Get out,' Kevin said. 'Mr shoot-'em-up?'

'Yeah, and Lenore's pretend boyfriend off and on for twenty years,' Clarence said.

Mattie stared at Clarence. 'Is this speculation or fact?'

'You mean did I see penetration? No, but he'd bring his "trainer" with him whenever he'd visit. Once the staff went home and it was just Lenore, the kids and me, you could tell they were a couple.'

'Because?'

'I've seen them kiss, hold hands. On occasion she'd have others over; you'd be amazed at the number of celebrities who live out here, and quite a few of them are gay. A lot of them, especially the actors, aren't open about that.'

'When did you last see Mr Gregory?' Mattie asked.

'He and the trainer were here a couple weeks ago. They were supposed to stay the weekend.'

'They didn't?'

'No. They left Saturday morning . . . what a frigging mess.'

'What happened?' Jamie asked.

'Mr Gregory and Lenore were fighting – and no, I didn't hear what it was about. I mean I heard something. He said, "I need you to do this for me." Whatever *it* was, she wasn't having it.'

'Any ideas?'

'No. I try not to eavesdrop on the family stuff. With her and Rachel that was impossible. Even the day staff can tell you about that.'

'I'll need a list of all of them. So tell me about the security for this place,' Mattie said.

'Right. It's not as good as you'd expect, and that was her doing.'

'Lenore's?'

'Yeah. The place is miked and all the doors and windows are alarmed, but the sound detectors only get turned on when the place is empty. She did not want anyone listening in. Same thing for video. I thought this place should have cameras; she didn't. She was scared that someone would see something, or hack the system, or that Rachel would do something provocative and post it to YouTube.'

'No video surveillance at all?' Mattie asked.

'The only camera she'd let me install is out by the gate. But look at this place, more than anything it's why she picked it. It's got natural borders. No one's coming across the river. There's a ten foot fence around the perimeter, with razor wire on top. There's thirty-two acres of forest that buffer the house, and the only road in and out has the gate.'

'No reporters? Fans?' Mattie asked.

'I used to think that would be an issue,' Clarence said. 'It wasn't. Most of her fans are older, not the fence-climbing types. She mostly stayed in the city, so if anyone wanted to see her they'd hang outside her apartment building or at the studio.'

'Where does the feed for the video go?' Mattie asked.

'I'll show you.' He walked them from the kitchen to a small study off of the living room. There was a monitor on the desk that showed the now open double-width gate. 'Here, how far back do you want to go?'

'Go hour by hour,' Mattie instructed.

They clustered around and watched the parade of vehicles in reverse. Kevin, then Mattie and Jamie, a crime scene van, Arvin's truck, a Grenville cruiser and the first crime scene van.

Mattie scanned the time and date on the bottom of the screen as they saw the first responders come through the gate. 'Who opens the gate?' she asked.

'Usually me. You want to see?'

'Sure.'

He paused the tape and went back to the live feed. He pressed a button on what looked like a garage door remote on a braided lanyard. 'This is the microphone, and then this opens and closes it.'

'How many of those are there?'

'Quite a few. We keep them in all the cars and there's at least three in the main house, one in the cabana and I always have this one on me.'

'That's a lot,' she commented. 'Do you know exactly how many?'

He shook his head. 'No, trouble is they're easy to lose. I can't tell you how many times I had to give Rachel mine. I was thinking that next time I ordered them I'd try to get GPS chips installed; at least that way when she drops one at some nightclub we can track it down.'

Mattie nodded. 'Rachel and Richard: what was their relationship like?'

'Not an easy answer. You guys want more coffee?'

They all declined, and Mattie waited.

Clarence looked back at the screen. 'Crap.'

There was silence.

'Everything's going to come out, isn't it?'

'Pretty much,' Mattie said. 'So this is another secret?'

'They're not bad kids. And for what it's worth, I can't believe Rachel killed him. Torture him, make his life miserable in other ways, but not this.' He stared at the screen, the image frozen on the closed gate. 'They were having sex.'

'With who?' Jamie asked.

'Each other, and for a long time . . . years.'

'Is this fact or speculation?' Mattie asked.

'I'd say ninety-nine percent sure it's fact. I always thought that Richard went along with it to keep her happy.'

'You weren't kidding about the secrets,' Mattie said. 'Is that all of them?'

Clarence turned and faced her. 'One more . . . and it's a doozy. She was going to have a baby.'

'Rachel?' Jamie asked.

'No. Lenore.'

FIFTEEN

'Is it Grenville?' Lil asked Ada, who was propped in bed with a cup of tea. It was five a.m. Neither of them had gotten much sleep, the news of Richard's murder kicking up so many bad memories of their own recent brushes with death . . . and with murderers.

Lil was on her laptop trying to work on her column, while simultaneously surfing the Internet for details on Lenore's, and now her son's, murder.

'Did it say where they've taken Rachel?' Ada asked. 'That poor girl.'

'It just said into custody. So here, I guess.'

Ada pictured the too-thin blonde whose moods shifted with the wind. 'It's not us, is it? That crack that Aaron made . . .'

'Please.' Lil stared at the screen. 'It looks like they think she killed her mother and her brother.'

'Horrible,' Ada said. 'And if she's pregnant and in jail . . . it's too awful. I can't see her surviving this. She seemed fragile. For what it's worth, I don't think she killed her brother. Not that I had more than a fifteen minute chat with her. She struck me as the kind of girl who'd hurt herself but not someone else.'

'Are the two that far apart?' Lil asked.

'I think they are,' Ada said. 'We've both been around the block; people behave kind of like you'd expect. Sure, people have secrets, so what's on the surface isn't always what you get. So let's just say it wasn't Rachel . . . who else would profit from Richard Parks' death?'

Lil sat on the edge of the bed. 'Ada, we're not getting involved in this.'

'We already are. And don't even pretend that you're not curious. So play along . . . I don't think it's Rachel . . . so who?'

'Well,' Lil said, abandoning any reticence. 'You've started with an assumption that could be dead wrong.'

'Which was?'

'You said "profit from his death". What if the motive has nothing to do with money?'

'You're right. But there's so much of it. If it's not money, we've got what? Revenge, jealousy, crazy stalker. And of course, are the two murders separate or related?'

'I'll make the assumption this time,' Lil said. 'Mother and son killed a day apart – these two things go together.'

'Agreed, and if Rachel's not the killer, then is she also a target?'

Lil looked at Ada. 'Oh God.' She grabbed her phone off the nightstand and called Kevin Simpson's cell. After she'd dialed she looked at the clock and was about to disconnect when he picked up.

'Hello?'

'Hi Kevin, I'm sorry to call so early.'

'Mrs Campbell?'

'Yes, dear. Look, I know this is none of my business, but Ada and I were talking about Richard Parks.'

He chuckled. 'Of course you were.'

She ignored him. 'Dear, sarcasm doesn't suit you. Anyway, let's for argument's sake say Rachel didn't kill him. Until we know why both Lenore Parks and her son were murdered, I think she could be in terrible danger.'

'She's safe.'

Lil paused. 'Who's heading the investigation?'

'Mattie Perez.'

'Wonderful! Is she there?'

'Mrs Campbell—'

'Yes, I know, Kevin, this is none of my business,' she said, thinking *you have to give to get*. 'But both Ada and I have spent the past couple days around the Parks family. We might have information that Mattie would want. Just tell her I called. It won't hurt my feelings if she says no, but please just ask.'

'Fine.' His tone letting her know it wasn't fine at all. 'I'll ask her.'

Lil held on the line and looked at Ada. 'You do realize,' she said, 'there's something very wrong with us.'

'I know nothing of the sort. If you get her on the phone, invite her for lunch.'

'Good idea.' And she heard the familiar rasp of the detective's voice.

'Lil?'

'Hi Mattie. Can't keep away from our lovely town.'

'No. So it's not even six in the morning. Please tell me the two of you don't have a scanner by the bed.'

'Not by the bed, although it could be fun.'

'So . . . is this a call from you the reporter, or you the concerned citizen, or . . . ?'

'The nosy neighbor,' Lil said, rounding out the options. 'A bit of all of them,' and she laid out her and Ada's whirlwind two days with Lenore Parks Productions.

'You actually saw her wheeled out?' Mattie asked.

'Yes, and the strangest thing . . . they held the meeting anyway. The company president was just shot and it was business as usual.'

'And now the acting CEO is dead,' Mattie commented. 'What did you think of Rachel?'

'Let me put Ada on,' she said. 'I barely talked with the girl. You know she's pregnant?'

'What?' Mattie 'said.

'Yeah, I'm pretty sure.'

'Hell, no. Kevin!'

Lil listened to Mattie over the line. 'Did they do a physical on Rachel Parks?'

'No. Just a search, and the routine screening stuff. Why?'

'She could be pregnant.'

'Crap, no.'

'Yup.'

'Mrs Campbell told you that? How does she know this stuff?'

'Beats me. But you need to get a doc in and probably a shrink as well. I've got a bad feeling about her in lock-up. We might want to think about a locked unit someplace.'

'Like a psych hospital.'

'It might be better.'

Ada's cell rang from inside her pocketbook. 'That can't be good,' she said, getting out of bed. She pulled it out, but didn't recognize the number on the read-out. 'Hello?'

'Morning, Ada.' It was Melanie.

Ada figured that, regardless of what Barry had said, she was about to be told that her short-lived career in reality TV had ended.

'We're about five minutes away. Do you want a bagel, breakfast sandwich, English muffin?'

Ada was flummoxed. 'So the show must go on?'

'Of course. If Lenore were alive nothing would stop her from taping. She even taped on Nine Eleven . . . in Manhattan. So, bagel?'

'Sure.'

'Great, see you in a few.'

Lil came up to her, phone in hand. 'You want to talk to Mattie?'

Ada nodded; she felt dazed. 'Sure . . . hi Mattie.'

'Feels like Old Home Week,' the detective commented. 'Lil said you had a conversation with Rachel Parks yesterday.'

'I did,' and she gave the detective a synopsis.

'What did you think of the two of them together?'

Ada caught the nuance in Mattie's voice. She thought back to the brother and sister duo at the cemetery. 'There was tension between them, but I wouldn't say it was hostile. He seemed very protective, and also . . . what's the word? Not that he was scared, but sort of on eggshells. And Lil told you about her pregnancy theory?'

'I'm still trying to process that one,' Mattie admitted. 'Incest resulting in a pregnancy. It's fairly heavy, and then add in that these are the children of a major celebrity.'

'I'll tell you this,' Ada said. 'They seemed genuinely close, possibly too close. Admittedly, I talked to the girl for maybe fifteen minutes, but she's deeply troubled, very intelligent and the kind of person whose mood changes in a heartbeat.'

'Act first, think later?'

'I think so. That's certainly how they portray her in the tabloids. Richard seemed reserved, kind of her polar opposite.'

'What do you think of the incest theory?' Mattie asked.

Ada remembered the looks between brother and sister, like they had their own silent language. 'It's possible. There was something about them. Lil said that when she first saw them she thought they were boyfriend and girlfriend. I don't know if this matters, or if and how it's connected, but they're going ahead with shooting this reality show.'

'Seriously?'

'Yeah. The crew will be here in a few minutes. And about that, here's an interesting tidbit. Richard Parks didn't want them filming this, and he certainly didn't want them using his mother's estate.'

'What are you talking about?'

Ada told her about the argument between Richard and Rachel. She hesitated before adding the piece about Richard yelling at Barry Stromstein. 'I didn't actually hear it, but I could see that Barry seemed upset, and Richard looked like his head was about to explode. It's understandable, the guy's mother is murdered and some-one's proposing to film a show about selling off her furniture.'

'You gals really are a piece of work,' Mattie commented.

'Don't say it. We're painfully aware of how morbid this all is.'

'I'll need to talk to this Barry.'

'Should I have him call you?' Ada asked.

'No. I prefer the surprise. So it looks like we'll be catching up later.'

Ada thought about Lil's lunch suggestion but, based on yesterday's shooting schedule, she realized anything before sundown wouldn't work. 'You with Jamie?' she asked.

'Yeah.'

'The two of you want a home-cooked meal tonight?'

Mattie laughed. 'I'm assuming we're talking Lil's cooking and not yours.'

'I'll have you know I am very skilled at the microwave.'

'No doubt. And yes, that would be great if we have time. Let's confirm later.'

SIXTEEN

Tromping through the woods of Lenore's estate with Kevin Simpson and Clarence Braithwaite, Mattie's thoughts played over the evolving investigation. She now knew that her original assumption – Rachel Parks shot and killed her brother, and possibly her mother as well – was wrong. The trail of blood from Richard's bedroom to hers was the first tip, followed by the absence of any powder residue on Rachel's blood-smeared hands. An hour ago she'd made the decision to have the girl transferred by ambulance to an area hospital. She'd called Rachel's psychiatrist, Dr Amos Ebert. He'd prefaced their conversation with, 'As her psychiatrist I can certainly listen to anything you have to say, but without a release I can't tell you much.'

She'd told him about how Rachel had acted in her cell. 'Spaced out like she's not quite there.'

'She dissociates,' he'd said. 'When the going gets too hard, she has the ability to check out. She's done it since she was a kid.'

'Like split personality?' Mattie had asked.

Ebert had coughed. 'That's dangerous territory, detective. And not something I'd bring up within earshot of Rachel. It's too easy to make people with borderline pathology decide they're Sybil. It's called hysterical conversion and, once you flip that switch, it's a free fall down the rabbit hole.'

As the conversation had progressed, she'd found him more accommodating than expected. He'd sounded shocked by the circumstances of Richard's death. 'She'll need to be someplace safe. I'd recommend Silver Glen: it's close, they know her and I have admitting privileges there.'

'Can they handle someone pregnant?' Mattie had asked.

There was a pause on Dr Ebert's end. 'She told you about that?'

'Not exactly, but I'll take what you just said as confirmation. Wherever we send her, they're going to need to test her. How far along is she?'

'At least a couple months. I'd had her on a mood stabilizer and she'd insisted on stopping it. At the time I didn't connect A and B. To be honest, I just found out after her latest public meltdown. They tested her in the emergency room. I'll make sure they test her again when she gets to Silver Glen. What a mess.'

'I think that's an understatement,' Mattie had replied, wondering if he knew about the alleged incestuous relationship between the brother and sister.

'I'll give you this for free, Rachel has never been seriously violent toward anyone other than herself. She'd get furious with her mother and, having had the two of them in sessions together, I couldn't blame her. But murder? No. Rachel wanted to make Lenore suffer, to find creative ways to embarrass her publicly. Death would have been letting her off the hook. And Richard . . . this is horrible. He was the only person that she really cared about, and who cared about her.'

'Did you know about Lenore's plan to have more children? Did Rachel?'

'Detective, I would love to give you all this information,' he'd said. 'At this point I can't. See if you can get Rachel to sign a release. If she's not going to be charged, I'd have no problems filling in some of the blanks about life in the Parks home.'

'I'd appreciate that. Or maybe she'd be willing to talk to me with you in the room.'

'I'd be OK with that. I'll call ahead to Silver Glen, make sure they have a bed, and tell them to get ready for her. Based on past visits, the fewer people who know she's there, the better.'

They exchanged numbers and hung up. From Ebert's hesitation, she was convinced that he did know of Lenore's bizarre plan to have more children, which according to Clarence involved frozen eggs, a sperm donor and a surrogate.

Now, as she walked the perimeter of the heavily wooded property with Clarence and Kevin, they came to the next piece of the puzzle.

'This wasn't here a week ago,' Clarence said, as they examined cut edges of the chain-link fence. The sharp metal was bright and free from oxidation where it had been snipped.

Mattie peered through the jagged opening; not fifty feet away was a road with a broad shoulder. Lots of places to park a car in the woods. She pulled out her cell and called the head of the crime scene team.

'It's got to be someone local,' Kevin said.

'Why's that?' Mattie asked, piecing together a probable sequence of events.

'Who else would know that Route Twelve touches Lenore's land?'

'Anyone who wants to look it up on Google Earth.'

'Sure,' Kevin said, 'but would they know it's a chain-link fence and that security is minimal?'

'It still doesn't mean someone local. It does mean someone who's been here before. And Clarence, you're telling me that she used this place like a TV set.'

'Pretty much,' he said. 'At least once a month in good weather you'd have crews down here, staged dinner parties with celebrities, pool parties. She always did her holiday specials from here. You name it and she'd film it.'

'They were filming yesterday,' Kevin offered.

'What are you talking about?' Clarence asked.

'They're shooting a reality show in Grenville.' He looked at Mattie. 'Your friend Ada Strauss is somehow involved.'

Mattie nodded. 'Yeah, she told me.' Cell in hand, she tapped Jamie's number. Her partner picked up.

'How's she doing?' Mattie asked; she'd had Jamie accompany Rachel Parks to Silver Glen Hospital.

'Not good. I think whatever bubble she's been in burst about thirty minutes ago. She won't stop crying.'

'Has she said anything?'

'Not about the murder,' Jamie said. 'I don't think I've ever seen someone in such pain. She keeps saying she wants to die.'

'I'm assuming they've got her on a suicide watch,' Mattie said, fearful that the only potential witness could wind up dead like her brother and mother.

'Oh yeah, and I've arranged to have a pair of uniformed officers outside her room. Which I might add is not making me popular with the staff here.'

'Has Dr Ebert gotten there yet?'

'No, you want me to call you when he does?'

'Yeah.' She was about to hang up.

'Mattie?'

'Yeah?'

'They dipped her urine when we got here. She is pregnant.'

'Seems to be a lot of that going around.'

She hung up and looked from the fence to the road and back to Clarence and Kevin. 'Clarence, any chance you keep a log of people coming and going?'

'No, but I never erase the video from the front gate. We could go back and see everyone who's been here.' He pointed to the fence. 'At least everyone who comes in through the gate.'

'OK, if you wouldn't mind going through them with someone from the CSI Team. We'll need to take them as evidence, but if you could put names to faces that would be a help. And that other thing . . . Lenore's surrogate. You have no idea who the girl is?'

'No,' he said, 'and the whole thing seemed so far-fetched, but if you knew Lenore and how she operated . . . I have no reason not to believe it. Why would she make something like that up?'

'Did she say what the delivery date was?'

'Late summer. She wanted to do a series of *Lenore Says* on early childcare. I was supposed to get the nursery set up.'

'She was fifty-two,' Mattie said. 'Any idea why she'd want more children?'

'God only knows. Here's what I think. The shows where she had Rachel and Richard had two of her all-time highest ratings. I think this whole "let's thaw out a couple of my eggs, get a surrogate and do the Mommy thing again" was for ratings.'

'Who would know the details?' Mattie asked. 'If this is true, then Rachel isn't the only natural heir to a few hundred million dollars.'

'I guess whoever did the procedure, Lenore's obstetrician. The surrogate could be anyone.'

She looked at Clarence. 'I get the sense you knew Lenore better than most. Make a guess.'

He nodded. 'It would have to be someone she could control. Someone who wouldn't go to the tabloids. So if I were going to guess, it would be an employee. And because it's Lenore and everything winds up on her show . . . Although . . .'

'What?'

'I'm trying to think if she'd want the public to know. She never revealed, at least publicly, who the sperm donor was for Richard and Rachel.'

'And?'

'I'm trying to think like her. If she never revealed who the father was, maybe she wanted to keep the surrogate's identity hidden. The media is fickle. What if the surrogate came off more sympathetic than Lenore, or if it looked like Lenore was taking advantage of some young girl? But it's one hell of a secret to keep. The pay-off for the surrogate would have to be huge. Either money or something else, like your own TV show. Lenore was surrounded by people who'd do a lot more than have her children if it meant getting ahead in the business.'

'Good thoughts, Clarence. If you come up with more let me know. You said Lenore never publicly revealed who Rachel and Richard's biological father or fathers were. Do you know?'

'Not for certain, but I'd put money on John Gregory. You can see it in Richard – same eyes, similar facial features. It's less clear with Rachel, or maybe Lenore used different sperm donors.' He shook his head.

'Could that have been what they were fighting about?' Mattie asked.

'You lost me,' he said.

'You said that Mr Gregory and his . . . "trainer" left early, that there was some kind of fight between him and Lenore. If all of this is true and he's a closeted actor trying to maintain a straight image, it seems that fathering a kid or two would help. Or maybe he wanted to let Rachel and Richard know that they had a father, or . . .'

'It's possible.' Clarence nodded. 'It makes sense but, like I said, if it wasn't what Lenore wanted, it wasn't going to happen.'

SEVENTEEN

'Damn shame,' Barry said to Melanie as he stared through the viewfinder at the set they'd thrown together in the ballroom of the Grenville Suites Hotel. Seated at a table was Ada in a vintage pale pink and black chiffon dress, and next to her was a local dealer whose idea of on-screen attire included striped suspenders and a red bow tie. The stage was littered with hastily gathered pieces of antique furniture, silver and porcelain. 'She looks great.'

'She does,' Melanie said, looking at how natural Ada was, 'but this one's useless. Too stiff, and the voice . . .' She shouted to the stage, 'Thanks so much, we'll let you know.' She looked to the back of the room, deliberately avoiding eye contact with the man in the bow tie and suspenders.

'My numbers are on my résumé,' he said.

'Yes, thank you,' Melanie said without turning. 'Next!' She glanced at Barry. 'There's no way we can use the mansion?'

'I don't see how. It's a fucking crime scene.'

'Shit! We both know that using Lenore's estate would shoot this thing through the roof. There's got to be a way.'

'I don't know. Richard wanted to pull the plug, and Rachel . . . that girl is one messed up chick.'

'Yeah,' Melanie said. 'One messed up chick with keys to the house. Where do you think they've stashed her?'

'Don't know and we need to find out.'

'And LPP?' she asked.

'No clue. They'll cobble together something, but Melanie, this show is our ticket. If we can get this pilot shot. Even if LPP were to go up in smoke, I think there's half a dozen studios that would jump for this.'

'I know,' and she left Barry with the cameraman and headed toward the next audition. This one looked better – handsome, late thirties, sandy blond, expensive-looking haircut, navy blazer, good build, even features. She grabbed his CV and headshot from the assistant. 'Mr Jacobs.' She extended her hand. 'So, you're the owner of Grenville Antiques.'

'Yes.' He glanced toward the stage and nodded toward Ada.

'You know Mrs Strauss?'

'Yes.'

'OK,' she laughed, 'I'm sensing there's some history.'

'A little.' He inhaled deeply as Ada left the stage and walked toward them.

'Hello Tolliver.'

'Mrs Strauss.'

Melanie looked at the handsome man with his perfect-for-the-camera face and whiff of an English accent. Of the two dozen interviews they'd already whipped through, this Tolliver at least looked and sounded the part. 'What am I missing?' She glanced at Ada and then back to Tolliver Jacobs.

'Ada,' he said, 'can we please just bury the past?'

Ada's jaw twitched. 'Fine. No reason you can't have the same shot as everyone else.'

'OK then,' Melanie said. She looked at Tolliver and figured she'd get the skinny from Ada after his audition. It would figure that the first real candidate would have some deal-breaking flaw. *Then again*, she thought, *a little on-screen tension could heat things up*. 'This is the set-up, Mr Jacobs . . .'

'Tolliver,' he said, displaying perfect teeth.

'Tolliver, there's a variety of items on the stage; pick whatever strikes your fancy and then explain it to Ada while we film. You want to make it as fascinating as possible, but don't turn into a grad student talking about his dissertation.'

He nodded. 'You want me to sell it.'

'Exactly.' She walked them to the stage.

Melanie explained the marks where Tolliver was to stand or sit. 'But feel free to move around; we'll follow. Also, the closer you can get to Ada the better. Even if it feels unnatural, it won't read that way on the camera. Got it?'

'Got it.' He eyed Ada. After Melanie walked off he whispered, 'Are we good?'

She looked up at him, unable to forget his past behavior, but also putting it into a more accepting context. Three years back Tolliver's partner had been murdered. He'd been devastated. What subsequently unfolded was a tragic story. Yes, in the midst of this Tolliver had behaved badly by seriously undervaluing a painting that had belonged to Ada's friend. He admitted what he'd done and, at the end of the day, Evie's heirs got an unexpected windfall from the sale of said painting. 'I'm very good,' she said. 'This is to see how you do.'

'Thank you,' he whispered back. 'You have no idea how much I need this.' He glanced around the stage. 'How do you feel about early American furniture?' His gaze landed on a small eighteenth-century cherry games table.

'Your pick,' she said.

Barry watched the monitor as the good-looking man with the perfect hair and right outfit walked Ada and the viewing audience through the wonders of a two hundred fifty-year-old drop-leaf table. Ever since he'd first heard her on the phone, he was impressed by Ada's ease. She knew which questions to ask, the ones the audience would want answered. Her face was expressive, but with the subtle nuance that was perfect for TV. So too were her movements, graceful without a lot of hand waving or gesturing. This Tolliver guy wasn't half bad, and having some eye candy for the ladies and gay viewers would be a plus. Maybe create a situation where he'd have his shirt off – of course that could be a stretch on an antique appraisal show.

Melanie, at the monitor next to him, was nodding. 'He's a keeper,' she said.

'Agreed; one down, and now we need at least a couple more to flesh out the season.'

'If we get a season.'

Her words triggered a rush of anxiety. 'This will work,' he said, not at all certain of that. Not even sure if Lenore Parks Productions was still open for business.

His cell vibrated. He pulled it out and saw Jeanine's number. 'Hey babe.'

'I just heard about Richard Parks,' she said, her voice coming through the speaker phone in her car with a slight echo.

'Yeah, it's pretty awful.'

'Barry . . .' She hesitated.

'What?'

'I'm on the road, about half an hour away. I need to see you.'

'OK,' his anxiety suddenly back. 'What's wrong?' expecting this to be the moment his too-beautiful wife would tell him that she'd been seeing someone else, someone more successful, someone able to give her all the things she deserved.

'Sweetie. You can't hide anything from me. "What's wrong?" What's wrong is you're freaking out and pretending everything's OK. What's wrong is I need to be with you. We'll get through this. Barry, you are brilliant and creative and Lenore was lucky to have you.'

'I love you,' he said.

'I know that, and it's not what you say, it's what you do. I love you too. Ashley, say hi to Daddy.'

'Hi Daddy.'

Barry smiled. 'Hi sweetie. Jeanine, we're doing auditions. It's dull stuff.'

'To you maybe. Don't try to talk me out of this. You need us there and you know it. Plus it's a beautiful day, and I want to see my handsome, albeit stressed out, husband.'

'You got half of that right,' he said.

She laughed. 'So you're not stressed out? I'll see you soon. Blow Daddy a kiss.' The line clicked off.

He stared at his iPhone, savoring the dual air kisses from his wife and daughter. It was nearly eleven, time enough for the LPP powers that be to have made a statement. Question was, did he want to hear it? He stared at the stage, and then at the monitor next to Melanie. Ada had just asked the big question, 'So what's it worth?' Her timing was flawless, leaving a long enough pause for the audience to try and guess before the expert.

He leaned in to hear Tolliver's response. He was good, starting with the high figure if the table had never been refinished, and finally coming out with the retail and insurance values.

'Perfect!' Melanie said. She looked to Barry. 'Agreed?'

'Yeah, that's one.'

'Mr Stromstein?' A woman's voice from the back of the room.

Barry turned and saw a short woman with curly dark hair in a navy suit, and the chunky chief of police he'd met yesterday. He swallowed and stood. 'Chief Simpson, good morning.'

Kevin Simpson waved to the stage. 'Hi, Mrs Strauss, Tolliver.'

Ada stared back. 'Kevin?'

Kevin looked back at Barry. 'So you're already filming the show?'

'Auditions,' Barry said, wondering what the hell the chief of police was doing here.

'Cool. This is Detective Mattie Perez with the State Major Crime Unit.'

'Hello.' Mattie extended her hand.

They shook.

Barry felt unsettled by the intensity of the woman's gaze. Like kids in a staring contest. She didn't blink.

He looked away. 'How can I help?' he asked.

'Is there someplace we can talk in private?' she asked.

Barry's nerves were in overdrive. Why would a detective investigating Richard Parks' murder want to talk to him? He'd heard that Rachel shot her brother, which on the one hand got the meddling duo out of his hair, and on the other quite possibly meant the death of any active LPP projects. He wanted to tell this detective he didn't have the time, that he was in the middle of auditions. But somehow her request didn't seem optional, and pissing off the local police who could make or break the show was all kinds of wrong. 'Sure, we could go to my room.' He turned back. 'Melanie, go on without me. You know what we need.'

'No problem, boss.'

Mattie took in Barry's lavish suite – at least five hundred bucks a night. His clothes were casual, but from his hand-stitched loafers to the iconic polo player on his chest, they weren't cheap. His eyes seemed in constant motion; his anxiety was palpable. She wondered at its source as he directed her and Kevin Simpson to comfortable leather club chairs. He sat across from them.

'A couple people,' she said, 'saw you and Richard Parks in a pretty heated discussion yesterday.'

Barry swallowed. 'Yeah.' He leaned forward in his chair.

'What was it about?'

'This show,' he said. 'Richard was pretty pissed off.'

'Because?'

'Take your pick. I was an easy target. His sister, who by all accounts hated Lenore, had decided to use *Final Reckoning* as an FU to her mother.'

'What do you mean?' Mattie asked.

He explained the show's premise. 'Every week we have experts go through the estate of someone who's just died. They present proposals, or outright offers, to the heirs and then dispose of the belongings. It all gets tallied and the heirs get the cash. Rachel's idea was to use Lenore's estate – or at least stuff from her house in Shiloh – for the pilot. She was very excited about the idea. And while I'm the first to admit it was beyond bad taste, the ratings would be unreal.'

'Richard wasn't on board with that.'

'Hardly.'

'But if it was Rachel's idea, why get mad at you?'

'I'm convenient,' he said. 'I had the sense that Richard didn't want to start something with Rachel. The girl has a reputation for not liking the word "no".'

'What did Richard want you to do?'

'Pull the plug.'

'On the episode or the show?' she asked.

'The whole thing.'

'Obviously you didn't.'

'No,' he said, rubbing fingers on his forehead. He looked to Kevin and then back to Mattie. He realized that she was the one running the show.

'And yesterday,' Mattie continued, 'Richard Parks was the acting CEO of LPP. Seems like if he said to pull the plug that's what would happen.'

'It's splitting hairs.' Barry sighed. 'He wanted *me* to pull the plug, not him. That way he could tell Rachel the show wasn't working and it wouldn't be his fault. Crap – I mean, she even wanted a producing credit.'

'What does that mean?' Kevin asked.

Barry laughed. 'It depends. I'm a producer and basically I do everything. If Rachel wants to be a producer, she gets the credit and I do everything possible to keep her away from the shoot. Can I ask where she is?'

'A hospital,' Mattie replied.

'Did she kill him?' he asked.

'Too soon to say.' Mattie's focus never left Barry. 'What I don't understand is why they were even at the cemetery.'

'I don't know,' Barry said. 'Maybe this is where they're planning to bury her. Although the way Rachel was talking, it was like she wanted to purge the house of everything connected with Lenore and start over. I'm not saying this right. It's speculation, but it was like she wanted to set up house. She said something about raising a family here. Honestly, I don't know the girl and, by all accounts, she's pretty crazy.'

Mattie switched topics. 'Can you walk me through your whereabouts yesterday through till today?'

'Great . . . my alibi.' He gave a nervous smile and proceeded to recreate his every moment.

As she listened, she realized a few things. First, if Barry was to be believed, his entire afternoon through early a.m. was accounted for in a series of interconnected meetings and work sessions, all related to this show. Were there gaps in time long enough for him to drive out to Lenore's estate, cut the fence, creepy crawl through the woods and shoot Richard? Possible, but unlikely with the tightly packed contents of his day.

'You've been to Lenore's mansion,' said Mattie.

'Sure, a bunch of times. We'd shoot episodes of *Lenore Says*, and she'd do company parties at least twice a year. Attendance was mandatory.'

'Altogether how many times have you been there?'

'Couple dozen, I guess.'

'And these parties, how many people are we talking about?'

'Usually it was the execs, producers and assorted wives and partners. In the summer she'd invite entire families and the kids could use the pool.'

As Mattie did the math, there was a knock at the door.

A woman's musical voice, 'Barry?'

Barry smiled. 'My wife,' he said, and got up and walked to the door.

A little girl with blond curls shot through. 'Daddy!'

Mattie watched as Barry scooped up his daughter, the joy on his face evident, and she couldn't help but smile and think about her own son, Oscar, when he'd been that age. The woman who came in behind the little girl made Mattie's breath catch. Mattie had long ago made peace with her looks; she was short, struggled with an extra ten to fifteen pounds around her middle and had hair like a poodle. As a teen she'd been horribly insecure, always feeling judged by others and always judging herself. She stared at Barry's wife. Without doubt, she was the most beautiful woman she'd ever seen, tall and willowy with massive waves of reddish blond hair that framed her delicate face and fanned out around her shoulders. She brushed a stray lock back as she hugged her husband and daughter. Her lips on his, her long fingers twined in his hair. Mattie heard Barry moan.

The little girl laughed and complained, 'Mommy, it tickles.'

Barry's wife pulled back and playfully brushed her hair across her daughter's face.

The child's laughter was free and infectious.

Mattie felt her own smile and looked at Kevin. She felt like telling him to pick his jaw off the ground. 'You have a beautiful family,' she said.

The woman looked up, seeing Mattie and Kevin. 'I'm sorry,' she said. 'I didn't know you were in a meeting.'

'More of an interrogation,' he said. 'Jeanine, this is Detective Perez and Police Chief Simpson. They were asking me about Richard and Rachel.'

'Oh.' The smile left her face. 'Are you OK?'

'Fine.' Still holding his little girl on his arm, he touched the side of his wife's cheek gently with his fingers.

'We're about done,' Mattie said, finding it hard to look away from Jeanine Stromstein, now struck by the intense green of her eyes. 'Mr Stromstein, we may have some more questions, and I'll want to interview everyone associated with *Final Reckoning*, at least everyone who was here yesterday. Were you here?' she asked Jeanine.

'No,' Jeanine said. 'We just drove down from the city. Is Barry a suspect?'

Her bluntness made Mattie pause. 'No, not at the moment.' She felt awkward in front of this woman who looked like she'd stepped out of a Pre-Raphaelite masterpiece. But awkward wasn't enough to let her forget who she was, or what she was here to do. And between Barry and Clarence's statements she now knew that many hundreds, possibly thousands, of people – including Barry's gorgeous wife – would have had enough familiarity with Lenore's estate to plot out Richard's murder. 'Ms Stromstein, seeing that you're here, would you mind running through *your* whereabouts from yesterday afternoon until now?'

EIGHTEEN

As psychiatric hospitals went, Rachel ranked Silver Glen at the top. From the bucolic surroundings with walking trails and stone benches to the quaint bridges over rushing streams. Even the rooms looked almost normal. If you could get around the breakaway hardware, designed to fall off the wall if more than ten pounds' pressure was applied, and the furniture bolted to the floor. From the brochures she knew that the windows, if broken, would turn into a fine powder. Still, as a teen she'd found ways to hurt herself here. One time she'd gouged her arm with a stick, not realizing that all the bacteria would enter her bloodstream and necessitate a two week hospitalization hooked to intravenous antibiotics. The only other psych place that was OK was Betty Ford. That had been a giggle. Not that she really had a drug and alcohol problem, at least not that she saw. That stay had been Lenore's idea, and for once mother and daughter had been kind of in agreement. Now, free from all drugs, legal or otherwise, she felt more out of it than after a romp at her favorite club.

She tried to focus. 'No,' she breathed, when a thought too painful to bring to memory whispered at the edges of her consciousness. She felt trapped and helpless. She curled her arms tightly around her legs and thought of techniques she'd been taught to pull herself back into reality. 'No.' Because what would happen to her if she could feel any of those things? 'Richard.' Her heart raced, and frantic thoughts whirred like a band saw.

'Rachel,' a man's voice called to her. She heard it, but it wasn't close.

'Rachel.' The voice was persistent, and she sensed movement in the room.

She curled her arms tighter, her chin tucked to her chest, her hair like a blanket over her eyes. *Rachel isn't here*, she thought. *Rachel is on vacation.* She flashed on one therapist, a group leader, who was big into visualizations. But not ones that would bring you to reality, ones where you'd imagine beautiful places and put yourself there. She pictured turquoise waters and warm sun, how it would feel on her face, her chest. She heard gulls and the gentle rush and retreat of the waves on soft white sand. She smelled salt and the hint of clams and mussels dropped from above by gulls and black-headed cormorants.

'Rachel.'

He wasn't giving up. But the beach was real, and maybe she wasn't alone. She gasped as the visual formed, a man rising from the surf in her private cove. His skin dripping with water, his dark hair slicked back, his blue eyes. *Richard.* His blood, and the warp and weave of her visualization began to unravel. Frantic, she tried to piece the cloth back together. That therapist's words ran through her head. *The brain doesn't know the difference between real and imaginary if you do it well enough.* Richard was staring at her, the hole in his chest, like a third eye, watching her. 'Richard.'

'Rachel, I need you to pull out of it,' the man's voice said.

His words snuck beneath the waves and the gulls. She felt numb and paralyzed; the warm sand and gentle waters did nothing as she froze in her brother's gaze. 'Help me,' she called to him. He seemed caught, unmoving, his lower limbs below the surf, while blood pulsed from his chest. 'Help me.'

'I will,' the man said. 'I need you to focus, Rachel. I want you to think of your breath and follow it in and out. Just the breath, nothing else. You don't see or hear anything other than your breath. Follow it in and follow it out.'

The man's voice was familiar – Dr Ebert. She felt a juvenile surge of rebellion but, caught between Richard's blood and the frightening emotions that tore at her like harpies, she surrendered to the voice's magnetic pull. *My breath, yes, I can do that. Nothing else, just the breath in and the breath out.*

'Good,' Dr Ebert encouraged. 'Keep riding the breath, and when you're ready I'd like you to feel your weight against the mattress, see how it molds and sinks in. See how the breath going in and out changes that. Observe the subtleties.'

The cove and Richard retreated. Her fears were held at bay by her focus.

'Perfect. Well done. Now listen to my voice, and when I tell you to open your eyes, I'd like you to do that. Is that OK?'

'Yeah.'

'Good, now Rachel open your eyes. We're going to get through this. You are going to get through this.'

She cracked her eyes open, and through the curtain of her hair saw Dr Amos Ebert's broad dark face.

'It's OK,' he said. His voice was soft and deep.

'It's not,' she said, too frightened to move, knowing that the minute reality found her, it would hurl her into an emotional free fall.

'You're right,' he said. 'And even so, you're going to survive this.'

'He's dead. Richard is dead.' She heard the words through her lips. It didn't sound like her. They seemed far away, some other woman speaking them. She saw him standing in the cove, and then more real. He was banging on her door, and then stumbling through. At first she thought it was some horrible joke, but Richard never played pranks – that was her.

'Tell me everything that you're thinking,' Dr Ebert urged. 'You're in a safe place; nothing and no one can hurt you here.'

'He was shot,' she said. She felt air rush through her lips. 'He came into my room. There was blood on his chest, his hands.'

'Yes, and what did you do?'

'I went to him.' Her words like steps on wafer-thin ice. 'There was too much blood. I put my hand on the wound.' She felt the blood, warm and sticky. She felt his pulse as his life bled out. 'He died there. I held him as he died.' She knew he was gone, she cradled him, feeling the softness of his hair against her arms. 'He was dead when I called nine one one. But I wouldn't leave him, because what if he'd died when I wasn't there?'

'That was the kind thing to do. To comfort him.'

'I knew. He was leaving me. I wouldn't leave him.' A tear formed, and then another. 'I wouldn't ever leave him. Why?'

'I don't know,' Dr Ebert said, his eyes fixed on Rachel.

'Why would someone do that to Richard?' From beneath the curtain of her hair she looked at Ebert. 'I'm the bitch. It should have been me.'

Ebert felt relief that she'd come back from her dissociative state. There'd been times – especially when she was in her early teens – when she'd zone out for days. He knew to tread carefully. The girl was exquisitely sensitive to rejection. Her brother's death, while tragic, could easily be the thing that made her follow through on her frequent impulses and threats to end her life. He also knew that if she ignored the pain and the grief, they would emerge in twisted and dangerous ways. 'Tell me about Richard.'

Her tears fell. 'He was perfect. Lenore should have stopped with him. He could handle her . . . he could handle me.' She made eye contact with her psychiatrist. 'You know I'm pregnant.'

'Yes.'

'It's Richard's baby.'

In his early fifties, with over twenty years under his belt as a psychiatrist, little shocked Amos Ebert. He schooled his expression while searching for an appropriate response, discarding the ones that came first to mind, such as *What the fuck? Are you insane?* or the obvious *How the hell did that happen?* He settled on 'Is this something you want?'

'Yeah. No one's going to talk me out of it.'

'Rachel, it's your body and your decision.'

'People will judge me.'

'If you tell them your brother was the father, that's true.' He'd worked with Rachel for nearly ten years. Had sessions with both her and Lenore – those had taxed his considerable talents. He'd met Richard on numerous occasions. Sitting here now with Rachel he realized that this very intelligent girl had deliberately, and until recently successfully, concealed at least one important aspect of her life. 'How long had you and Richard been intimate?'

'What makes you assume that?' she said, her green eyes wide, the hint of a smile on her lips. 'I could be more like Lenore than you think. You know, the turkey baster method.'

'I don't think so,' he said, remembering her staid brother. Probably the only person in the world who genuinely cared for Rachel.

'You're right,' she said. 'And it wasn't his fault. I'm the had one. He never wanted to do it. He would have stopped if I'd let him.'

Dr Ebert listened to classic Rachel, self-hating and vulnerable. This made sense. On more than one occasion – the first time when she was twelve – Rachel had attempted to seduce him. Her efforts had been clumsy and motivated by an intense need to feel wanted, to fill an aching void and stem her emotional free fall. Resisting and redirecting her urges without leaving her feeling rejected took skill, which her young brother would not have had. Now, in the setting of Richard's murder, and her pregnancy, this material needed to be explored. 'When did you and Richard start—'

'Fucking?'

He gave her the hint of a smile. 'I was going for something softer.'

'I was twelve and he was fifteen.'

Ebert held his breath. Had she revealed any of this when she was still a minor, he would have been bound to report it to youth services. She was now nineteen and that wouldn't be necessary. 'So all this time?'

'No. Like I said, it was me. He did it for me. I was always the instigator. It would make me feel better, at least for a little. I'm such a piece of shit. What sort of person makes her brother do that?'

'One in a lot of pain,' he offered. 'I am curious as to why this is the first time you've brought this up.'

'Yeah.' She pushed back against the wall and ran her fingers through her hair, pulling it off her face. 'Dr Ebert, you've been good to me, and I know I've pulled a lot of stunts. Like even now, I'm sure you had appointments and stuff, and here you are in the middle of the day . . . and yes, I know Mom had you on a retainer. And when all of this is figured out, I still want you to be my psychiatrist.'

He felt a question in her words. 'I'm not going anywhere, Rachel.'

'Good. I couldn't tell you before.'

'Because of your ages?'

'Yeah. I'm crazy, but I'm not stupid.'

He laughed. 'No, you are definitely not stupid. So, going with that, let's talk about what comes next.'

Her mouth gaped. She saw Richard, the blood. She felt him in her arms, his soft hair.

'Rachel,' Ebert said. His voice direct. 'Stay in the present. Tell me what's going on.'

They were interrupted by a knock at the door.

He shouted back, 'We're in session.'

The door opened. 'I'm sorry.' A male nurse in Silver Glen navy scrubs poked his head in the door. 'There's a detective who wants to talk to Rachel.'

Rachel blinked. She saw Dr Ebert and the nurse. She also saw Richard's blue eyes staring into hers, as if it were happening again.

'Not a good time,' Ebert said. 'She's not ready for that.'

'No,' Rachel said. 'Is it that woman?'

'It's a Detective Perez.'

'Short, dark poodle hair, kind of stocky?' Rachel asked.

'Yeah.'

She looked at Ebert. 'I'll talk to her.'

'You're certain?' Ebert asked.

'Yeah.' As the nurse left, she added, 'But I'm not going to tell her about Richard and me, and I don't want you to either.'

'You got it.'

'Don't write it down anywhere. This has got to stay secret . . . God.'

'What?'

'I'm turning into my mother. You'll stay?'

'I think it's a good idea.'

The door opened and the nurse returned with Detective Perez. She looked at Dr Ebert seated in front of the platform bed and then at Rachel, pressed back against the wall.

'I want Dr Ebert here,' Rachel said, looking at Mattie.

Mattie nodded and extended her hand. She and the doctor shook. 'Do you have a card?' she asked, offering him one of hers.

'Yes.'

She tucked his away and looked around the sparsely furnished room for a place to sit.

'I'll get a chair,' the nurse said from the door.

'They don't let you have things that aren't bolted down,' Rachel offered. 'Or maybe it's just me. I've been here before . . . my reputation precedes me.' She smiled at Ebert.

'How are you doing?' Mattie asked.

'Honestly, I don't know.' She glanced at Ebert. 'I'm not suicidal, not now.'

'Good,' he said, as the nurse returned with a chunky wooden chair.

'Let me know when you're done,' the nurse said. 'I'll come and take it away.'

'Thanks.' Mattie waited for the nurse to leave. She glanced around the room, noting the dome camera in the ceiling. 'They tape the patients?' she asked the psychiatrist.

'Sometimes. If they're particularly concerned that someone might try to hurt themselves, but it's not routine.'

'Are they taping now?' she asked.

'Yes, but just video, not audio.'

'I see.' She wondered if a subpoena for the tapes of Rachel would bear fruit. The hospital would push back with patient confidentiality. 'Rachel, I need to ask you about last night and I'd like to tape this interview. Will you be OK with that?'

'We'll see,' Rachel said.

'Is that a yes or a no?'

'Sure, go ahead. Yes.'

Mattie pulled out a tiny digital recorder and clicked it on. 'This is Detective Mattie Perez.' She stated the time and date, who was present and where they were. 'Rachel, I'd like you to tell me every thing you remember about last night.'

Rachel's shoulders slumped and her hair fell forward. 'I didn't hear anything, no gunshot. He just came into my room. I was sleeping.'

'Who came in?' Mattie asked.

'Richard. I heard him at the door.' *Rachel felt the room shift as Richard's hand fumbled at her door, pulling her from sleep. 'Rachel,' he called out. His voice was wrong; she could hear his pain. 'Are you OK?' he asked.* 'He asked me if I was OK, and he was dying. Those were his last words.' *She heard him fall, his knee landing too hard. That was the instant she knew, even before she turned on the light. The sound of his knees hitting the wood floor, that's when she knew he was dying. She hadn't even seen the blood yet.* 'Isn't that strange? I knew it was awful, and then I was out of bed and he was on the floor.' *Her hands in his hair, on his chest.* 'There was so much blood. I remembered you're supposed to apply pressure, and I did. I felt his heart beating and the blood just pushed out into my hand. I knew I was supposed to call nine one one, but

I couldn't just leave him. He was looking at me, I think he wanted to speak, but it was too late. We just stared into each other's eyes. I loved him so much.' Her shoulders heaved and she sobbed. 'Richard, how could you leave me?'

Dr Ebert leaned forward. 'Good girl,' he said. 'You've got to feel this.'

'It hurts.' Her mouth twisted.

'I know. It has to,' he said. He glanced at the detective. There were tears in his eyes.

'Can I continue?' Mattie asked, prepared to terminate the interview if the doctor felt it would be too much.

'Rachel?' he asked.

She swallowed and accepted the box of tissues he held. She blew her nose. 'He had the softest hair,' she said, 'and the bluest eyes. We always figured they were our father's eyes. I, of course, got Lenore's.'

'Who is your father?' Mattie asked.

'That's top secret,' Rachel said. 'Sorry, that was bitchy. I don't know. It was on my list of things to do to figure that out. We had our suspicions. There's a queer actor Mom was besties with. He has dark hair and beautiful eyes like Richard.' Rachel stared at the detective. 'I'm sure you know by now that Lenore was a dyke, another well-guarded secret.'

Mattie nodded. 'Did you know she was planning to have another child, possibly more than one, using a surrogate?'

Rachel started. 'You're kidding . . . who? Did it actually happen? Is this a theory or fact? It's pure Lenore, but who's the surrogate?'

'It seems likely, but no, I'm not one hundred percent certain. I was hoping you might know.'

'Isn't that a kick in the pants? Richard – I bet she told him, and screw him for not telling me.'

'You and your mom fought a lot.'

'Yeah, and no, I didn't kill her.' Rachel looked to her doctor. 'Why Richard?' She glanced from him back to the detective. 'Why him and not me? It wasn't a robbery. Why?' *And again she was there, hands slick with blood, staring into his beautiful eyes as his life went out.* 'Why Richard? It should have been me. It should have been me.'

Ebert's voice was soft. 'It wasn't you, Rachel. It's terrible and it's done. There's nothing that can bring your brother back.'

His words rolled in her head. *It's terrible and it's done. There's nothing that can bring your brother back.* She railed against the truth. 'No,' she wanted to scream, to rip herself open and tear out this pain. *There's nothing that can bring your brother back.* But then something happened. Like a switch thrown in her head: . . . *nothing that can bring your brother back.* There was a bright light, and what was up was now down, black was white. *Bring your brother back.* She opened her eyes, which had been tightly clenched. She looked from the concerned face of the short detective to Dr Ebert's broad features and close-cropped black hair. She noted he was going gray around the temples, and wondered how old he was. Despite all their years together she knew so little about him. That would change, she told herself. She paused and listened to the silence. *Bring your brother back. Yes,* she thought, *that's exactly what I'll do.*

'Dr Ebert,' she said, everything suddenly clear, as though she were a camera and the scene had just come into crystalline focus. 'When we finish this interview, I'd like you to discharge me. I'm not a threat to myself or anyone else. It's time to go home.'

NINETEEN

Rachel didn't want to question the white light that flooded her head as she gazed out of the Bentley at the rolling hills. Everything had changed. She'd never believed in God, or given much thought to an afterlife. She'd assumed you die and rot in the ground, the end. Yes, there'd been her flirtation with Satanism, but that had been to tick off Lenore, who promptly stole the idea and did an episode of *Lenore Says* on goth fashion for Halloween, deftly turning Rachel's rebellion into black lace place mats and candy satchels stitched with safety pins. This was real, and she knew better than to share what had happened – was happening – to her with Dr Ebert. The last two hours of her life, unlike anything she'd ever experienced. Of course, Dr Ebert didn't want her to leave Silver Glen.

Even the detective had expressed concerns. Although hers had less to do with Rachel's mental status and more to do with her physical safety. 'Your mother and brother have just been murdered,' she'd said. 'The motive is unclear; you'll be safer in a protected environment.'

'I'll be fine,' Rachel had said, knowing that was true. 'If whoever killed Richard and Mom wanted me dead, they could have taken me out last night. I wasn't the target.'

'We don't know that,' the detective had replied, and Rachel had consented to officers patrolling the grounds of the Shiloh estate, the white light in her head telling her it would be better to negotiate than try to impose her will.

Ebert had been more forceful, but even he'd eventually backed down.

'It's OK,' Rachel had said. 'I swear I have no intention of hurting myself, or anyone else. I need to go home. I have a lot to take care of.' She didn't want to question this assurance, this sense of clarity. She sure as hell wasn't going to share what was really happening. Richard wasn't dead, not really; he was alive and well and growing in her belly. She would give birth to him. The thought made her giggle.

'You OK back there?' Clarence Braithwaite asked from behind the wheel.

'Better than OK,' she said, catching his eye in the rear-view mirror. There was another mystery, she thought. *Clarence has been around your entire life; he's covered for you on more than one occasion; he always kept Lenore's secrets.* Like Ebert, he knew to resist her adolescent attempts at seduction. Today she'd called him on his cell, asked if he could pick her up. There'd been no hesitation, no 'I'm in the middle of something else'. He'd just wanted to know where and when. The white light made things so clear – Clarence could be trusted. 'What are your plans?' she asked him.

'What do you mean?'

'I'd like you to stay; whatever Mom was paying, I'll make sure you get a raise.'

'Thanks,' he said. 'How you holding up?' he asked.

'I'm going to get through this,' she said, wishing she had someone to confide in. Someone who wouldn't judge and think she was crazy. The person who popped to mind was that kind woman with the intense eyes she'd met in the cemetery. As Rachel pictured her, she seemed to be a piece of the white light, and if she really listened there was a voice, Richard's voice. 'Do you think they're still filming that new show?'

Clarence cleared his throat. 'Yeah. I got a couple calls from a field producer and then from his assistant, wanting to film at the mansion.'

'Are they there?'

'Rachel, it's a crime scene.'

She let the white light mull the information. 'But that's perfect.'

He stared back at her and nodded. 'Can I say something you might not like?'

'Sure.'

'That's something your mom would have said.'

In the past those would have been fighting words. Fragments of vicious fights with Lenore, Rachel screaming, *I'm nothing like you! You're the most hateful self-centered bitch. I hope you die!'* But the white light would have none of that. The past was the past. 'You're right,' she said. 'End of the day, I am my mother's daughter. Only I want to do this better.'

He didn't ask for clarification, his eyes fixed on the back roads to Shiloh.

'So where are they filming?' she asked.

He pulled out his cell. 'I've got their numbers in my history. You want me to find out?'

She had no hesitation; this was what the light wanted. 'Yes. And wherever they are, that's where we should head.' And then she had another epiphany. 'Clarence, did you know that Lenore was planning on having more kids?'

'Yeah.'

'So she told you?'

'She did. I was supposed to set up the nursery. It's going to be twins.'

Rachel touched her belly – her brother inside, the due date six months away. 'Who's carrying them and when are they due?'

'I don't know . . . and in six months.'

'Did my brother know?'

Clarence hesitated. 'I'm not sure.'

'I'm thinking yes. So there's some poor woman out there with two of Lenore's babies and no Lenore . . . Interesting.'

*　　*　　*

Ada breathed in the cool spring air, glad to be off her feet, her gaze focused on the crocuses that edged the gardens around the bluestone patio where she'd had lunch earlier with the crew. They were on a five minute break. They'd been filming hopeful antique dealers since seven a.m.; now it was nearly four. Her jaw ached from smiling and three hours back she'd abandoned her pumps for a pair of hotel slippers. From now on, she'd be sure to bring her own.

Barry Stromstein had popped in and out, told everyone they were doing a 'fabulous job'. When Ada had asked about the status of the show in light of Richard Parks' murder, he'd been evasive. At one point he'd appeared with a stunning woman and little girl. From Melanie she'd learned that this was his family, and that he'd met his wife, Jeanine, when she'd been a contestant on one of his previous shows, *Model Behavior*.

Reflecting back through the day she smiled. Every dealer in the state, and quite a few from outside, wanted a spot on *Final Reckoning*. Their eagerness was palpable, but sadly their on-screen talent was negligible. She wished Lil were here. It was fun and exhausting, and being around Melanie and the crew was pure adrenaline. She watched a pair of robins land beneath a redbud and peck at the ground. Lost in thought, she didn't hear Rachel approach.

'Ada?'

'Rachel!' She looked up at the blonde girl, who seemed so young in jeans, T-shirt and a leather jacket, her face free of make-up and her hair in a messy ponytail. Her green eyes were bright and luminous. 'How are you?'

'Can I join you?' she asked.

'Of course.' Ada looked over to where Rachel had come from and saw a tall dark-haired man hanging back about fifty feet. 'Who's he?'

'Clarence,' she said. 'He works for us . . . kind of a friend, I guess.'

'I'm so sorry about Richard,' Ada offered, Rachel's sudden appearance adding to the day's surreal quality.

Rachel took the chair next to hers and sat with her hands on her stomach. 'I loved him so much,' she said, 'more than anyone.'

Ada felt at a loss for words. 'He loved you too. Anyone could see that.'

'I know, and I realize how much I've taken for granted. Not just him.' She looked back at Clarence. 'I think I've gone my entire life without really seeing. There's good people here,' her gaze turning back to Ada. 'It's like this is the first day I'm seeing that. Like I've been blind, and suddenly things I couldn't see are clear.'

'You've been through some shocks,' Ada said. 'Sometimes that bring things into focus.'

Rachel snorted. 'Shock therapy. You know Mom wanted me to have that. My psychiatrist said no. He said it wouldn't work for what I have. He's another one, Dr Ebert. I think you'd like him. Although he's pretty ticked at me right now for leaving the hospital AMA.'

Ada looked from Rachel to her own slipper-covered feet. She wondered if perhaps she should give this Dr Ebert a call. Something about Rachel felt wrong, the expression in her eyes a bit too intense. And where exactly had she been that she'd left against medical advice? 'I don't mean to be rude, Rachel. But what are you doing here?'

'You're not rude. You're looking at somebody who has everything . . . and absolutely nothing. I'm looking at someone who has absolutely everything. I'd like to know what that's like. And for the first time in my life, I think it might be possible for me too.'

'I've had a good life,' Ada admitted. 'I still do, but everyone has problems and hard times.'

'Do you?' Rachel asked.

'Of course. Just a couple days ago I was in a pretty big funk over my sixty-fifth birthday.'

'Happy birthday.'

'Thanks, and I feel like a moron for comparing my pity pot with the tragedies you're facing.'

'No, there's nothing you could say that would make me think bad of you. I'm really glad you're doing this show.'

'I'm not so certain it's going to happen,' Ada admitted.

Rachel's eyes widened. 'Trust me, it will happen. It has to.'

Ada felt the hairs on the back of her neck. Something about Rachel's tone, the intensity in her eyes, like there was a fire inside of her. 'Why is this show so important?' Ada asked.

'That's a good question. Can you keep a secret?'

Ada was torn, but being at heart a curious person she couldn't resist. 'Of course.'

'My brother's not really dead.'

This is not good, Ada thought, keeping the panic off her face. 'What do you mean?'

'He's inside of me.'

'Of course he is,' Ada said, trying to put a normative spin on things. 'He'll always be with you.'

'No,' Rachel said, 'I mean really inside of me. He's guiding me. And here's the funny thing.'

Ada braced, wondering on what planet this would be considered funny.

'I think Lenore's in here too . . .'

Ada stared back. She shuddered, seeing a subtle shift in Rachel's expression, her eyes, the shape of her jaw; for a moment it was like seeing Lenore Parks. She struggled to find her voice, alarmed that, while seemingly calm, Rachel was barking mad. *Mad enough to kill her mother and her brother?* 'How does this show figure into that?'

'I need to keep everyone happy. I understand that now. My whole life has been just one fight after another. But now we're all together. I'm going to have a baby. I'm sure it will be a boy and I'll name him Richard. It'll be like giving birth to my own brother. And the show will be for Lenore. She'll get to do her thing. I'll make us a home. I hope we're going to be really good friends, Ada. I really do. I'm so happy you're doing this show. It's going to be awesome, and even Richard would have to agree that if we do this in the mansion where he was killed, the ratings will be ridiculous.' She smiled, did Lenore's trademark head bob and winked.

Ada's breath caught. It was pure Lenore.

'Ada!'

She turned at the sound of Melanie's voice. She'd lost track of time, the conversation with Rachel having made her forget the dozens of hopeful dealers still to get their shot at fame, or at least a spot on a reality show. She was trying to make sense of Rachel's ramblings – Richard and Lenore were inside of her? She wanted to make a home? *Is she talking in metaphors?*

Melanie spoke into her Bluetooth. 'Found her . . .' She looked from Ada to Rachel, not having recognized the celebrity at first with her toned down hair and outfit. 'Tell everyone to take another fifteen, but not a second longer. Is Barry there? OK, no, that's fine.'

Rachel cleared her throat. 'You're with the show.'

'Hi.' Melanie shifted her clipboard and extended her hand. 'Melanie Taft, I'm the assistant field producer.'

They shook.

'I'm so sorry about your brother and, of course, Lenore,' Melanie said.

'Thank you.' Rachel smiled. 'So what are you shooting today?'

'Auditions for the experts.'

'Mom always said casting shows is where you make or break them. And Ada, forgive me for what I'm about to say.'

Ada, rarely at a loss for words, marveled at Rachel's sudden poise. Her posture erect, her approach to Melanie was clearly that of an employer to an employee.

'They have to be exhibitionists, people who can ignore the camera and be completely relaxed and hopefully a little unstable. Then, you've got to have eye candy.'

Ada coughed. 'Like sixty-five-year-old grandmothers?'

'Ada,' Rachel said, her expression intense. 'You bring something important – class. This show runs the risk of being in horrible taste, which is not necessarily a bad thing for reality TV. But certain lines can be approached, but not crossed. We're going to be showing people at their rawest and most emotional. Someone's died and now we've got to liquidate their estate. I can see why Lenore gave this the green light. Even the name – *Final Reckoning.*'

'People will trust you,' Melanie added. 'Even watching you with the dealers. We'll have one camera on you at all times, one on them and one on the item. It's your face and reactions the audience will want to see. In a sense you're the voice of the viewer.' And to Rachel, 'You can't imagine what a godsend this one is.'

'I see it,' Rachel said. 'She's the mother everyone wishes they had. I don't know if Barry mentioned this, but I've decided to attach myself to this show as an executive producer.'

Melanie, who'd spent a good portion of her day coming up with creative ways to throw obstacles in front of contestants, seemed stunned. 'Really?'

'Is there a problem with that?'

'No. Just, Barry didn't mention it.'

'I'll talk to him. So when were you hoping to get into the mansion?'

Melanie's eyes widened. 'You're still OK with that?'

'OK? It was my idea. We'd be stupid not to, and the sooner the better.' She turned to Ada. 'We'll get ratings higher than the

Kardashian wedding. Who wouldn't be interested? The trick,' looking to Melanie, 'will be in the editing.'

Ada looked between the two women and then at Clarence, who hung in the background, now stomping out a cigarette on the ground. 'It's a crime scene,' she said.

'That'll make it better,' Rachel said, and then, to Melanie, 'We should get rolls of that yellow crime scene tape, just leave bits and pieces scattered around to remind the audience. So where is Barry? I need to talk with him and see how things are going. Maybe we should all plan on a dinner meeting. Give me a chance to meet the crew and hash some things through with Barry.'

Melanie, who'd earlier told Ada to plan on taping well into the night, immediately shifted to follow Rachel's cue. 'How's eight?'

Rachel looked at Ada. 'I'd like you to be there and, if you want to, bring your girlfriend?'

'Love to,' Ada said, thinking that if she were about to visit Narnia she'd want Lil along for the ride. 'Could I bring my grandson, Aaron? He's playing hookey from UConn and I know he'd want to get an inside look at this.'

'Absolutely, and you know where we should do it – what's that place right on the green? You know, the one with the awful food but amazing ambience.'

'The Greenery,' Ada said.

'That's the one. Melanie, reserve a big enough room, if necessary get the whole restaurant. And give me Barry's numbers. I need to see where things are at.'

TWENTY

Mattie sat back in the too-familiar Grenville police chief's office, it's prior occupant's awards and photos with politicians and celebrities replaced by Kevin Simpson's fishing-themed decor or 'Kevin with Trout', as her partner Jamie had dubbed it. It was hard not to compare the former chief – competent and corrupt – to good-natured Kevin, who knew everyone and everything.

The three of them – Jamie, Kevin and Mattie – sat around his desk focused on the phone, which was on speaker. Kevin's computer monitor was turned so that the two detectives could view the ballistics report on Lenore's murder.

'It's a match.' Detective Jean Murphy's voice came through the speaker.

'It is, and we've got the gun,' Mattie said, looking at the bagged and tagged nine millimeter Glock on Kevin's desk. 'So we'll go with the assumption: same gun, same shooter.'

This time a man's voice – Detective Scott Baker – 'It's a seventeen C Gen three. It's what I carry.'

'You and half the NYPD,' Detective Murphy answered. 'What I don't get is, why leave it in Richard Parks' bed? It was deliberate. And absolutely no fingerprints?'

'None,' Mattie said. 'Kind of a clumsy attempt to frame Rachel.'

'Maybe they were done with it,' Kevin offered. 'Didn't want to have it around.'

'It's possible,' Detective Baker said. 'Although I still like your idea of keeping Rachel locked away.'

'I tried,' Mattie said. 'But her doctor said he couldn't hold her, and she's not a suspect. At least she's allowing a uniformed presence around the mansion, which by the way is a security nightmare. You'd think someone of Lenore's stature would have had a better system.'

'They don't need them,' Kevin said. 'You'd be amazed at the number of celebrities in Grenville and Shiloh. That's why they like it here. People don't bother them. For Lenore, putting the gate up and a fence around her perimeter was good enough. Or it was before yesterday.'

'So, in both cases,' Mattie said, 'the killer shot for the heart. He, possibly she, hit Lenore's aorta and Richard's left lung and ventricle. Death would have come in a matter of minutes. In the case of Lenore, from a distance of twenty-five feet. Richard's was at close range.'

'So twenty-five feet with a Glock,' Detective Murphy added, 'and a single shot, says someone's a practiced marksman.'

'Yeah, and from how you've described Lenore's schedule,' Mattie continued, 'someone knew exactly where she'd be.'

'Yeah,' said Detective Baker. 'Apparently on days she shot two episodes, her every minute was mapped out. The tough part is there was no secret about that. We've got a list of over three hundred people who'd have had access to her schedule.'

'But not Richard,' Mattie added. 'He's in a meeting at LPP Tuesday night. Over two hundred executives were in that meeting. Lots of them aware they're about to get the ax.'

'Yeah, the tension in that room,' Detective Murphy said, 'was thick. People were sweating. They all wanted to know if they still had jobs.'

'Did they?' Jamie asked.

'No,' Murphy replied. 'And with Richard's death the top executives at LPP have started laying off everyone associated with *Lenore Says*. Monday morning half of them are to going to find their belongings in boxes.'

'That quick?' Mattie asked.

'Yeah, apparently the cash drain is huge. And if there's not a product and sponsors, their CFO wants to pull the plug fast. Which speaks against one of the producers or crew members wanting to kill Lenore. Their livelihood depended on her being alive and able to get in front of a camera.'

'True,' Mattie said, 'but not all the plugs are getting pulled, correct?'

'That's right,' Detective Murphy replied. 'LPP has a dozen reality shows on the air, and another dozen in production.'

'Like *Final Reckoning*,' Mattie said. 'Frankly, that's the common denominator in the two murders, or it could be.'

'Agreed,' Detective Baker said. 'And here's a strange thing: there's absolutely no documentation, at least none that LPP is willing to divulge, that talks about that show. Apparently this Barry Stromstein decided to put the ball in motion all on his own. He'd had a meeting with Lenore the morning she was shot. Word is he was one bad idea away from getting canned.'

'And,' Mattie said, 'witnesses saw him and Richard having words . . . or at least Richard was having words with Barry. Richard wasn't keen on the show, and this is where things get freaky. Rachel Parks wanted to have Lenore's estate featured on the show, as in selling her mom's things.'

'Seriously?' Detective Murphy asked. 'That's—'

'Yeah,' Mattie continued. 'Richard and Rachel were not seeing eye to eye on that. So since we're talking motive and access, we've got to look at Barry Stromstein and his cast and crew.'

'So the motive would be what?' Kevin asked.

'A hit TV show,' Mattie offered. 'Staying employed.'

'It doesn't sit quite right,' Detective Baker said. 'Think about it: yes, this Barry guy is off trying to make a show, possibly without the necessary approval. For all he knows both he and his crew have pink slips waiting.'

'Do they?' Mattie asked.

'Not yet,' Detective Murphy replied. 'Seems Rachel Parks has taken an interest in the project.'

Kevin grunted. 'You're not kidding. She was on the phone not an hour ago wondering when the CSI team would be finished, so they could start setting up the house for shooting.'

'What did you tell her?' Mattie asked.

'That I'd get back to her. You guys are running this show – you tell me.'

'Interesting,' Mattie said.

'What are you thinking?' Detective Murphy asked over the speaker.

'Everything leads us back to this creepy show,' Mattie said. 'There's way too many connections for this to be coincidence. At the very least whoever killed Lenore and Richard are insiders who are familiar with both LPP headquarters and Lenore's Shiloh mansion.'

'And her schedule,' Detective Murphy interjected.

'Even the security, or lack thereof, around the estate,' Jamie added.

'The mansion's been used in dozens of episodes of *Lenore Says*,' said Kevin.

'Right . . .' Mattie said. 'Kevin, if they want to shoot that show, I'm thinking we should let them. The CSI team can get everything wrapped up tonight. I could be wrong, but I think there's something about this show that's connected to the murders.'

'You want to hear something funny?' Kevin asked.

'Sure,' Mattie said.

'When I was on the phone with Rachel, she asked me not to clean up a thing. She said, "leave all the crime scene stuff", but here's the kicker. She said, "leave the blood".'

'What were you thinking?' Jamie asked Mattie as they headed to their black SUV.

'It's this show,' she said. 'The more I think about it, who really profits from this?'

'That Barry guy,' Jamie said, 'and I suppose anyone associated with the show, if it becomes a hit, including our adorable Ada.'

Mattie chuckled. 'Yeah, I can see that. Although for someone living in a retirement community she does seem always to be in the middle of homicides.'

'She *is* in the middle of this show,' Jamie offered.

'True, and that is a beautiful thing.'

'Because—' Jamie stopped. She clicked the button on her key ring for the locks. 'You've got to be kidding?'

'It is convenient,' Mattie said as she yanked the passenger side door open.

'Mattie, we've been working together three years now?'

'Close to, rookie. You got something you want to say?'

'Just an observation,' the young detective said. 'Last time we were in this town your friends Lil and Ada were extremely helpful.'

'They were.'

'And they got hurt.'

Mattie paused. 'I don't remember that.'

'Not physically, not that time. But remember what happened. That horrible woman posted pictures of the two of them in bed.'

Mattie swallowed; discussions of Lil and Ada's relationship made her nervous. 'I'd forgotten about that.'

'I hadn't,' Jamie said. 'I think they're two of the most courageous people I've ever met. So if you want her to try and get information, you know Ada'll do it. Everything here looks so pretty, but we both know it's just window dressing. This is a double murder and we still don't know the motive. And if you're right and the killer is connected to this show, Ada's in the middle of something dangerous.'

'You don't think she's already digging?'

Jamie chuckled. 'I didn't say that. I think that's under the heading of leopard, spots . . . changing.'

'We should talk to her, but I hear you. We should do it on the DL.'

Jamie glanced at Mattie as they headed north toward Shiloh for a last look at Lenore's estate before opening it up to the cast and crew of *Final Reckoning*. 'It can't be easy for them,' she said.

'For who?'

'Lil and Ada. Think of all the shit I get? The only reason they didn't can my ass was because you were willing to be my partner. Even before I came out, everyone just assumed I was gay.'

Mattie really wished Jamie would change the subject. 'You're a good detective. It shouldn't matter.'

'It shouldn't, and it does,' Jamie said. She felt Mattie's discomfort and, not for the first time, wondered at its source. She knew Mattie had married young, had a son, Oscar, who was in a graduate program at UConn. Beyond that, Mattie didn't talk about her personal life. 'I asked Patty to marry me.'

'Congratulations,' Mattie said, wondering how much longer it would take to get to the estate. Without doubt Jamie had grown into her favorite partner. Their first year together she'd been more of a mentor and supervisor. But not now; the woman was smart, had good instincts and an uncanny ability to see below the surface of a person's words. She didn't care that she was gay. *So why does this conversation make you squirm?* 'What made you pop the question?'

Jamie slowed as they passed the stretch of road where the chain-link fence had been cut. 'Beyond that I love her and want to spend my life with her, it's a lot of practical things. We both want kids, and we're looking for a house. I have a brother who thinks I'm going to hell for being gay and Patty has a brother-in-law who won't let her near his own kids. Her sister's a wimp who just lets him do that. All I can think is that if something were to happen to either one of us, we'd have no protection. Those assholes could come in and try to take it all. While same-sex marriage still only counts at the state level, with the repeal of "Don't Ask, Don't Tell" and DOMA, maybe it'll become federally recognized.' She paused. 'I'm thinking about what the New York detectives said.'

'Which part?' Mattie asked, relieved to be back on the more comfortable topic of murder.

'About how many people despised Lenore. Not just disliked, but actively hated or feared her.'

'Like Barry,' Mattie said as the locked gate to Lenore's estate came into view. There were news vans parked in front of it and uniformed Grenville officers. Jamie showed her badge through the windshield and the gate opened.

'The problem is, his alibi is good. We could probably poke a hole through the time Lenore was shot, but we've got half a dozen witnesses saying he was holed up in meetings through two a.m. the night Richard was killed. The bigger question is how many Barrys are out there?'

'They're getting a subpoena for LPP's human resources records. It could be many.'

'Revenge is a good motive,' Jamie said as she eased the SUV behind a CSI van. 'And then there's the big secrets of Lenore being gay and possibly having more children.'

Mattie swallowed. 'Yeah.'

'New York says there were at least three girlfriends, and Clarence can probably confirm that. So there's a potential jealousy angle.'

'Then why go after her son?' Mattie asked. 'I think that motive can go lower on the list.'

'Probably right. Still, I'm keeping it on mine. And then we've got our mystery surrogate. Maybe she wasn't happy with the deal, or decided she wants to keep the kids. In terms of the money trail, by killing Lenore and Richard you've bumped off two of the three natural heirs . . . but then why not take out Rachel? Here's a thought: with so many people hating Lenore, it's almost like they could have raised an office pool to hire a hit man.'

Mattie snorted. 'That would be a first.'

Jamie laughed as she opened the door. 'Think about it . . . but no, I keep getting hung up on the part where, yes, they hated her and were afraid of her, but she was also the one putting fat paychecks into their pockets.' She looked at the mansion and then back at Mattie. 'You're right.'

'About what?'

'Ada. She's on the inside of the LPP machine; maybe she can find out what makes it tick.'

TWENTY-ONE

Barry couldn't decide if he were the luckiest producer in television history or the most screwed. 'Oh God, no,' he whispered under his breath. He plastered on a smile as Rachel Parks sauntered down the staircase of the mansion. *What has she done? She's crazy, absolutely out of her fucking mind.*

At the foot of the stair two cameras captured her advance. The girl was an expert, having studied at the serpent's breast. Her expression was subtle, her eyes lovely like her mother's, with a hint of sadness, her black dress clinging to her curves without being sluttish. Her face was dewy and young, but what was freakish was she'd dyed her hair auburn – just like Lenore's, like seeing the mother brought back to life thirty years younger.

Rachel paused two steps from the bottom, one hand gracefully holding the railing. She'd wanted to start the show with an introduction. Barry was leery, but had quickly discovered that what Rachel wanted, Rachel got – *like mother like daughter.*

He glanced at his crew, most of them with him since LA and *Model Behavior.* He had managed to keep them employed and on the cusp of what might be the hottest new show in TV. That it might simultaneously bring reality TV to a new low in taste was irrelevant.

In addition to his inner circle, the mansion was crawling with over a hundred LPP employees, many of them on the verge of being laid off; this shoot was an eleventh hour reprieve from the unemployment line.

'Thank you for coming,' Rachel said. She looked down and then straight into a camera.

Barry checked the monitor as she paused, her eyes wide. He held his breath, not knowing if the girl could deliver. If she couldn't he had lots of tricks, but if she could . . . He bit his lip.

'My mother had so many beautiful things.' Another wistful pause. 'But she's gone, and so is my brother. Things are just things and it's time for me to start anew. Welcome to my home, to where Lenore raised me and my brother Richard. We've had lots of film crews and lots of good times over the years. Some of you watched, and saw Lenore do everything here, from stuffing a turkey to hosting parties for A-list Hollywood.' She shook her head and gave a small, sad laugh. 'I could tell you stories about those. But now, it's a new chapter and, much as I loved my mother, her taste' – she swept her hand upward as a camera followed, panning over the lavish second story landing with its gilt mirror and Louis Quatorze furnishings – 'is not mine. So, in the spirit of my mother, who was a television innovator, I'd like to welcome you to *Final Reckoning.*

'To get us started, I'd like to introduce my dear friend and the show's hostess, Ada Strauss.'

Barry called 'Cut'. He looked at Rachel on the monitors. She was perfect. He stuffed back the excitement; *this is going to work. This is really going to work.* He gave Melanie instructions to get the next scene set, both of them having gone the last forty-eight hours with almost no sleep and an untold amount of coffee and energy drinks. Last night had been pure insanity once they'd realized that Rachel was serious about moving forward with the shoot, Lenore's estate and the mansion. The roadblock of it being a crime scene had evaporated with a single call to the accommodating chief of police. But once it became clear that this was a go, Barry knew he was over his head, with no storyboards, no shoot schedule, inadequate equipment and crew . . . and no one could ever know that. Yes, they'd worked out the broad strokes of the show, but the details and logistics, plus the lack of an approved budget . . . Melanie had summed it up nicely. 'Shoot first and ask questions later.'

He looked up as Rachel walked toward him. Her appearance was freaking him out, like Lenore back from the grave. *Why would she dye her hair like that?* How would the audience react? And did it matter? This was a freak show, his freak show, and welcome to it.

'How was I?' she asked.

'Perfect,' he admitted.

'Really?'

'Yeah.'

'Good, and you got everything and everyone we asked for?'

'I did, thank you.'

Rachel smiled. 'Hey, we're in this together. You've produced a show before; I haven't. If we need something you have to let me know. We're partners, Barry. If something's not going right, you need to let me know.'

He blinked. Yes, she looked like Lenore, but that's as far as the comparison went. Yesterday afternoon, when it became clear that the shoot could actually move forward, Barry had been thrown. Still in the middle of casting, they'd not scripted the episode. It was fly by the seat of your pants taken to new heights. That was followed by the realization that his small crew and creative team weren't equipped to handle a set of the magnitude of Lenore's estate. It was Rachel who'd bluntly asked, 'What do you need,

Barry?' Not since his one hit show, *Model Behavior*, and maybe the early days with Lenore, could he remember feeling valued. It was a rush, and he didn't want to think about it for fear it might vanish. *You're back*, he thought. *You're going to be on top.* 'Thanks Rachel, it's going to be a really long day. You let me know if you need breaks.'

'I'm too wired,' she said. 'This is amazing. I always felt jealous of the film crews and how everyone knew what they were doing. And then when the show would go on the air and I'd see how perfect everything looked . . . that's what's going to happen here, isn't it?'

He smiled. 'Yes, the miracle of editing. We'll film a couple hundred hours and then hack it down to forty-one minutes.'

'It's got to be exciting,' she said. 'I mean I know it's about selling dead people's stuff, but this has got to be a hit.'

'Rachel,' he said, 'your doing this pretty much guarantees that.'

She laughed. 'Thanks, and we both know that people will think I'm the biggest "C" in the world.'

Barry looked at her. 'Not necessarily,' he said. 'Call it editing, call it producing, but you'll come off however you want me to have you come off.'

'I want to come off like her,' she said without hesitation.

'Lenore.'

'Yeah. Think of all the things she did. She televised herself getting knocked up, and did it like . . . like shooting a cover for *Town and Country*.'

He considered his words. Prior to the last two days, he'd had no real contact with Rachel Parks. But people talked, and Rachel was one of the darling train wrecks of the tabloids, not to mention fodder for office gossip. Now it appeared she was his new work partner. 'Is that why you dyed your hair?'

'Do you think it's too much?'

'It looks good, but it does make you look like a younger and prettier Lenore. It'll be a shock for some . . . but in reality TV that's a good thing.'

'I thought so. This whole thing . . . Oh look, there's Ada. You're the one who picked her, aren't you? She looks awesome.'

'Yes,' remembering how only two days ago she'd thought his choice of hostess was too old.

'I'm going to say hello, and Barry, remember: if you need

anything, let me know. I intend to pull my weight. You'll be the one who knows what to do. I'll be the one to make sure it happens.'

'Good deal,' he said and, weirdly enough, he meant it. He watched as Rachel greeted Ada. The young woman threw her arms around the elder, whom they'd again dressed in Chanel; the make-up apron was still around her neck. He turned away. The next scene to be shot was critical. In it, Ada would briefly explain to Rachel – as she would to the heirs of each week's episode – what the show entailed.

Melanie came up to him. 'This next scene makes or breaks the show,' she commented, as though reading his thoughts.

'Yeah, you read Daryl's script.'

'Yeah, and made a few changes.' She glanced at Ada and Rachel. 'I bet we don't need it.'

'I hope you're right, but make sure she can see the teleprompter anyway.'

Barry turned at the sound of the front door opening. His anger surged. People needed to respect the 'Do Not Disturb, Filming in Progress' signs. Just as quickly as his temper flared, it came down. 'Jeanine, Ashley, what are you guys doing here?'

'I hope you don't mind,' Jeanine said. 'We've been out all day. I'm in love. This town . . . the farms, the houses . . .'

Barry, even a decade into their relationship, got lost in her emerald eyes. He sensed her excitement. 'Something's up; what is it?'

'This place, Barry. I don't know how to describe it.'

'Horsies, Daddy,' said Ashley. 'And ponies, and we saw moo cows, and they let me pet the baby chicks. They were so soft.'

'We stopped at a farm that has a petting zoo,' Jeanine explained. 'It's owned by a husband and wife who raise exotic animals, ostriches, zebras. They even have kangaroos. This whole town . . .'

He marveled at how the light through the front windows created halos in her fiery hair. He often wondered why she'd abandoned her modeling career. Yes, Hollywood and New York were filled with gorgeous women. But with Jeanine it went beyond the surface, and she also had the rare ability to show her inner grace on film. If he'd had his way she'd have been the winner and not first runner up on *Model Behavior*. To be fair, in a totally uncharacteristic way, Jeanine had choked in the final competition. It was an underwater photo shoot with the two remaining contestants in mermaid drag. Jeanine, who'd proven herself a strong swimmer and diver in prior episodes, seemed unable to stay down long enough to get the necessary shots. She'd then further damaged her chances by sobbing on screen, like all of the other silly girls who'd gone home, wailing that the task was too hard.

The audience had given the win to an insipid redneck teen with a back story involving a mother so obese she had to be craned out of her bedroom and a father who got his own short-lived reality show about backwoods hunting, entitled *Coon Hunt*, which was hastily cancelled when it was discovered he was an active member of the KKK. When the final results had been tallied, Barry had seriously considered giving the win to Jeanine anyway. But one thing he knew – you can fake anything in TV, just don't mess with the FCC rules concerning game shows. And while *Model Behavior* was a reality show it was still a contest, with a six-figure cash prize and a year's contract with a top agency. He looked at little Ashley, who was gazing wide-eyed at all the activity in the grand foyer. 'You're having a good time,' he said.

'Barry, do you know what houses go for here? What we paid for' – she picked her words carefully, not wanting Ashley's impressionable ears to pick up anything they shouldn't – 'our little apartment . . . We could have something wonderful here. And did you know that Grenville has one of the top-rated public school systems in the country?'

'I didn't. So what are you saying? You want to move?'

'Do you know how many Hollywood A-listers have homes out here? It wouldn't hurt your career. Imagine Ashley growing up here, with space, and kids who aren't afraid to leave their homes. There are real neighborhoods. We were driving around, and . . .' She shook her head. 'I know you like New York and all, but . . .'

'If this show takes off . . .' He looked back at Melanie, who was shepherding Rachel and Ada into the paneled library for the critical next scene. 'You'd really consider leaving New York?'

'Barry, if it was what you wanted, I'd do it in a heartbeat. Think about it; this is a real place. We could raise our family here. Maybe another baby, maybe two.'

He looked at Ashley. 'You like it here, sweetheart?'

'They had a baby kangaroo,' the little girl answered. 'His name was Poppy.'

Barry laughed, knowing a three-year-old's 'yes' when he heard it. 'Jeanine, you're serious.'

'Yeah. The clothes, the Birkin bags, none of that matters.'

'Don't say that,' he said, wondering what he ever did to deserve her.

'I never cared about that stuff. You know that and, yes, I understand that we have to look a certain way, and I want to. But think about it. Even from that side of things, Grenville is hot. Half of the west coast have houses here so their kids can grow up outside of Hollywood. Think about it – you, me, Ashley . . . maybe a Baby Barry.'

He snorted. 'I will not saddle a child with the name Barry.'

'You know what I'm saying. Flowers in the spring, a fire in the fireplace, actually knowing our neighbors. Our kids getting on a yellow school bus in the morning.'

'I do.' The dream she painted was one that he could sign up for. He looked at the beehive of activity around them. His eye caught on a piece of crime scene tape. It hadn't been left by the police, but rolls had been strewn by one of the interns to make the reality of a murder scene more real. There was every indication this show would be a hit. 'It's a hell of a gamble, Jeanine. We could buy something here and find out the show wasn't going to get picked up. Or that no one wants to watch it. It might be better to rent something. Do a month to month lease.'

'We could,' she said. She glanced at their daughter and gently shook her head. Her voice soft and just for his ears. 'I don't think a lot of moves are good for her, but if you think it best.'

She was right. 'How's this . . . you meet with a realtor in the morning and get a better feel. If you see something you think is perfect, call me and we'll figure this out.'

'I love you so much,' and her hands were on his face, her lips on his. She pulled back. 'So much.'

'I love you too.'

Not to be left out, Ashley chimed, 'Love you, Daddy.'

'Come on, Ashley,' Jeanine said, her fingers entwined with Barry's. 'Let's go look at houses while Daddy works.' She brushed his cheek with a final kiss and whispered, 'I will follow you to the ends of the earth, but for now let's stop in Connecticut.'

He watched them leave, feeling the loss of her touch. He caught

a final scent of her citrusy perfume and turned back to the show
he'd not fully realized was in chaos.

Melanie, in one of her standard shooting outfits – camo pants
with lots of pockets, a silk T-shirt and a khaki vest with more pockets
– was coming toward him across the foyer.

'What's wrong?' he asked.

'Nothing, I mean nothing this second. They're setting up.' She
glanced back. 'Barry, I'm freaking out. We have no storyboard.'

'I know,' he said, 'and—'

'You don't have to say it. We're working through the night . . .
again.'

'We have to,' he said with a smile. To all the world – or at least
to the couple hundred LPP employees who'd descended on Grenville
and Shiloh – he was a TV producer in his element, smoothly handling
the reins of what they all hoped would be their salvation, a long-
running hit show. 'Just because we don't have a clue on Friday
afternoon doesn't mean we won't have one by sun-up Saturday.'

'I can handle that,' she said, standing by his side. 'The premise
is basic: three experts give their opinion and offer quotes to Rachel.
We'll need to throw in a couple twists. Ethan thought about maybe
holding an estate sale. Set up tents, put the stuff on the driveway.
Or one of the dealers was talking about an on-site auction. Can you
imagine?'

'Lenore would shit bricks.'

'I know,' she said. 'It's in awful taste.'

'Yeah, it's perfect. The logistics, though; we need to shoot this
fast.'

Melanie's expression slipped and her worry showed. 'What's with
Rachel's dye job? It's freaking me out.'

'I don't know,' he admitted. 'But, unlike what her brother felt,
she wants this to move forward.'

Melanie's voice lowered further. 'I think she did it. I don't know
why or how the cops let her out. But look at her. It's like fucking
All about Eve. She kills Lenore and then . . . turns into her. Which
maybe I can handle. But here's what's got *me* shitting bricks.' Her
smile stayed fixed as a crew member approached.

'Ms Taft, they told me to let you know they're ready to start.'

'Too fabulous. I'll be right there.' As soon as he was out of
earshot she whispered, 'What has me really scared . . .'

'That someone else will get shot?' he offered.

'No. Strange, I'd not even thought about that. Mostly because I figured she did it and, as long as she gets her way, things should run smooth. But that's the kicker. What little I've seen of Rachel Parks has shown me she's unpredictable. Yesterday she's Rachel, today she's Lenore. When she wakes up tomorrow, who's she gonna be? And how the fuck are we going to deal with it?'

Ada was waiting with Rachel in the library for the next take; she was exhausted. She'd been at this since six a.m. It was nearly seven p.m. and all she wanted was a hot bath, something to eat that wasn't from the food service truck, and Lil. They'd been told this was the last scene of the day; that was five thirty, but a series of delays – mostly problems with the lighting – had left them frozen in their spots.

'How are you holding up?' Ada asked, long past the shock of Rachel's dye job and jarring resemblance to Lenore.

'Tired,' she admitted, '. . . and sad.'

'You're thinking about Richard?'

'Yeah, I'm starting to rethink this whole thing. But then I look around . . .'

The make-up woman reappeared, as she'd done at thirty-minute intervals throughout the day. She hovered first around Rachel, patting down the shiny spots on her nose and brow, and then did the same with Ada. She whispered, 'I heard them say we'll be out of here in an hour, if you can get this done in one or two takes.'

Ada chuckled, amused at how people took her for a professional actress, or whatever a TV hostess was. 'I'll do my best.'

'And not just Richard,' Rachel said. 'I never realized what all this meant. I just assumed Lenore was the world's biggest narcissist and needed this, like some kind of mirror to see how important she was. I still think that's true . . . to a point.'

'What's changed?' Ada asked, wanting to know what made Rachel tick. She knew the girl was mentally ill, but for the life of her she couldn't put a name to her array of symptoms. Possibly bipolar, with all the hot and cold, but incredibly raw, with moods that could be tripped by the careless word of a crew member. She'd flare hot, scream viciously at the object of her displeasure, and after a while come back to earth, unperturbed and unapologetic. The net result was that everyone treated her like a ticking bomb. The question behind all of it was, when she did explode could it . . . would it . . . did it . . . include murder?

'It's who she was.' Rachel sounded weary. 'Mom needed this to exist. Richard understood that and I think, in his Richard way, had made peace with it. He knew we were accessories to Lenore. I never understood that, or maybe I did. I just wouldn't accept it. But you want to know something?'

'What's that?'

'Just wanting something to be true doesn't make it so.'

'Correct,' Ada said.

Rachel looked through the library's open door to where Melanie and Barry were having a discussion. 'They don't have this planned out,' she said.

'How can you tell?'

'They're going too fast. A single episode of *Lenore Says* could take months to prepare. By the time they got to filming everything was set. And yes, I know with reality TV the premise is you're watching real life, but that's not how it works.'

Ada chuckled. 'Yes, I got that memo.'

'I wonder if he's up to this?' she said.

'Barry?'

'Yeah. He does have a track record or I would never have hired him.'

'You hired Barry?'

'I'm sorry.' She shook her head. 'I meant Lenore. And I know what she'd be doing right about now.' She stood up. 'I'll be right back.'

Ada shifted in her chair to watch as Rachel strode out to have words with Barry and Melanie. She saw Barry's eyes widen and his expression go from anxious, through a hastily concealed flash of anger, to panic. He was flushed and red-faced as Rachel turned back to Ada. She smiled, and in a clear voice called out, 'OK, people, we're shooting in five. Let's get this in the can.' She looked at Ada and, with Lenore's head bob and wink, said, 'Let's do this in one take, so we can all go home and get some rest.'

TWENTY-TWO

From their vantage on the edge of the fountain, Detectives Jamie Plank and Mattie Perez surveyed the mansion's brightly illuminated drive as the fleet of LPP personnel packed and dispersed to area hotels and B and Bs. It was ten p.m.

Parked among the vehicles were six of Grenville's twelve cruisers, most of the officers on overtime. They were augmented by six state vehicles and twelve troopers.

'For one spoiled celebrity I have no trouble getting the manpower to babysit,' Mattie mused. 'But when the locals were getting targeted, nada.'

'Hey,' Jamie said, her tone deadpan as she mimicked the tag line from a mandatory sensitivity seminar they'd endured. '*It's the people that make the case* . . . You think she's in danger?'

'She's the last Parks standing. Unless we count our supposed test-tube babies. Either she did it or she's a target. I think it's the latter, or she's smarter than we give her credit for. Could she have hired someone? Absolutely, but she wasn't the shooter. Either way, she needs to be watched.'

'There's Mrs Strauss,' Jamie said, as Ada and her grandson appeared at the front door. 'You wanted to talk to her.'

'Yeah,' Mattie said, 'but not here.'

'Right.'

They watched as Ada and Aaron got into his vintage blue Mercedes with its patches of sanded, but not yet painted, body filler.

'It's like end of shift at a factory,' Jamie said, as the stream of cast and crew exited the brick mansion.

'Or rats on a sinking ship,' Mattie commented. Throughout the day they'd been on the phone with their New York counterparts, who in turn had been digging into the workings of LPP. Once word had gotten out that there was a pilot being shot, everyone wanted to get attached. That Rachel was on board as a producer, according to LPP's head of HR, was a huge draw.

'Could this have been predicted?' Jamie asked.

'What?'

'This – the scale of this show? Is this the motive?'

Mattie nodded. 'I'm not certain, but it's on the board.'

'There's Stromstein,' Jamie said, as Barry, a canvas bag over one shoulder and a lawyer's wheeled briefcase trailing from his other hand, appeared in the doorway. He was in animated conversation with his assistant producer, Melanie. 'He looks angry.'

'Yeah,' Mattie agreed. 'Wonder why?'

'You know,' Jamie said. 'We could—'

'Not without a warrant,' Mattie said, referring to her partner's enthusiasm for the high-tech listening device 'the Little Whisperer', which could only be used with a judge's say so.

'He gains the most,' Jamie said.

'If the show's a hit, yes.'

'You said always to follow the money.'

'Yeah, and his alibi is tight and, according to the New York team, his crew was all together in a series of planning meetings when Lenore was shot. Can they swear to the occasional bathroom break?'

'More than enough time to zip up to the penthouse and plug Lenore,' said Jamie.

'Absolutely. Or it could have been a group effort.'

'That's a stretch,' Jamie said.

'I know,' Mattie agreed. 'I keep getting this insane thought.'

'You going to share?'

'Sure, it's like this. You know how we're forever getting hit up for ten or twenty bucks for someone's retirement, or when somebody's in the hospital?'

'Yeah?'

'Well, everyone hated Lenore. And the ones that didn't hate her were afraid of her.'

'Maybe not the girlfriends,' Jamie offered.

'Maybe not, until they found out they weren't exclusive. So, what if everyone kicked a grand toward getting rid of her? That way everyone's conveniently in meetings, or on a shoot out of town.'

'Or at the hospital like Rachel and Richard. It's a bit left field, and a lot of cutting off your nose to spite your face. But maybe . . .' Jamie looked at Barry, 'some could see a life at LPP without the L . . . like him. I'd like to know what has him so flustered. Should we ask?'

Mattie thought about it. Their previous interview with Mr Stromstein had yielded little. 'I've got a better idea. Let's go visit the ladies and see what Ada found out. If something's going on behind the scenes, she'll know about it.'

Jamie chuckled. 'Yeah, better than the Little Whisperer, and no warrant required.'

'It was awesome!' Aaron said, as he and Ada met Lil at the door.

'Exhausting,' Ada said, as the two women kissed.

'The kettle's on,' Lil said.

'Lovely.'

'How many cups of tea do you drink a day?' Aaron asked.

'I don't count,' Ada said, as she sank to the hall seat and eased off her pumps. 'I'm bringing slippers tomorrow.' She laid her head back and closed her eyes. She winced as the phone rang.

'It hasn't stopped,' Lil said from the kitchen. 'I've been letting it go to the machine.'

'Who's calling?'

'Everyone; there's a general sense that you've become a TV mogul. Who knew that half of Grenville was dying to get on air?' Lil passed Ada her tea.

A familiar voice came over the machine. 'Hi guys, it's Mattie Perez. I realize it's late.'

Before she could say more, Lil grabbed the handset. 'Mattie, how are you? Sorry the dinner thing didn't work out.'

'Yeah, the day kind of got away from all of us. Any chance Jamie and I could still stop by and ask Ada a few questions?'

Lil stared at Ada who, despite her exhaustion, looked adorable in her blue suit, with her spiked hair. 'She's about done in . . .'

'We're right outside.'

'Of course you are, so come on up.' And then to Ada, who was sipping tea with her eyes shut, 'We've got company.'

'Really?'

The phone rang.

'I'll turn the ringer off,' Lil said.

There was a knock at the door.

'Aaron?' Ada asked, not wanting to move.

He went to let the detectives in as a girl's voice came through the answering machine.

'Ada? Are you there?'

Ada strained, hearing what sounded like a child . . . a frightened one.

'Ada . . . Mrs Strauss. Are you there? Ada? Ada?' the girl's frightened voice called out.

'It's Rachel,' Ada said. 'Something's wrong. Lil, pick up.' She looked up. 'Mattie, Jamie, come on in.' She put a finger to her lips and pointed to Lil.

'Rachel?' Lil spoke into the phone.

'Is Ada there?'

Lil shook her head and looked at Ada. 'Hold on.' She passed the handset.

Ada took it and put it on speaker. 'Rachel, what's wrong?'

'I'm scared.'

Ada felt the young woman's fright through the line but couldn't understand the breathy child's voice. 'What's happening, Rachel?'

'I'm being silly.' Her voice was like that of a lisping five-year-old. 'All these policemen . . . but I'm scared. Can you come over?'

Ada was torn. It had been an exhausting day. Admittedly, most of it was spent with Rachel, learning all about what it was like to grow up as Lenore's unloved daughter. 'Why are you scared?'

'It's dark, and Richard isn't here. I'm scared. There are people here. I don't know them.'

Ada looked at Lil and twirled a finger around her ear. Rachel was making no sense, and what was with the little girl routine? 'It's late, dear, and I just got home. The police will keep you safe. That's their job.' Ada listened to the sound of her own voice, like she was talking to a five-year-old. 'The policemen are there to keep you safe.'

'Could I come over?' she asked. 'Clarence will drive me. Please?'

Ada felt trapped. On the one hand this was fascinating. On the other, no way did she want to invite Rachel's kind of trouble into their home. And having spent the last couple days around Rachel she knew that the woman could not handle frustration. Telling her 'no' was a sure way to set her off. 'I'm not certain that's a good idea.'

'Please. I can't stay here. I won't stay here.' Her scared five-year-old shifted to a petulant one. 'I want to stay with you and Lil. Please. Please.'

'Sure,' Ada said. She felt something tighten in her gut. 'Get a pen and I'll give you the address.'

Lil stared at Ada and slowly mouthed, *are you insane?*

Ada shrugged.

Rachel giggled. 'It'll be like a sleepover.'

'Yes,' Ada said, and she gave her the address.

Mattie had her phone out as Ada hung up.

'Where are we putting her?' Aaron asked.

Ada looked to Lil. 'The couch in the living room?'

'I guess. Ada, what's going on? Why in God's name did you say yes?'

Ada winced. 'I'm not a good person at this moment, Lil.'

'What are you talking about? You just offered our home to a near stranger. With double emphasis on the *strange*. For all we know she killed her mother and her brother.'

'I know. I think I'm becoming one of them,' Ada said. 'This is terrible.'

Lil sat next to her and took her hand. 'Do you have a secret?'

'I'm a bad person,' Ada admitted. 'I'm ashamed to say what I was thinking.'

'Really?' Aaron asked, listening in. 'Now you've got to say.'

'Yeah, I didn't want to get her angry. Rachel's got a hair-trigger temper, it's like she goes from zero to a thousand in a heartbeat.'

'So? You were more than kind with her on the phone,' Lil said.

'It's what was running through my head, that if I make her mad this will all end. I'll be off the show.'

'Oh,' Lil said, her mouth in an O. 'Bitten by the bug?'

'I guess. It's not like anything was all that glamorous. We spent most of the day just sitting and waiting, but it's exciting, Lil. Even now, I'm exhausted, but I can't wait to go back. Everyone is so young and enthusiastic.'

Lil butted her forehead against Ada's. She whispered, 'You're allowed. Think of Rachel as your crazy boss. I've got my editor, who as we both know can be an opinionated prig. Sometimes you have to do a little kissing up. That's life.'

While Lil, Ada and Aaron made plans for Rachel Parks' sleepover, Mattie was giving instructions over the line. 'If she moves, stick with her.' She gave the address for Lil and Ada's condos. 'This is too bizarre,' she said, to whoever was on the line. 'I've got the

number of her shrink; maybe this will make sense to him.' She hung
up and looked at Jamie. 'She hasn't moved,' she said.

'What do you mean?' Ada asked.

'Rachel's still where you guys were shooting. That was Kevin
Simpson. He says she's sitting in the chair sucking her thumb. She's
certifiable. She should never have been allowed to leave Silver Glen.'

'It's got to be an act,' Jamie said.

'Then she doesn't let up,' said Aaron. He looked at his grandmother. 'You were with her all day . . .'

'I was,' Ada said. 'I guess we'll be babysitting whoever she thinks
she is tonight too.' She looked at Mattie. 'I don't feel equipped.
You said you had her psychiatrist's number. Do you think it's too
late to call?'

'Probably,' Mattie admitted, 'but this isn't the time for niceties.'

'Agreed,' Lil said. 'Aaron, would you mind getting some linens
and making up the sofa bed in the living room?'

'You don't want to put her in the guest room?'

Ada shook her head. 'Absolutely not.' Between their two condos
they had six bedrooms. In Ada's, two were taken by Aaron and her
mother and the third had become the repository of decades in the
garment industry. In Lil's, the master was their bedroom, one was
Lil's office and the third was for guests. The thought of Rachel in
their home was scary enough. She glanced at Lil. 'It's better to have
her in the open.'

'No problem,' Aaron said, his focus split between his grandmother
and wanting to eavesdrop on Mattie's phone conversation with
Rachel's shrink.

'Dr Ebert. Hi, it's Detective Perez. I hate to bother you, but we've
got a situation with Rachel.'

Amos Ebert eased out of bed. His wife looked at him and mouthed,
Rachel?

He nodded and headed into his home office in their Upper West
Side home. 'Is she OK?' he asked, feeling his anxiety spike as it
did with late night calls. Sometimes from Lenore or Richard, sometimes from emergency room doctors and social workers, but usually
from Rachel.

'She's been acting strange all day,' Detective Perez said. 'She's
insisting on spending the night with a woman she just a met a couple

days ago . . . she's dyed her hair to look like her mother. We just got off the phone with her and she's sounding like she's five.'

Ebert listened. 'Where is she now?'

'About to leave the mansion to spend the night with two women she just met in Grenville.'

'Is she alone?' he asked.

'No. She's on round-the-clock security.'

He felt his anxiety ease. At least she hadn't hurt herself, and this other stuff . . . he'd worked so hard to keep this from happening, to keep the hysterical aspect of her personality disorder from fracturing into distinct 'as if' personalities. 'I should never have let her leave Silver Glen.'

'She didn't give you much choice,' Mattie said.

'True. Look, I'm in the city, I can be out there in an hour and a half, two tops.'

'I don't know if that's necessary,' Mattie said. 'Can you at least tell us what we're dealing with? I mean, is she safe?'

'She's never hurt anyone other than herself, if that's what you mean.'

'So you've said. But what's with all the different people?'

'Rachel dissociates. It's like spacing out but even more so. I think with the trauma of seeing her brother die, and having it so close to her mother's murder, she's literally splitting apart. Rachel has Borderline Personality Disorder, and she has a strong histrionic streak.'

'Translation, please,' Mattie said.

'The borderline is like she's always in an emotional mine field. The slightest rejection, misperceived insult, frustration . . . anything can set her off to where she's unable to contain her emotions – rage, self-loathing, depression. It's extreme, and before all of this she had made progress, fewer trips to the emergency room, less cutting, fewer drugs and less alcohol.' Dr Ebert looked at the framed diplomas above his desk. It was nearly midnight. He wondered if this were a breach of the doctor–patient relationship. 'Here's the thing; Rachel is a hysteric. What that means is she's an incredibly good hypnotic subject. In a sense that's what dissociation is, self-hypnosis. She's able to shut down and wall herself away if things get too hot. Sometimes she does it because she's frightened of what will happen if she feels her emotions.'

'But the little girl stuff, and dying her hair?'

'That's what I was trying to avoid.'

'I'm missing something.'

'Borderlines who are also hysterics can turn into multiple personalities.'

'So you are talking about the *Sybil* thing.'

'Yeah, and if she's headed in that direction I need to do something about it. Because once someone starts naming and identifying different personalities the whole thing takes on a life of its own, and it can take years to undo.'

'I'm missing something. Is it real or not?'

A vein pulsed on his forehead. 'Depends how you look at it. Rachel is adept at self-hypnosis. If she tells herself she's Lenore – she's Lenore. This little girl is some remembered construct of a younger self. Detective Perez, I've been with Rachel for a long time. In the past when these personalities emerged, I've been able to help her put them back, let her conceptualize them as part of who she is as a whole. Right now, maybe it's the extreme stress, the loss of Richard, pregnancy hormones . . . it's gone further than in the past. I'll be there as soon as I can.'

'That would be good,' Mattie said, as she tried to think through the doctor's explanation of Rachel's mercurial shifts.

Ebert paused, thinking through the logistics of getting his car from the garage at this hour. 'You did say she's under observation.'

'Oh yeah,' Mattie said. 'There's a couple dozen state and local police at the estate.'

'Good. So someone's actually watching her, as in line-of-sight.'

Mattie's breath caught. 'I don't know that for certain. Why?'

'History,' he said. 'I suggest you check and request that a couple of those officers keep their eyes on her at all times. I'll be there as soon as I can.'

They disconnected and Mattie immediately rang Kevin Simpson.

'It's bad,' were Kevin's first words. 'I was just about to call.'

Mattie braced as Ebert's last warning, possibly prophetic, rang in her head.

'She's gone,' Kevin said. 'Or she's hiding. Or . . . someone took her.'

'How long?' Mattie asked.

'Not more than five minutes. She went to her bedroom to pack a bag. One of the officers went in to check on her, the door to the deck was open, she was gone.'

Mattie stared at Jamie. 'Kevin,' she said, trying to keep her voice calm. 'Comb every inch of that mansion and the grounds. Five minutes isn't a lot. Did anyone hear anything?'

'No . . . the officer who was with her left her at the bedroom door. Rachel said she just needed to get a few things and she wanted to change.'

'Kevin, just find her. Call in everyone you need. If we don't have her back in fifteen minutes, I'll see what I can do in shaking loose some more manpower from the state.'

'There's more,' he said.

'What?'

'In her bathroom. There's blood, a lot of it.'

The pit in Mattie's gut deepened. 'Every inch, Kevin. Find her.' And what she wouldn't say . . . *or her body.*

'What about dogs?' he asked.

'Do it. I'll get there as soon as I can.'

Mattie looked from Jamie to Lil and Ada. She was about to tell Jamie that they needed to get back to the mansion, and then remembered why they'd come here. 'Ada, something happened today between Rachel and the producer.'

'Yes, late this afternoon. Rachel was worried that Barry didn't have things figured out for tomorrow's shoot.'

'What did she do about that?'

'I didn't hear the details, but you could tell she was angry.'

'How did he handle it?'

Ada recalled the way Barry's face turned red as Rachel had laid into him. 'What could he do? She's the boss. He wasn't happy.'

'And you didn't hear any of it?'

'No, but I remembered feeling bad for him. She did it in front of everyone. So I'm sure when you ask around, people heard. It must have been humiliating.'

'Right.' Mattie looked to Jamie.

'Kind of a pattern,' her partner said. 'Sort of the same thing happened between Barry and Richard Parks, and possibly between him and Lenore.'

'This is not good,' Mattie said, her annoyance at Rachel's

disappearance replaced by something more ominous. 'Call him,' she said. 'Lil, Ada, fun as always. We need to get a move on.'

'And if she shows up?' Ada asked.

'Do not let her out of your sight and call immediately. And she might need medical attention, but call me first.'

TWENTY-THREE

B y two a.m. Mattie's worst fears were becoming reality. Rachel Parks had left, or been abducted . . . or worse, from the mansion. All of the Parks' vehicles were accounted for.

Rachel had said she was going to call Clarence and have him drive her to Lil and Ada's. That call never happened. And Rachel's bathroom, where Mattie now stood with Dr Ebert, was spattered with blood, a lot of it. Mattie examined the droplets and smears against the white ceramic of the tub. Streaks of dark red with pooling by the drain, drops on the floor and bloody finger- and handprints on the sink, which were small and definitely female. There was no evidence that she'd packed a bag and her iPhone was by the bed, hooked to a charger.

'Could she have done this to herself?' she asked the psychiatrist.

'Yes,' he said. 'She cuts, usually on her upper arms and inner thigh. The only times she went for her wrists were when she wanted Lenore to see.'

'This much?' Mattie asked. She looked for the means and saw no razor or box cutter, the preferred implements of cutters she'd encountered through the years.

Dr Ebert, who even in the middle of the night managed to look professional in a navy blazer over a striped button-down shirt, shook his head. 'She's a superficial cutter. And she cleans up afterward. She doesn't want people to know when she does it, and it fills her with horrible shame.'

'You've actually seen—'

'A couple times. When she was fourteen Lenore and I thought it might be helpful to have me stay for a few weeks. We were working on an intensive therapy. So yes, I've been in this same bathroom after she's cut. So the good news, if there's any, is this is where she'd go to cut. The bad news is that she's tidy, and this isn't.'

Mattie mulled through his words. 'You said she didn't want people to know. Anyone in particular?'

'Her brother,' he answered without pause.

'And he's dead,' Mattie said. 'Maybe that's why it's such a mess. Her reason to hide it is gone.'

'It's possible.' He stared at the congealed blood near the tub drain. 'It's too much. She's gone too far.'

Mattie's cell rang. She picked up. It was Kevin Simpson.

'I'm outside with the search and rescue team. We got a pooch,' he said.

'Bring them up. They can get the scent from here.' She glanced at her watch – two twenty-four in the morning. Over two hours since Rachel had disappeared. *Not good*, none of this was good. 'If she cut herself, where's the razor?'

Ebert's dark eyes met her. 'That's what I'm worried about. She's got it with her. This isn't her pattern.'

A powerful tan-and-black German shepherd entered Rachel's bedroom, its leash tight in the grip of a thin brunet in a dark green parka and khakis with a canine search and rescue patch on her shoulder. Kevin Simpson was behind her.

'This is Officer Margaret James,' he said.

'And this is Perry,' the handler said, indicating the dog. 'This is the missing woman's room?'

'Yeah,' Mattie said. 'There's blood in the bathroom.'

'That should do.' She walked Perry to Rachel's bed. She gave the one word command, 'Scent,' and then walked the dog to the bathroom. 'Scent.' She looked back at Mattie. 'We're good to go.'

'OK to follow?' Mattie asked.

'Not a problem, just stay a bit behind.' She stroked the top of the dog's head. 'Perry, find.'

The dog's posture shifted, ears up, tail back, and his nose, like a pointer, shifted from the bathroom to the door leading to the deck. With Margaret giving him his lead he headed for the door.

Mattie, Dr Ebert and Kevin trailed behind.

Having checked when they'd first arrived, Mattie knew that the door was unlocked. Her earlier suspicions that this was how Rachel left, or was taken, were now confirmed by Perry the dog. Her anxiety surged as she remembered how this was also the mode of access and egress for Richard Parks' murderer.

The dog didn't hesitate as he trotted down the steps, his pace slowed only by his handler. 'If it was light, I'd let him off the leash,' Margaret explained as they all pulled out flashlights. The dog headed straight toward the pool and then past the cabana.

Mattie noted lengths of crime scene tape strewn on the ground, most of it added by the film crew. There were empty coffee cups and plates at the tables that surrounded the pool, and here and there cigarette butts.

The dog trotted around the cabana. His nose pointed into the darkened woods that encircled the mansion.

The pit in Mattie's stomach tightened; she could guess where they were headed. She heard the rushing water of the river to their right. With their beams trained on the ground they slowed their pace to avoid tripping on roots and rocks. Perry's eager snuffles and the noise of crickets did little to calm her. Fifteen minutes later and they were at the break in the chain-link fence.

Perry butted his nose against the metal and looked back at Margaret.

'Good boy.' She turned to Mattie. 'Keep going?'

'Yeah.' Her cell rang. It was Jamie. They'd split up after leaving Lil and Ada's. 'What you got?'

'An airtight alibi for Barry Stromstein. And you?'

'We're at the spot in the fence where Richard's killer came and left.'

'Crap,' Jamie said.

'I know. So tell me about this alibi.'

And Jamie, who was at the Grenville Suites Hotel, told Mattie that Barry and company had been holed up all night working on storyboards for the day's shooting.

'No breaks?' Mattie asked.

'Not long enough to get out there and abduct, or whatever. So I've been doing the bed count thing.'

'And?'

'More than one person can possibly handle. A lot of horny twenty- and thirty-year-olds in a hotel in the country. Apparently there were not enough rooms to go around.'

'Any notable absences?'

'Nothing leaping out. It's weird, this whole vibe.'

Mattie watched as Kevin held back the fence for the dog, the trainer and Dr Ebert to pass through. Kevin looked at her and, still talking to Jamie, she eased through. 'What do you mean weird?' Mattie looked at Perry as he sniffed the road's edge. The dog looked up. His posture stiffened.

'Not good,' Margaret said.

Mattie didn't need to hear it. 'The trail ends? She got in a car, didn't she?'

The dog handler nodded. 'It looks that way.'

Mattie shook her head as Jamie offered her impression of the LPP all-nighter at the hotel. She stared down the road, where the dog's nose pointed like a compass. Rachel could be anywhere. She could be dead.

The dog started down the road and then stopped. He sniffed the ground and then raised his head.

'That's odd,' Margaret said.

'What?' Mattie asked, her cell to her ear as she walked next to the handler. She threw her beam over the road and saw fresh skid marks. 'They left in a hurry.' She swept the light in a circle; dense woods on either side of the road that led from Lenore's back to Grenville, or to the interstate. Increasingly, this looked as though Rachel did not leave of her own volition. 'Go back,' she said to Jamie. 'What did you just say?'

'Which part?' Jamie asked.

'About making things tough for the contestants?'

'They call it FWT or FWC, Fucking with the Talent or with the Contestants. Apparently it's a thing you do in reality shows to keep them interesting. They throw unexpected obstacles at the talent. Which I guess in the case of *Final Reckoning* are the dealers competing for Lenore's estate.'

'So things they won't see coming,' Mattie said, wondering if this weren't a complete goose chase. The girl was missing and her chief suspect, and his crew, were all present and accounted for. Which left a few hundred people who hated and/or were afraid of Lenore, but other than revenge wouldn't directly profit from her death. 'FWT,' she muttered, as Kevin called for a car to meet them. 'So what do they have planned?'

'That's just it,' Jamie said. 'And I wonder if it matters. But I get the sense that nothing is planned. According to one of the grips, shows like this go through a development process that's at least a couple months long, sometimes years. Every episode is planned out, and even though it's supposed to be live action and spontaneous, it's mostly scripted. Although they're careful not to say so.'

'We knew this,' Mattie said. The New York detectives had confirmed that, prior to Monday, *Final Reckoning* hadn't existed. 'What am I missing?'

'This,' Jamie said. 'When word got out that Rachel was missing, I heard more than one crew member say it had to be the FWT.'

'And when Barry found out?'

'He wasn't heartbroken.'

'The show must go on?'

'Yup, although . . .' Jamie seemed pensive on the line. 'If Rachel is dead, who's left? If we go back to the basics – you know, follow the money – then who stands to profit? We've got a handful of cousins in the Carolinas, none of whom is named in the will. So even if they stand to inherit, it will be well over a year, maybe several, before her estate clears probate. Chances are the lawyers would see more than any heirs.'

'Plus two unborn babies that we're not even sure exist,' Mattie said.

'Not trying to be funny,' Jamie said, 'I'm thinking they'll have an alibi.'

'We've got to find this surrogate,' Mattie said.

'According to Detective Murphy, Lenore's Park Avenue obstetrician won't release anything. Even with a subpoena he can fight it under doctor–patient privilege. With Lenore dead, why would he care?'

'Good question; so someone else is involved. Someone who doesn't want him leaking the information. But we know a few things. Lenore needed to be in control. Going with that, the surrogate is someone she'd have under her thumb. Someone she could control. She's going to be an LPP employee, and I'd be willing to bet money she's right under our noses.'

TWENTY-FOUR

'Lil.' Ada put down her vampire novel, unable to focus. It was four a.m. on Saturday morning and neither woman could sleep. Their faces glowed by the light of their iPads. 'I can't stop thinking about Rachel.'

'I know,' Lil said, her mind going too fast for sleep. She listened to the night noises – crickets and frogs. A couple hours back she'd called Mattie, who'd been close-lipped. She knew from experience that the detective wouldn't give her the full story, not unless she had something to trade. 'Where would she go?'

'That's the thing. We don't really know her. Just weird bits of her and her brother, and then he's killed and she's calling, sounding like she's five. What if it's an act? And I know it's irrational, but I feel responsible. If I hadn't come up with this stupid idea, none of this would have happened.'

'Ada, Lenore had already been shot when we got to the city. This isn't our doing.'

'I said it wasn't rational, but I can't shake it. The more I think about how Rachel acted yesterday, the more I realize we shouldn't have been shooting that damn show. Lil, she was pretending to be her mother. Although I don't know if "pretend" is the right word. It's almost like she was Lenore, if that makes any sense. I keep seeing her in my head. She's obviously unstable . . . and all day long—'

'What?' Lil asked.

'All day long,' Ada pressed back against the headboard, 'we were being filmed all day long.'

'Isn't that the point?'

'I don't know. We did takes and there'd be multiple cameras. But even between takes I'd see that the red lights were on. At first it bothered me, and then, yeah . . . that's the point of a reality show.'

Lil pondered. 'So the show, and then . . . was anything happening?'

Ada shook her head. 'I drank a lot of tea and Rachel talked . . . a lot. And they filmed it all.'

'What was she talking about?' Lil asked.

'If I were to sum it up, she was weirdly hopeful, but not quite right. She's excited about having a baby and would talk about her brother and her mother, but it all felt disconnected. I thought she might be in shock and that it had just not hit her yet. But maybe that's not it.'

'Give me some specifics.'

Ada gazed at the sliders. 'She said that they were *always* with her, Richard and Lenore.'

'That doesn't sound so odd.'

'What if she meant it literally? Like she really thinks they're still there and not some idea of the dearly departed watching over her? There was other stuff, and to be honest I tuned her out at times. I don't usually do that.'

'Ada, you were with her the whole day. You got there at five a.m., and they didn't wrap till after ten. Which . . . what will they do without Rachel?'

'I'd say pull the plug, but what do you want to bet Melanie will be here in an hour with coffee and bagels? I know why I tuned her out,' Ada said.

'Why?'

'Listening to her made me feel worse. Because I know she's crazy, so I sat and nodded and spaced out. And thinking back through the day, it was when she started to talk about her new life. That's what's killing me.'

'What? I'm missing something.'

'The cameras: what if this show turns into some horrible documentary of Rachel's meltdown? It's going to come off like a freak show, from her physical transformation to these rambles about her mother and brother. This is why I feel like crap. I'm a part of it. Oh Lil . . .'

'Ada, you've done nothing wrong.'

'I'm not so sure of that. And where is she?' She pushed back the covers and got out of bed. 'I can't stand this. Lil, we've got to do something.'

'I know . . .' And Lil was up and headed toward the closet.

'There are probably dozens of police out looking for her,' Ada said. 'So what's two more middle-aged women?'

Lil stopped. She looked at Ada, who was throwing on a Prussian blue track suit. 'I love you so much,' she said.

Ada chuckled. 'That's because no one else will go with you, in the dead of night, to find a missing heiress.'

'There is that . . . Oh my goodness.'

'What?' Ada said.

'I'm married to Nancy Drew.'

'She was gay?' Ada asked.

'I often wondered. Did she have a boyfriend?'

'We both know that doesn't mean a thing. Look at Lenore.'

'There's so much information we're missing,' Lil commented. 'To start, with Richard dead do we know for certain that Rachel is the heir?'

'She's the natural heir. Whether or not Lenore structured things differently, we don't know. If Rachel were my daughter, I'd set up a trust. The thought of her with that much money . . . not good.' Fully dressed, Ada caught a glimpse of the two of them in the mirror on the back of the closet door. Her in a blue track suit and Lil in a burgundy one. She snorted. 'We look like two of the Power Rangers.'

'I never understood that show. My girls watched it.'

'Part of me feels like we're running away,' Ada said.

'From the film crew, from *Final Reckoning*?'

'Don't laugh, but yes, and we should hurry.'

Lil grabbed her keys and the satchel with her camera and laptop from her nightstand. 'Maybe that's what Rachel did,' she said. 'Maybe she realized this whole thing is in bad taste and, rather than be a part of it, she bolted.'

'It's a thought,' Ada said. They headed to the front door. 'We should tell Aaron we're going out. He's going to be so disappointed.' Ada stopped, her hand on the knob.

There was a light knock on the other side.

Lil looked over Ada's shoulder and turned on the outdoor light. 'Speak of the devil.'

'Aaron.' Ada opened the door to see her grandson, freshly showered, in jeans and a red hoodie.

He looked from his grandmother to Lil. 'What are you two up to?'

'Going for a drive,' Ada said.

'I see that.' His tone was suspicious. 'Grandma, you've got a seven o'clock call, which means hair and make-up no later than five.'

'Aaron, why are you out here?' she asked.

'I wanted to be ready when they came.'

'It's four a.m.'

'I don't want to miss them.'

Ada looked into her grandson's eyes. His excitement was obvious. On the list of people she loved in this world, his name would be one of the top four out of her mouth. She glanced back at Lil. 'We want to drive around, and maybe see what's happened to Rachel.'

'But didn't Mattie want you to stay here in case she turns up?' he asked, having had a first hand view of how Ada and Lil intruded into police investigations, at times with terrifying results.

'You'll be here,' Ada said. She stepped into the cool pre-dawn air.

'You're running away,' he said.

'Don't be silly,' Ada said.

'They'll film it anyway.'

'I figured that,' she said. 'Huh? Aaron, you're the same age as Rachel.'

'Yeah, but my mom's not a bazillionaire and, sadly, I do know who my father is.'

'True, but if you were to sneak out of the house in the middle of the night, where would you go?'

'You mean if I were Rachel? 'Cause where I'd go and where a crazy celebutante would go . . . although, maybe not so different. Around here there's not a lot of options, and Connecticut clubs close at one or two. So if she went partying, unless there's some kind of after hours scene in Grenville, which there isn't, the closest would be Brattlebury. And that's not her scene.'

'What are you thinking, Ada?' Lil asked.

'I'm thinking about what we know of Rachel from the press. She's always getting picked up by the cops or getting thrown out of nightclubs. Even crazy people have habits. So if it's the middle of the night and she's missing, maybe she went clubbing.'

Lil nodded. 'Or the part of her that likes to go clubbing wanted a night out. But like you said, it's Grenville and Shiloh. A couple restaurants have bars, but nothing in town stays open past midnight.'

'Then what Aaron said: let's think out of town – Brattlebury, or even Hartford. Rachel was raised here, she'll know where to go.'

'It's not New York,' Aaron offered. 'Although in the middle of the night, she could be in Manhattan in ninety minutes. And the two of you are not going to downtown Brattlebury or Hartford at four a.m.'

Ada caught their reflection in the hall mirror, two ageing Power Rangers; he had a point. 'Here's a thought.' She headed back toward Lil's office and settled behind the computer. She clicked on the browser as the other two followed. She typed in *Rachel Parks* and was offered four million hits. She refined the search and added the word *nightclub*. And finally, *after hours*. That got her down to thirty-seven hundred.

Lil grabbed a pad and pen and took notes. 'That one,' she said, noting a blog entry with a picture of Rachel apparently passed out on the sidewalk. 'What's the date?'

'April 23rd,' Ada said. 'The day Lenore was shot.' She read it aloud. 'Brooklyn nightclub owner Casio Gomez was philosophical when asked about the latest celebrity meltdown at his trendy Park Slope club, Murielle's. He said it was "the price of success", although whether he was referring to the bad-girl behavior of Rachel Parks, or his nightclub, was unclear. Mr Gomez did point out that Murielle's has a strict no-drinking policy for anyone under age and that at no time was Ms Parks served alcohol. One late night . . . er, early morning, reveler gave a first hand account of the famous train wreck's behavior. "She might not have been drinking, but she was high as a kite."'

Ada paused. She looked at the pictures of Rachel, her dress hiked up and not wearing underwear. And then at related posts and comments, where people had offered their two bits about that night. 'She knew she was pregnant.'

'Drugs and alcohol are not so good for a developing fetus,' Lil offered. 'Especially in the first trimester. And from everything you've said, she intends to keep the baby.'

'Yeah, but even today – I mean yesterday – when we were shooting, everyone, myself included, was drinking a lot of caffeine. She had either water or herb tea.' She scrolled back to a couple earlier entries.

'But you said she dyed her hair,' Lil said. 'Most OBs discourage that. A certain amount of the ammonia gets absorbed through the scalp.'

'I asked her about that. She said it was henna and the OB told her that it was fine.'

'So that's not adding up,' Aaron said. 'Either she's taking care of her unborn child or she's not. Or maybe she's not even pregnant and the whole thing is a publicity stunt.'

Ada shook her head. 'She is pregnant. I heard her talk with her doctor. And I do think she's taking care of the baby.' She stared at the screen. 'Here's another at the same club, two weeks earlier.' There were pictures of Rachel and her brother seated with a couple of young actresses. They looked happy and healthy. In one, Rachel's head was thrown back and she was laughing at something her brother had said. Clicking back to the browser she found several more sightings of Rachel Parks at the same club. Clearly it was a favorite.

'Aaron, how late do after hours clubs go?' Lil asked.

'Speaking as someone who's been to a total of two raves and one after hours club, I'd say things break up around six or seven in the morning. Kind of the vampire thing: when the sun comes up it's time to crawl back home.'

Lil and Ada exchanged glances. 'She could be in New York,' Ada said.

'Or turn up here,' Lil added.

'Or turn up dead,' Aaron offered.

Ada shuddered. 'Let's not think that. For all of Rachel's issues, there's a sweetness to her. And I can't help but think of how alone she must feel. We should split up.'

'I'll drive to Brooklyn,' Lil said, as she looked down at her outfit. 'This isn't going to get me in, is it?' She looked at Aaron.

'No. Wear black and bring your press card and camera,' he offered. 'I should go with you.'

Ada looked at her grandson, aware that his heart was set on spending the day with the film crew.

'You don't have to,' Lil said, aware of what he was about to sacrifice.

'Yeah, I do,' he said. 'It's fine. I don't think the cast and crew of *Final Reckoning* will miss me.'

Ada got up and gave him a peck on the cheek. 'I don't care what anyone says, you're the best grandson ever.'

'Gee, thanks. We should get a move on.' He looked at Lil. 'Meet you at my car in five?'

'Sure,' and Lil headed back for a quick change, somewhat clueless about what to wear to a club that catered to night-prowling New Yorkers.

'Why the change of heart?' Ada asked Aaron.

He pushed back his bangs. 'It's fun and all, and I think you should milk this for everything it's worth, but they're not real.'

'Who's not real?'

'Any of them. It's like they're all desperate for something. And they turn on each other and are constantly trying to make points with that Barry guy, or with Melanie. But behind their backs they say awful things. Who wants to be part of that?'

Ada nodded. 'It is exciting, though.'

'Yeah, but I don't think I want that. So, overall, I'd say it's been a good learning experience. But not for me.'

Lil reappeared, having done a lightning change into fitted black jeans, black turtle neck, flats and a black leather car coat she'd swiped from Ada's side of the closet. Her silver-blond hair was tied back in a ponytail.

Aaron snorted and Ada raised an eyebrow.

'I'm trying,' Lil said.

'It's fine,' Aaron offered. 'Sort of like a sixties hipster; I'll call you Dieter.'

After they'd left, Ada sipped tea and searched the Internet. The condo felt empty and she wondered if the show would go on. She thought about what Aaron had said about the cast and crew. Yes, she'd felt it, the desperation, but also the excitement. She looked at pictures of Rachel, invariably in a nightclub. Some were with her brother; several were of her unconscious or being carted out on a stretcher; and others showed her in designer gowns at award shows. There was even one with her, at age eleven, on *Lenore Says*. There was much darker material as well. Evidence of a porn tape, but whenever she clicked a link it was to find the offending material had been removed.

'Interesting.' She looked at the dates of the postings, over two years old. 'Horrible,' she said aloud, realizing Rachel would have been a minor. But their presence – now absence – raised questions. Who posted them? Who took them down? Who shot the video and who was she with? From there the questions grew darker. She'd been a minor, and whoever had posted or shared the video had committed a serious crime. Even viewing it, which she had nearly done, would be a violation of federal law. Had the authorities

removed the postings from the Internet? Her mother? Her brother?
A family lawyer?

She clicked on YouTube and entered Rachel's name. Lots of small
videos, mostly shot with camera phones. Engrossed in her task, she
started at the sound of the doorbell and then the phone.

She picked up on her way to the door. 'We're here,' Melanie chirped
over the line.

'That's one question answered,' Ada said.

'What are you talking about?' Melanie asked, as Ada opened the
door.

'Has Rachel been found?' she asked.

'No, but don't worry, we're prepared for all contingencies.'

Ada looked at the smiling brunet. Her face was scrubbed, her
eyes bright. She was ready for a day of shooting and was *prepared
for all contingencies.* That statement brought home the awful possibility
that Rachel might not be found, at least not alive.

TWENTY-FIVE

At six a.m. Lil lucked out and found a parking spot for her
Lincoln a block from Murielle's, the nightclub where Rachel
had been hours before Lenore was shot. 'This is nothing
like I remember,' she said, as they got out.

'You've been to Brooklyn?' Aaron asked.

'Ages ago. I went with some friends from college to a party. It
looked nothing like this. It's all so clean . . . it looks expensive.'

'It is,' he said. 'Almost as bad as Manhattan. It's a damn shame
that Grandma couldn't have hung on to Great Grandma Rose's
apartment on Delancey.'

'It wasn't an option,' Lil said.

'Come on, Dieter, there are ways.'

'Don't be a brat.' She glanced at the GPS app on her iPhone.
The address for the nightclub showed they were close.

'There,' Aaron said, indicating a broad store front with black
curtains in the windows and a single light over the door. 'That's the
address.'

'Yeah,' Lil said, recognizing it from the picture of Rachel on the sidewalk. Only then there'd been a crowd and an ambulance. 'It's so quiet.'

'Yeah, weird.' They crossed the street, and Aaron tried the door. 'Locked.' He knocked and looked for a bell. 'Maybe there's a secret code or something.'

Lil strained to hear any noise or music, but there was just traffic in the background, and a distant subway.

Aaron knocked again.

'They're closed,' said a woman out walking her miniature dachshund.

'On a Friday? That's odd,' Lil said.

'Closed as in shut down,' the woman said. 'Under-age drinking. They'll pay a fine and be open by tonight.' She bent down to scoop up her dog's leavings in a plastic bag. 'Good girl, Millie.'

'How long have they been closed?'

'Since the night that Parks girl got carted out. I guess she's nineteen, and drinking age in New York is twenty-one.'

'You don't know who owns this place, do you?' Lil asked.

'I do,' she said. 'Why?' She deposited the plastic bag in the nearby garbage can.

'I'm a reporter,' Lil said. 'I'm working on a story about Lenore and her kids.'

'I can make a call. Who do you write for?'

'I've got a syndicated column,' Lil said.

'Would I know it?'

'It's about antiques. Lenore's production company is in my hometown shooting a reality show . . .'

'Where her brother was shot?' the woman asked.

'Yes.'

'Interesting. And why are you tracking down Rachel's haunts?'

'Not certain,' Lil said. 'Kind of why I'm here.'

Aaron squatted and started to play with the long-haired black dog.

'Hmmm. I'm May, by the way, and this slice of cuteness is Millie.'

'She is gorgeous.'

'Yes,' May said, 'and she knows it.' She tapped the screen of her cell and hold it to her ear. 'Casio, I'm outside with a lady reporter from Connecticut. She's doing a piece on Rachel.'

Even from a distance Lil and Aaron could hear loud swearing in an Italian accent through the phone. May held it away from her ear. She mouthed, *not looking good.* 'Casio, is that a yes or a no?' There was silence. 'He's coming down.'

'He lives here?' Lil asked.

'He and his wife own the building. Murielle's is kind of a local institution and he's pissed at getting shut down.'

They heard deadbolts turn. The door opened on to a short dark-haired man with a couple days' growth on his chin. He looked at May, and then to Lil and Aaron. He squinted against the light. 'Who are you?' he asked.

'Lil Campbell,' she said and extended her hand. 'And this is my assistant, Aaron Gurston.'

'Huh . . .' He hung back in the door. 'What do you want to know?'

'About the night, I guess the early morning, that Rachel got hauled away.'

'Bitch,' he snorted, followed by several choice words in Italian. 'And the worst part was she didn't have a drop of alcohol, at least nothing served here. My bartenders know to check and we card everyone. They know Rachel, and if they want to keep their jobs they'd never serve her.'

'You use a bracelet system?' Aaron asked, and before Lil could ask for clarification, he added, 'So if you're under age you get one color and if you're legal you get another.'

'Yes. We did not serve alcohol to Rachel Parks. I don't know what twisted game that bitch was playing, but she wasn't drunk. If you write the truth I'll give you the number for our bouncer; he saw the whole thing. He told me she left the club without stumbling, and just lay down on the sidewalk. He tried to get her up, but she wouldn't move. And because she's famous people started taking pictures, someone called nine one one and now my club is closed for a liquor violation. And there's not a damn thing I can do.' The man's face turned red. 'They want to fine me fifty thousand dollars! We never served her alcohol, and there's nothing I can do to prove it.'

Lil stared at the man. 'I believe you,' she said, thinking of her conversation with Ada. Rachel knew she was pregnant; she wasn't drinking. 'I might be able to help.'

'How?' The man opened the door wider, affording them a glimpse of high ceilings and a long corridor.

'Do you have a card?' Lil asked. She fished out one of her own.

'Not on me,' he said. 'I'll give you my cell. I'm Casio Gomez . . . this is my club, and if you can get me out of a fifty thousand dollar fine and get me back open, you'll get a lifetime membership.'

May snorted.

'What?' he said.

'Seems like she'd be getting the short end of the deal.'

'If I can get you proof that Rachel Parks wasn't drinking,' said Lil, 'do you think that would do it?'

'What kind of proof?'

'I imagine they did a breathalyzer on the ambulance and probably a toxicology screen in the emergency room. The trick is going to be getting protected medical information.'

Casio's shoulders slumped. 'The girl used drugs, lots of them. And what if she'd been drinking before she came to the club?'

'Then it won't work,' Lil admitted. 'But I've got good reason to think – and what you just told me about the doorman makes sense – Rachel Parks was sober as a judge when she lay down on your sidewalk. What I don't understand is why she did it.'

Back in the car, Lil had Aaron drive as she made calls on the speaker phone, first to Ada. 'Have they found her?'

'No, and the show goes on,' Ada said. 'I'm in Lenore's bathroom getting my hair and make-up done,' she added, to let Lil know their conversation wasn't private. 'And by bathroom I mean something the size of one of our condos. She has an entire beauty parlor in here.'

Speaking softly, Lil gave her the upshot on the visit to Murielle's.

'Excuse me,' Ada said. 'Guys' – she was talking to James the hairdresser and Gretchen the make-up artist – 'I need five minutes of privacy.' There was a pause on the line. 'OK Lil, Rachel's psychiatrist is with Mattie. I'm sure he can get copies of all of her medical stuff. And if Mattie doesn't know this part . . . I'll tell her. It's bizarre. Why would Rachel just lay down on the sidewalk?'

'For attention,' Lil said.

'From whom? Her mother? The papers? Her brother?'

'It could have been for an alibi,' Aaron chimed in from behind the wheel. 'If she's in the emergency room when someone kills her mother, no one can say she did it.'

'Smart boy,' Ada said. 'Let's take it further. We know that Richard was her guardian angel.'

'Not to mention some less savory brother and sister goings on,' Lil added.

'Yes, well. A bit of a fallen angel then. But if she were in the emergency room, Richard would come to her rescue. He always did. So not only is it her alibi, but his as well. The two of them were in the hospital the morning Lenore was shot. And if the whole thing was a ruse on Rachel's part, maybe it wasn't for attention, at least not this time.'

'So they hired someone to kill their mother?' Aaron asked. 'Then who killed Richard? And for all we know, Rachel . . .'

'Don't say it,' Ada whispered.

'It's a possibility,' Lil said. 'She could be dead, and if we follow this through then maybe the killer is cleaning up loose ends, as in anyone that could implicate him or her.'

'It doesn't sit right,' Ada said. 'Look, give Mattie a call and try to track down those medical records; let's at least see if this much is right.'

'So how are they planning to film without Rachel?' Lil asked.

'Melanie says they've got more than enough from yesterday. She says they can cut and slice till no one would ever know. Don't ask me how . . . and you want to know what they're planning? Apparently it was even Rachel's idea.'

'What?' Lil and Aaron said in unison.

'A tag sale, even though they're calling it an estate sale, but we both know it's the same thing. The ad is going in today's paper, and tomorrow they're going to hold it right here in the driveway. They're going to film the whole thing and at the end of the day tally up the takings. To keep it from being totally gruesome, Rachel wants the proceeds to go to charity. Today we film the three dealers who think they're competing to liquidate Lenore's estate.'

'But if they've already decided to hold an estate sale?' Lil was perplexed.

'Surprise!' Ada said. 'I don't know how this is going to play out, but we have three dealers chomping at the bit to get on TV, and whoever wins could come off looking like an incompetent fool.'

'Grandma,' Aaron said, as he took the turn for the Brooklyn Bridge, 'what about you?'

'Good question, and I'm not entirely happy with the answer – I am having fun.'

Aaron snorted. 'I love you Grandma, but you do realize you are one very twisted woman. You both are.'

'Lil,' Ada said. 'Call me if you learn anything new.'

'Will do. I want to go back to the LPP building.'

'Why?'

'Well, if we're doing the Miss Marple thing – and let's face it, we long ago passed the point of innocence – I want to walk in the footsteps of Lenore's shooter.'

'You know,' Ada said, 'speaking of footsteps, and I don't know if this matters, but I'm thinking about everything Rachel did yesterday . . . not just the way she looked, and not just her mannerisms, but putting it all together. There are times when I truly believe she thought she was her mother. And the more I think about it, this show, and holding an estate sale in front of a multi-million dollar mansion and then giving the proceeds to charity – it's pure Lenore. Tacky as hell, but making it seem piss elegant in the end.'

'I think you're right,' Lil said. 'I don't think Rachel's dead,' she added, and the thought lifted her spirits. 'If she faked being drunk, for whatever reason, it's no stretch to think this is another stunt.'

'Last question,' Ada said. 'I've now got hair, make-up and Peggy the wardrobe lady all giving me the stink eye, but why, Lil? Why, in God's name, would she disappear?'

'I think I have the answer,' Lil said. 'So I'll answer your question with the one we should have been asking all along: what would Lenore do?'

Ada hung up, and accepted her third cup of tea from a young man whose job description likely included a line or two on beverage preparation. That he had no hesitation about popping into Lenore's show-stopping bathroom seemed typical for this bunch. She mused over Lil's parting question: *what would Lenore do?* The answer was obvious: anything and everything for ratings.

As Gretchen, the make-up lady, finished applying a layer of miracle spackle, she thought about the more curious question of why Rachel would pretend to be drunk.

'OK,' Gretchen said, and she pulled off the shiny smock.

Ada looked in the mirror at the elegant woman with her flawless make-up, dressed in a black lace slip. 'It's good,' she said, gently touching one of the stiff peaks of her hair.

'Careful,' warned James, the hairdresser.

She smiled. 'I really like it. You have to teach me how to do this.'

'It's mostly the product,' he admitted. 'And I have a secret or two.'

'Would you share?' she asked.

'Please, if this show is a hit I'm sticking with you like glue. You'll never have to do your own hair again.'

'Did the two of you know Lenore well?' she asked, looking from James to Gretchen.

'Not much,' James said. 'She had her own team, although your dresser was hers for years.'

'Peggy?' And then it clicked. 'She's the one who found Lenore after she was shot.'

'Yes,' Gretchen said as she assembled her touch-up kit. 'Peggy Stark.' She was about to say more when the heavyset woman with the elaborate braid down her back appeared, pushing a garment rack. Under her breath Gretchen added, 'Speak of the devil.' She turned from Ada. 'Hi, Peggy. She's looking good.'

Peggy maneuvered the rack flush against the wall and turned to Ada. A pair of wire-rimmed glasses sat on the end of her slightly upturned nose. She studied Ada, her expression serious. 'I was thinking green,' she said. She selected a voluminous hunter green silk dress with tulle petticoats and a tight bodice.

Ada regarded the garment. 'That doesn't look like one of mine.'

'It's not,' Peggy said, not meeting Ada's gaze. 'I got your measurements and have been doing a bit of shopping.'

'Really?' Ada said. 'It's beautiful. Is it new or old?'

'It's new, but retro,' Peggy said. She pushed a strand of hair behind her ear. 'It's by a young designer in Nolita. I sent him your picture and told him what we were going for. You won't need a slip with it, it's fully lined. No bra either.'

'It's lovely,' Ada said. She glanced at the open door, then at Gretchen and James, and finally at Peggy, who was holding the shimmering dress and looking at her expectantly. She had a moment's clarity and wondered if this were an important piece of things. Lenore lived without privacy. It wasn't just that she put her life on display for the viewing public, but that there was this whole other world of invisible people, like satellites around her star. *In for a penny*, she thought, and eased the slip's straps off her shoulders. It fluttered around her feet, leaving her in bra, panties and old-fashioned silk stockings and lace garter belt. She suppressed a giggle.

Peggy looked up at her as James and Gretchen went out, leaving the bathroom door wide open.

'You don't want to know,' Ada said.

'I might,' Peggy said.

'Always wear clean underwear,' Ada said, as she unhooked her bra.

'Absolutely,' Peggy said, as she unzipped the back of the dress and placed it on the tile floor. 'Probably best to step into it. You're in good shape,' she commented. 'Pilates?'

'Yoga,' Ada said, as Peggy eased the dress up. It cinched in tight around her waist and there was boning in the bodice that molded her breasts into the 1950s conical ideal of feminine perfection.

Peggy stepped back. 'Can you sit?'

'I'll try,' Ada said, looking at her reflection. 'It's gorgeous . . .' She eased back into the make-up chair.

'Lenore would practice in the mirror,' Peggy said. 'To see how the outfits would read on camera.'

'You knew her pretty well,' said Ada, as she turned in the chair from the half mirror above the vanity to the full-length gilt-framed one next to the door. She positioned her legs beneath her and had visions of black-and-white TV housewife June Cleaver waiting, with Martini in hand, for Ward to return from a day at the office.

'I knew Lenore,' said Peggy, the tone of her voice not inviting further discussion.

'What happens to this dress after the show?' Ada asked.

'You mean do you get to keep it?'

'Do I?'

'Not always, but when you talk to your agent that's the kind of thing you get worked into your contract. But this one you can keep. I told the designer if we used it we'd mention him on the show, and of course he gets credit at the end. It's a good deal for him.'

'I've been noticing that,' Ada commented. 'There seems to be a lot of . . . product placement?'

Peggy snorted. 'It's just getting started. Lenore was huge into product promotion. Commercials are becoming obsolete. Nowadays, everyone tapes the shows they want and then fast-forwards through the commercials. So to keep sponsors it's all about product placement. You'll see, if *Final Reckoning* is a hit, you'll be drinking soda out of a huge cup with the company name on it and we'll have top designers begging to dress you. There were some episodes of *Lenore Says* that were little more than infomercials.'

'I can't see how there could be much product placement in a show about appraising antiques.'

'Barry's no slouch,' Peggy said. 'Everything that gets filmed is a potential sponsor: the car you drive, the shoes you wear, the granola bar you have between takes, everything. And if a sponsor wants to get on the show and is willing to pay the bucks, it won't matter if the product doesn't fit. Let's say it's a tractor . . . you'll be doing a segment on vintage tractors.'

'Interesting. How much do sponsors pay?'

'Depends on the show and the ratings. You'll learn about that. I can tell you this, to get your logo on *Lenore Says* costs at least a quarter million. If you actually wanted the product used, it could be a million or more.'

Ada continued to pose in the mirror while surreptitiously studying Peggy Stark. She reminded her a bit of an old friend, Miriam Roth, the first girl she'd ever kissed. 'So you worked on *Lenore Says*?'

'For fourteen years.'

Ada heard bitterness in her voice. 'You don't sound happy about that.'

'Long and boring story,' Peggy said. She turned away from Ada and knelt down by the garment rack to select a pair of black pumps.

Ada's eyes took in the array of footwear. 'Not the green ones?'

'No,' Peggy said. 'Too matchy.'

Ada thought through the different reasons why mentioning Lenore would make Peggy shut down. 'Fourteen years, that's a lot of wardrobe changes. It's strange,' Ada said, trying to get her to open up. 'For someone who till a few days ago knew nothing about what goes on behind the scenes of a TV show, it's been a crash course. But you've been doing this for—'

'Forever.' The woman knelt in front of Ada and slipped on the shoes. Her experienced fingers smoothed the stockings to leave no wrinkles.

'I can't help being a little star struck,' Ada said. 'Lenore was huge.'

'She'd kill you if she heard you say that.'

'You know what I mean.'

'I do, but Lenore wasn't good with jokes, especially about herself,' Peggy said.

Encouraged, Ada pressed on. 'But she kind of set herself up for that. Everything about her looked so perfect . . . so polished. I suspect you had a hand in that.'

'Thank you,' Peggy said, as she retrieved a red enamel tool box from the base of the garment rack. She placed it on the marble countertop and opened it to reveal a fortune in jewelry, most of it vintage.

'Wow!' Ada stared in as Peggy removed the top tray and displayed a second layer of opened jewelry boxes – from Tiffany, Cartier, Bulgari. 'I'm assuming I don't get to keep these.'

'That would be correct,' Peggy chuckled. 'Although if you get big enough, everything is negotiable.' She stepped back and examined Ada. 'You have lovely bone structure, great neck. I'm thinking a pair of chandeliers, not too big, and maybe a statement bracelet.'

As she spoke, Ada continued to try and get a feel for this woman who would have had daily, and fairly intimate, access to Lenore. Playing a hunch, she offered a bit of herself. 'I think my girlfriend would be jealous to hear you say that.'

Peggy paused, and then pulled out a pair of exquisite Bulgari emerald and diamond earrings. 'The two of you been together long?'

'There's together and then there's together. We were friends first, and then it went on from there.'

'That's nice,' Peggy said. 'She's the tall blonde who was at the cemetery?'

'Lil, yes.'

'You make an attractive couple.'

'I think so – do you have someone?'

'No, and if you know someone good, I'm in the market.'

'Not to be completely crass,' Ada said, 'are we talking male or female?'

Peggy eased on the right carring. 'I'm gay,' she said. 'And I imagine you've heard the gossip about Lenore. One of the best-kept secrets that everyone knew.'

'Yeah, and yet she never acknowledged it.'

Peggy swallowed and stepped back. 'No, she didn't.'

And then Ada took another calculated leap. 'That must have been hard . . . for you.'

Peggy's lips drew back into a grimace. Her shoulders sagged and she started to sob.

Ada was out of the chair and quickly shut and locked the bathroom door. 'It's OK, Peggy.' Not certain as to the source of the woman's grief.

'You'd think,' she wheezed, 'that after the way she treated me, I wouldn't feel so . . . sad.'

'You were her girlfriend.'

'Once, but that's ancient history.'

'Sweetie,' Ada said. 'It's clear you still have feelings for her. That must have been hard. You just lost someone you cared for.'

Peggy shook her head. 'Please, I lost Lenore a long time ago.'

Ada quickly reassessed. If it wasn't Lenore's murder, then . . . 'Oh.'

'Yeah, big sad "Oh". I don't do this kind of thing. I'm thirty-eight, and you'd think I'd know enough just to move on, and now . . .'

'She's dead . . .' Ada said, trying to imagine Peggy with Lenore. There was a fourteen year age difference, and if Peggy had been Lenore's dresser, and sometime girlfriend, for years . . . Other pieces slipped into place.

'A bracelet,' Peggy said. She batted back tears and hunted through the lower section of the tool box.

'How old were you when you and Lenore . . .'

'Hooked up?' Peggy asked. She held a heavy gold bracelet in the shape of a jaguar, its eyes studded with emeralds. 'Twenty-two.' She opened the catch.

'Right or left?' Ada asked, realizing that Peggy's relationship with Lenore had probably ended years ago, but apparently the woman's flame hadn't gone out. 'Clearly it's none of my business, but why stay?'

'Job, bills, masochism . . . hope . . .'

'That you'd get back together?'

'Yeah, pathetic. And like I said, I'm in the market. At this point even my delusions of romance can't bring her back from the grave. Ada, I can't believe I'm spewing like this. It's not me.'

'You've been carrying this for years? How horrible. Do you think she knew?'

'That I still had a thing for her, was still in love with her? Yeah. Do I think it registered in any way? Absolutely not.' She looked down. 'She likes them young and pretty, and I was, and then I wasn't.'

'In the end,' Ada asked, 'did she have a girlfriend?'

Peggy put the red tool chest back together and closed it. 'Girlfriends, plural . . . I think the day I realized that was the day I should have run. Lenore wasn't exclusive. If you ask me, that's why she was shot. She treated the people who cared for her the most like dirt. She probably treated the wrong person like crap, and bang.'

'Not to pry, but how did you find out?'

'That I wasn't her one and only? I came up the booty trail and found her with another bunny.'

'Translation, please?'

'Lenore's private entrance and exit to LPP. She liked to come and go unobserved, and she liked her playmates to do the same. I told the cops all this. I'm probably still on their list of likely suspects. It's clear that whoever killed Lenore knew all about the booty trail. In through the garage, then up her elevator, shoot her and then leave the same way. The elevator opens outside her dressing room, where not even her security can see who's coming and going.'

'No attendant in the garage?'

'It's tiny, just Lenore and the top executives. You get in and out with a pass card.'

'Cameras?'

'You'd think so, but no. Lenore wanted to keep any records of her flings private.'

'She wasn't stupid,' Ada said. 'What about when the affairs ended? They'd still have the pass card, or would she ask for it back?'

Peggy snorted. 'She'd have the code changed, and they'd have a worthless piece of plastic.'

There was a loud rap at the bathroom door. Melanie's voice came from the other side. 'Ada, you ready?'

'Couple minutes,' she shouted. She grabbed tissues and handed them to Peggy. 'You're smudged,' she said.

'Thanks.'

Ada bit her bottom lip and watched as Peggy wiped away her eye liner. 'I can't imagine what that must have been like, seeing her with other people.'

'Not a picnic but, like I said, I was pretty, young and stupid.'

'No,' Ada said, 'getting your heart broken isn't stupid. It shows you've got a heart, and from what you say – and pretty much everyone else too – she didn't.' And then, figuring she'd not get the chance again, 'Do you know who her current girlfriends were?'

Peggy took a big breath. 'I don't know that I'd even use the term girlfriend, especially over the last few years. Now that I'm finally getting some clarity, you don't usually think about women in this way.'

'What way?'

'Predatory, like a man; she didn't have girlfriends and, looking back, maybe I thought of her as my girlfriend, and that was a mistake. I was pretty and I was young and that was all she cared about. It's like she wanted to have me and, once she did, she was on to the next . . . and when you're Lenore, you get what you want.'

Ada stared into the mirror, looking from her own flawless make-up and glamorous outfit to Peggy's red-rimmed eyes. 'By predatory, you're saying she'd use her position to get women to sleep with her.'

'Oh yeah. You want to get on a show? You want to get ahead? Well, you've got to give something to get something. That's entertainment.'

TWENTY-SIX

B arry looked between the monitor and the talent, Ada and that Tolliver guy. They were in Lenore's paneled library and this was the scene where each of the antique dealers made their pitch for the estate.

With too little sleep and too much caffeine, Barry was desperate to get this pilot into the can. 'Just forty-eight hours,' he muttered, still fuming over the latest bullshit phone call from LPP's Chief Financial Officer, Patty Corcoran, neither confirming nor denying that *Final Reckoning* had the green light. Although he was able to get her to cough up the funds for two more days of shooting – today and their balls-to-the-walls plans for tomorrow. It left him drained and scared. She'd informed him that three-quarters of the producers at LPP had been let go. 'If you're not producing revenue,' she'd said, 'LPP can't carry you through the reorganization. It's the new world order.' He'd counted; she'd used the word 'reorganize' over eight times in a five minute conversation. Between the lines, it was pretty clear that Patty had her eye on the CEO spot.

'We'll take it somewhere else,' Melanie said, having overheard the entire conversation. 'It's a fabulous concept. And thank God Rachel signed the paperwork before she did her vanishing act. Not to be morbid – well, maybe a bit – but can you imagine if she's dead? Think of the ratings. No way they won't run this. We'll place an "in memory of" screen for three seconds at the start or at the end, and we're good to go.'

Barry nodded, and watched as Tolliver made his pitch. Rachel was supposed to be in this scene as well. They'd either drop her in from previous footage or find some other work around. 'We just have to get through today and tomorrow . . . and how's that going?'

'Like planning a wedding in one day. It's insane, but with enough cameras we'll get what we need. We can use voice-overs and make stuff up, if we have to.'

'Run through it for me,' he said, rubbing his temples. Somewhere, someone was wearing perfume. He felt the beginnings of a migraine and, rather than wait, retrieved a pill from his jacket and popped it under his tongue.

'We've got a couple dozen interns putting signs up all over western Connecticut. You'd love 'em – *Lenore Says Come to My Estate Sale*. They're quite groovy and we've got ads in the evening and morning editions of the local papers, and *The New York Times*. Rachel went through all the stuff she wants to get rid of and, let me tell you, there was no love lost between her and her mother.'

'And it's all legal? She signed everything she had to?'

'Yeah, and if she hadn't?'

He smirked. 'What do you think?'

'Right. The tents arrive later this morning and we'll work through the night to get them set up. So we've got Tolliver and the other two wannabes to film, we've got to do the deliberation scene, pick one, get him or her to appraise the goods, tag it, set it out . . . I need a Valium . . . maybe some coke. I wonder if Carrie has any more of her son's Adderall.'

'Just delegate but, you know, don't trust anyone. This is our shot. If we don't take it . . .'

'I know, we won't have jobs come Monday.'

'We may still not, but if we can pull this off . . .'

'Who *wouldn't* watch it?'

'That one,' Barry said. He was pointing at Tolliver. 'He's the one we need for this.'

'Some eye candy.'

'Yeah. Get some footage of the other two. If they're any decent tell them we'll give them spots in future episodes.'

'Of course we will.' She winked. 'We'll be sure to do that.'

His cell vibrated; it was Jeanine. 'Hey babe.'

'Hey back. Shooting's going good?'

'It's going,' he said. 'How's my best girl and my second best girl?'

Jeanine chuckled. 'I'm not going to ask who gets top billing. Ashley, say hello to Daddy.'

'Hi Daddy, will you be home tonight? We're looking at houses, and with two acres you can have a horse.'

He heard Jeanine in the back. 'Honey, don't scare Daddy.'

'And for every acre and a half extra you can have an extra horse,'

Ashley informed him. 'Although Mommy says a pony is a good way to start. Am I going to get a pony?'

It threw Barry back to those wonderful memories of *Model Behavior*. Jeanine on that stallion, hair flying, limbs free – breathtaking stuff, and why she should have won.

Jeanine came back on the phone. 'Yes, apparently both Grenville and Shiloh have laws on the books that go back to the seventeen hundreds. The size of your parcel determines how many horses and various other livestock you can own.'

In spite of the crazy production schedules and his jangled nerves, he needed this call. 'You know, I'm not saying no.'

'I'm kidding about the horses,' she said.

'I'm not. You told me how much you loved to ride as a kid. Wouldn't that be something, if you could teach Ashley, if you could teach me?'

'Step at a time, baby,' she said. 'Somehow I can't see you mucking out stalls. You do your thing, I'll do mine. I'm telling the realtor we'll want a rental property for a year, but that it could change. I heard something strange, though.'

'What's that?'

'Someone said Rachel Parks is missing, as in maybe dead.'

'The girl's a nut job,' Barry said.

'But you need her for the show.'

'Jeanine, I'm going to make this work. Tell that realtor that we're buying, not renting. If LPP is too stupid to pick up this show, I know half a dozen studios that would jump for this concept.'

'Barry, I can wait. You don't have to do this for me.'

'Jeanine, I do it all for you, for us. Tell that realtor nothing less than five acres; if I got the math right then we can each have a horse. I'll get a nag and call her Lenore.'

She snorted. 'OK, any other requests?'

He paused and thought of what he might like in a country home. He laughed. 'I don't need to give this a second thought,' he said.

'Why's that?'

'Because you've never once let me down.' He thought back through their years together. 'Not once. You get whatever house you want. Buy us a shack; if you and Ashley are in it that's all I care about.'

There was silence on the line.

'You OK?' he asked.

'I am, and Barry . . . some day, if I do let you down, you need to know that everything I do is out of love for you and Ashley.'

'That just made me nervous.'

Her tone lightened. 'Don't be. I think you put me on too high a pedestal. It's bound to crack.'

'Never.'

After he hung up, he noticed his head was clear; all traces of the gathering migraine were gone. Jeanine's unconditional love was better than any medicine. He nodded at Melanie, who was supervising the shoot. They'd had Rachel and the dealers select a few choice antiques and pieces of Lenore memorabilia to feature on the show. This included one of her Emmys, which Rachel had teared up over as she'd said, 'Yes, for the children's sake, let's sell it.' And now she'd gone missing, was possibly dead, and the fucking cops were looking at him as a suspect, as if he had time to go around killing people. Although the day Lenore was shot, he remembered that sense of relief, that he could breathe, that maybe he could pull a rabbit out of his hat. It was a feeling that was repeated when Richard turned up dead. Rachel was another story. Yes, she was a nut job, but if she could be managed her instability made her ratings gold. Lost in a daydream of life as an A-list producer, he didn't see the two female detectives.

'Mr Stromstein,' the shorter and older one asked. 'We realize you're busy, but we have a few questions we need to run by you; is there someplace private we could go?'

His anger surged. He wanted to scream, *'Not fucking again!'* He didn't. He turned the corners of his lips into a pleasant half smile, a technique he'd learned when attending a meditation seminar. 'Of course.' He glanced back at Melanie and Ethan. They had things under control. He paused, noting that one of the other changes since losing Lenore, and then Richard, was that the sense of internal competition in his team was gone. Not even the hangers on who'd descended from LPP, all wanting to attach themselves to *Final Reckoning*, were vying to take his place. There was something else he saw in their eyes – hope. He took a deep breath and turned to the detectives. The last few days had been punctuated with their questions: *'Who might want Lenore dead?'*

'*Everyone.*'

'*Who would benefit from her death?*'

'*No one, at least not anyone who's still breathing. Rachel, maybe, but is she still breathing?*'

He caught the eye of the older one, Mattie something. And it hit him like a brick – *he*, Barry Stromstein, executive producer of *Final Reckoning*, was benefiting from the deaths of Lenore and Richard. *Oh shit!* he thought, realizing that, on this most impossible day, he'd need to find a criminal attorney. If these detectives couldn't find out who killed the bitch and her turkey baster son, *they'll think I did it*.

Mattie hung back in Lenore's elegant conservatory and let Jamie direct this new line of inquiry. She watched as Barry Stromstein glibly fielded the questions. She felt the sun on her back and neck through the beveled glass. The lush foliage and blooming exotic plants barely registered over the knot in her gut. It was the call from Ada Strauss, and her report of her conversation with Peggy Stark – Lenore's dresser and on-again, off-again lover – that had sent her mood spiraling. That Peggy was also the one who found Lenore made the information crucial. It bothered her. Mattie was no prude; years in domestic abuse followed by her current position with the state's major crime squad had exposed her to every shade of human despair and depravity. But this . . . this was the domain of men. This was what men did to women, not what women did to other women. But it wasn't just that. She felt haunted . . . ashamed . . . confused.

'What do you know of Lenore's love interests?' Jamie asked.

'I assume you're referring to the girls,' said Barry.

'Yes. How many; who were they?'

'I'm not the best person for this,' he admitted. 'We all knew, definitely her masseuse, possibly the Pilates girl; there was always someone. Blonde, pretty and tall, but she'd go for the brunets, too.'

'Would she pay them?' Jamie asked.

'Not in cash, but a job as a spokesmodel, maybe a spot on a design show, more under the heading of giving a struggling actress, director, writer . . . a needed boost.'

'Did you sleep with Lenore?' Jamie asked bluntly.

'No, not her type, not her gender.'

Mattie braced for what she knew would be the next question. Proud of how far Jamie had developed as an investigator, and somewhat shocked by how tightly their minds worked in sync.

'What about your team?' Jamie asked. 'Who on your team has had an affair, or whatever, with Lenore?'

Mattie saw Barry's neutral smile waver. They were on to something.

'Mr Stromstein?' Jamie pressed.

'I couldn't say.'

'Won't say,' said Jamie. 'Yet, when we find out that you did in fact know, you will be judged to have made the decision to obstruct a homicide investigation at this moment. That could be quite ugly, including accessory to murder. After all, who's really benefiting from Lenore's death?' Her gaze was fixed on him. 'Be careful here, Mr Stromstein. This is an important decision point. I'll pretend I did not ask the first time: who on your team has had sex with Lenore Parks?'

He stared at the ground. He said nothing. The seconds stretched, the silence of the conservatory wrapped them in a cocoon of warm sun and the sweet and earthy smells of potting soil and orchids. 'Melanie,' he said, his voice barely audible. 'My field producer, Melanie Taft, and while I don't know for certain, I'd say Carrie Melville.'

'So Melanie is a definite and Carrie a possible? What makes her a possible?'

'She's the only one who didn't come with me from LA. She was with my predecessor at LPP and Lenore specifically requested that I keep her. When people want those kind of favors, there's usually a reason.'

Mattie sensed Jamie's next question.

'I see. So, field producer; that was your title when we first met three days ago. Melanie was an assistant producer.'

'Yes.'

'I see. What is your title now, Mr Stromstein?'

He looked up. 'Executive producer.'

'What does that mean exactly?'

'It's just a title, a way of showing the chain of command.'

'And an executive producer would be higher than a field producer, and certainly higher than an assistant producer, correct?'

'Yes.'

'So it would be safe to say in the last few days, since the death of Lenore, and then of her son, both you and Melanie Taft have received promotions.'

'Yes.'

'Interesting; and this is while hundreds of LPP employees are being laid off. How did that happen?'

'I insisted on it,' he said.

'Gutsy move,' Jamie said. 'Who approved that?'

'The CFO, Patty . . . Patricia Corcoran. I didn't do anything wrong. This show has been all-consuming. I've been doing the work of an executive producer, I'll be damned if I don't get the credit. And Melanie has more than stepped up to the plate. I couldn't do this without her. She deserves the credit.'

'And I'm assuming there's more money involved?' Jamie asked.

'Yes and no. If the show's a hit I'll get a back-end cut and, yes, Melanie will get a raise. I didn't kill Lenore.' His face was red. 'And Melanie's time has been dedicated to getting this show off the ground. If you knew her, you'd know she's not the type to hurt anyone.'

Mattie again felt the workings of Jamie's mind and braced for the next line of inquiry.

'But she is the type to sleep with the boss,' Jamie said. 'From what we've learned that was standard LPP practice. Was she still sleeping with Lenore?'

'I don't know.'

'If Lenore asked her to carry her babies, would she do it? You know, be her surrogate?'

Barry looked startled. 'What? Of course not.'

'And Carrie?'

'I have no way of knowing that. Lenore was planning on having another child?'

Jamie stared at him, her expression tight-lipped. She let the silence stretch. '. . . Apparently so. No idea who the surrogate is, Mr Stromstein?'

Barry stared back. 'No . . . no.'

Jamie looked to Mattie, silently asking if she had any further questions. With twin surges of pride and relief, she realized that Jamie had mined this seam till it was dry, at least for now. She shook her head. 'I'm good.'

TWENTY-SEVEN

'**G**rueling,' Ada said to Lil, her mother and her grandson, all gathered in their cozy living room. 'It's like being back with Harry when we'd do fifteen-hour days preparing for the big sales.'

'You like it, though. I can tell,' Aaron said, looking between Ada and Lil seated together on the couch.

Ada smiled and sipped Scotch. 'I do. There's a lot of waiting around, and watching.'

'Mattie and Jamie were there,' Lil commented.

'Yes. I make them nervous,' Ada said.

'As you should,' Rose interjected. 'The two of you will get yourselves killed one of these days, and what am I going to do with two condos?'

'Get a boyfriend,' Aaron offered.

'Around here?' Rose shook her head. 'There's ten women for every man, and the few there are aren't much to look at.'

'What about Stan?' Ada asked.

'Just friends,' Rose said. 'I have no interest in taking care of an old man. You two need to be careful.'

Ada looked to Lil. 'Anything from your trip to LPP?'

'It's a ghost town,' Lil said. 'Yes, it was a Saturday, but apparently that shouldn't matter. The same guard was on, that retired cop, George. He was very philosophical, and quite chatty. He was also wondering if you might be up for a date. I let him know you were taken. At which point he asked me out.'

Ada chuckled. 'And?'

'I said I was also taken. But here's something interesting: Lenore had a private elevator that went straight to her suite from the garage. George said there's no way to tell who she gave pass cards to. Piecing it together I'd say it was to anyone she wanted to get in and out unobserved.'

'Peggy told me the same thing. It raises the likelihood that she was killed by an ex, doesn't it?'

'It does. But George, who's seen enough of the comings and goings, thinks this is the end of LPP. He felt Richard might have been able to hold things together, but certainly not Rachel.'

'Who might be dead,' Aaron added.

'Or might not,' Ada offered. 'With her history of the big fake-out, this might well be a grab for attention. Although that doesn't sit right.'

Lil nodded. 'I still think it's a question of "what would Lenore do?"'

'You might be right.'

'Aaron and I have been on and off the Internet all day,' Lil said. 'Rachel's disappearance is big news. And this estate sale is getting a ton of press.'

'I know,' Ada said. 'When we'd finished shooting and they were driving me home, there were cars lining the road to Lenore's. People are planning on sleeping over so they can be the first in.'

'It's all over the TV,' Rose said. 'There'll be riots if they're not careful.'

'Supposedly,' Ada said, 'the plan is to let in only a hundred people at a time. They'll start handing out tickets at eight a.m.'

'That's standard estate sale etiquette,' Lil said. 'What's for sale?'

'It's all staged, and according to Melanie most of it was selected by Rachel, but some of it is in very bad taste.'

'Such as?' Aaron asked.

'Personal photos, clothes, underwear.'

'You're kidding,' Rose said.

'No,' Ada said, 'things still in packages, but the idea of selling Lenore Parks' panties – crass. And then there's some good antiques. Rachel wanted . . . wants to redecorate the mansion completely. I can't help but think about that poor girl. If she's doing this as a stunt, then fine, I guess. But if something's happened to her . . . She's pregnant and fragile, at least I think so, though lord knows I've been fooled before.'

'And Tolliver won the expert slot for the week,' Lil commented.

'I wouldn't exactly call it a win. He was the most photogenic, and they've replaced his staff with extras from central casting, all young, all pretty. It's both fascinating and grotesque.'

'There will be some disgruntled employees at Grenville Antiques,' Lil said.

'To put it mildly,' Ada replied. 'And to add insult to injury, Tolliver is insisting his entire staff of appraisers be on hand for the shooting to feed lines to the talent.'

'The Cyrano de Bergerac method,' said Rose. 'So what you're saying is they're all a bunch of shysters.'

'I suppose,' Ada said, 'but creative and energetic . . .'

'And scared and desperate,' Lil added.

'And someone among them,' Aaron said, in the voice of a TV announcer, 'is a murderer.'

'It's not a joke, sweetheart,' Ada said. She looked at Lil. 'I snuck upstairs at one point and talked my way into Rachel's room.'

'Of course you did.'

'There was blood in her bathroom – quite a bit.'

The room was quiet.

'I was chatting with the trooper,' Ada continued. 'He told me that they had a dog team in that morning, but that the trail ended outside the estate. That she either got in a car, or was put in one. I'll tell you something else, and obviously I'm no expert on blood spatter, but nothing looked like she'd been dragged. There were droplets, and some finger smudges that were probably hers. We know she's a cutter, so I'm hoping – I can't believe I'm saying this – but I'm hoping that's what it was. She cut, maybe a little too deep. The part that's killing me is how scared she sounded on the phone. Aaron, can you get me another?' She held up her empty tumbler. 'I wonder if I'll get any sleep tonight.'

'I have Ambien,' Rose offered.

'On top of booze,' Ada said. 'You trying to kill me, Mother?'

'Don't say such a thing. I certainly see how the two of you became a couple. All this interest in cutting and murder and blood spatter . . .'

Ada completed her mother's sentence as Aaron returned with a generous three fingers of whiskey. 'And a sexually predatory talk show hostess, her damaged children, her corporation which might be finished—'

'Or might not,' Lil said. 'Think about it, right now Lenore Parks is more famous than ever. The show you're filming could get huge ratings.' She sounded pensive. 'You're going to be a celebrity, Ada.'

'I'm just the hostess.'

'True, but millions of people will know who you are once this thing airs. There are already thousands of Internet hits for you attached to this show.'

'Are you OK with that?' Ada asked. 'Because I'll tell you the truth, and I don't feel great about it, Lil. I'm thrilled your column has taken off the way it has, but—'

Lil smiled. 'I know, Ada, and it's OK. You've been a little jealous.'

Ada winced. 'I'd love to say it was something more noble, and your success is wonderful. It's just, for all those years I was the wind beneath Harry's wings.'

'No!' Rose interjected. 'You weren't just the cheering squad, you did the work. Don't think I didn't see it. Without you, Harry would have run Strauss's into the ground. He could charm the habit off a nun, but he had no head for business. That was you. You pushed the expansion into multiple stores. You got the volumes to where you could buy at the price point you needed. And it was you, Ada – because Harry's memory had already started to slip – who orchestrated the buy out at the height of the market. Harry was Harry, no more and no less. He could close the deal, but without you, there'd have been no deal to close.'

'Huh?' Ada stared at her mother.

'You think I didn't know? You think I'm not proud of what you've accomplished?' She looked from her daughter to Aaron, and then to Lil. 'Look at us. When I was born women couldn't even vote. And now, Aaron, God willing, you'll be able to marry the man of your dreams . . . as long as he's Jewish.'

'Would it be fine if these two got married?' he asked.

Rose fixed him with a water-blue stare. 'Of course, but young man, you know your primary motivation is that it would give your father a coronary.'

'No flies on you,' he said.

Rose grunted. She looked at Ada and Lil together on the couch. 'Times change, Ada. But the trouble with the two of you . . .'

Ada butted her shoulder against Lil's. 'I knew the other shoe would drop.'

'Stop it,' Rose said. 'The trouble with the two of you – OK, trouble's not the right word. It's synergy; alone you're both smart women, but what's happened . . . I think for the first time in both of your lives, you've each got a supportive spouse.'

Lil rested against Ada; Rose's words rang true. 'I loved Bradley,' she said. 'But you're right. The expectation, the role – and I suppose I never questioned it – was that I was there for him. Would he have been there for me if I'd wanted to go out and have a career? Or go back to school? I'd like to think so . . . it's just his career – he was everyone's doctor – was important. I was OK with being the woman behind the man.' She looked at Ada. 'It was having you in my life that gave me the confidence to start writing, to say yes, even if I wasn't certain I'd succeed. That was you – and I'll let *my* less than gracious thoughts show – I've been a little jealous of not having you around so much. The last few days with the show, I'd be working on a column and want to run something by you, and you're not there.'

'I'm sorry,' Ada said, her fingers twined through Lil's.

'No,' Lil said, 'don't be. As to our nosing into places we shouldn't go, your mother's right.'

'Duh,' Aaron chimed. 'I've seen what the two of you have for reading material. And since you've gotten your e-readers, I'm scared to think what the two of you have been downloading.'

'It's true,' Ada said. 'I sometimes look at Mattie and get a little twinge of "what if?". I think if I'd been born twenty years later, that's what I'd have wanted to do.'

'And that's the issue,' Lil said. She gently squeezed Ada's hand. 'We're not pros, we don't carry guns . . . and someone involved with this show – at least that's how it's shaping up – is a killer. I'm worried, Ada. What if you say or do something that puts you in their cross hairs? If anything were to happen to you . . .'

'Grandma, she's right,' Aaron said. 'What if the person who killed Lenore and Richard is watching you look at Rachel's bathroom and sees you talking to Detective Perez? What if they think you know something?'

Ada nodded. 'Good points, and curiosity killed the cat, but . . .' she paused. 'A few days ago I was feeling sort of sorry for myself, like I was just on the conveyor belt to the grave. I know, it's stupid and—'

'Now you're in the middle of yet another murder investigation,' Rose spat out.

'Yes, Mother, and let me finish my thought. I'm excited, and not just about the murder.' She looked at Aaron. 'You were there, the energy and creativity of those people. Yes, there's a lot that's ugly and probably all of the seven deadly sins have offices at LPP, but it's fascinating.'

'I get it,' Lil said. 'If it weren't for the murders, this would be an amazing opportunity.'

'It still is,' Ada said. 'Do you think that you and Aaron want to come to the shooting tomorrow?'

'Absolutely,' Lil said. 'Let's just not call it a shooting. And let's stick together. I'll have your back and you'll have mine.'

'I don't get an invitation?' Rose said.

'I didn't think you'd want one,' Ada admitted, 'after all this talk about putting our noses where they don't belong.'

'For the love of God, Ada. You're my daughter. Where do you think you get it from?'

TWENTY-EIGHT

Dressed in a vintage midnight-blue Dior gown with sapphires dangling from her ears and around her neck, Ada stood with Aaron on the second floor landing. Their focus was on Lenore's front-circle fountain, now obscured by four towering green-and-white striped banquet tents. Beyond those they glimpsed the barely restrained crowd that had gathered behind the gates. Dozens of cops and additional security in LPP blazers – mostly out-of-work actors – manned the blue barricades in front of the electric gates.

'There's thousands of them,' Aaron said. 'Ethan told me they're backed up to the highway. And they're only letting in a hundred at a time?'

'Ethan? You mean the cute twenty-five-year-old with the dreamy brown eyes and dimples?' she asked, noting the slight blush that spread across his cheeks.

'I don't even know if he's into me, or just being nice,' Aaron admitted. 'But he is Jewish. You look amazing, by the way. I always thought I had the hottest grandma.'

'Nice save,' she said. 'And yes, they gave out numbers and will let in a hundred at a time.' She looked at the circus-style tents, their contents concealed by canvas flaps. The entire morning, from being picked up in a stretch limo at four a.m. to driving past thousands of Lenore fans camped along the road, had felt surreal. Even now, with the sun just up, and dressed for something formal, she found it hard to focus.

'Ms Strauss.' A young intern approached. 'They need you on set.'

'OK.' She raised her eyebrows . . . 'What a strange day.'

'And it's just getting started,' Aaron said. 'Be careful.'

She nodded and, mindful of her make-up, kissed his cheek. 'You too . . .' The stiff satin of her dress crunched as she followed the intern down the sweeping stairs and out to the waiting camera crews. She thought back to that first day at LPP, seeing Lenore carted away, and then that manic pitch meeting. She glanced at Barry, who sat removed from the action in an open tent with his beautiful wife and their little girl. His daughter was dressed in pink with a pony on her jumper. His one-sentence tag line for this show popped to mind – '*Antiques Roadshow* meets *The Hunger Games* on the set of *Gilmore Girls*'.

She glanced at the camera crews positioned around the massive tents, at the crowds and the circulating security. Her anxiety surged. *This doesn't feel safe.* She looked for Lil and her mother, but couldn't spot them.

'Ms Strauss,' the intern prompted.

'I'm coming,' and she followed him to the tents.

He pulled back one of the canvas flaps and Ada got her first look at Lenore's estate sale. Each of the circus-style tents was connected, creating a seamless circle. The inner walls had been left open to leave the magnificent fountain visible and give the camera crews natural sunlight. 'You must have been working all night,' she said, as the intern directed her toward Melanie and the film crew she'd come to think of as hers.

'You have no idea,' he said, as they walked past tables covered with tagged tchotchkes and bibelots that had belonged to Lenore. She didn't know where to look. One tent was filled with furniture, some of which she recognized from the past two days. She glanced at the tags; the prices were high. *Who spends fifteen hundred dollars for a sterling tea pot at a tag sale?* But considering the provenance and the fact that proceeds were going to a children's charity, she figured people would pay. Another tent had racks of clothing which, under different circumstances, she would have liked to examine.

Other details competed for her attention, like the iron tent stakes that had been pounded through Lenore's drive, and several terracotta flower pots that had fallen into the pool around the fountain. There'd be thousands of dollars of repair work needed when the day was over. She winced when she saw a table covered with bras and panties. Admittedly they were still in their original packaging, but *why*? She was about to comment when Melanie greeted her.

'Ada, you look like a queen. Absolutely spectacular.'

Ada pointed at the table of underwear. 'Really? Lenore's underwear?'

'I know.' Melanie waggled her brows. 'Who knows if we'll use it, but today is about maximum footage. We have twelve crews!' she leaned in and whispered in Ada's ear. 'And a few plants.'

'Plants? What do you mean?'

'You'll see. It's going to be wild.'

Ada did not doubt that.

'I need to sit,' Rose said, unable to keep up with Lil as she zipped through the tents snapping pictures for her column.

Lil bit back her irritation. Rose had insisted on joining them, not thinking how grueling the day would be for her ninety-year-old body. 'I could take you back to the limo.'

'What, and leave me parked like a dog in the back of the house? Where's the fun in that? I want to see the chaos when they let everyone in. What about there?' She pointed to the dainty Moroccan-style tent in the corner of the estate where Barry and his family had set up.

'Fine, if they'll let you,' Lil said, and the two women tromped across the lawn.

Barry stood and waved. 'Lil,' he shouted. 'Glad you could make it. Our girl looks amazing.' Suddenly distracted, he looked toward the tents and spoke into a mouthpiece strapped to his chin.

Lil stopped and looked back toward the tents. Crew members were rolling up and tying the canvas walls to reveal the inside. Her eyes rested on the beautiful woman in blue satin. She did a double take. 'Ada?' She pulled out her camera.

Barry walked over to her. 'She's going to be a star. The camera loves her, and the stuff that comes out of her mouth . . .'

'She's my daughter,' Rose said. 'She gets it from me.'

'How wonderful!' he said, his eyes on Rose. 'I'm Barry Stromstein, one of the executive producers.'

'Rose Rimmelman,' she said. 'And how many executive producers are there?' she asked, her New York accent thick as if winding up to tell a joke that starts with, *How many executive producers does it take to screw in a light bulb?*

'Three, at the moment.'

Lil looked at him. 'You, who and who?'

'Me, Rachel and the LPP CFO, Patty Corcoran.'

'I don't think I've met her,' Lil said, curious that he'd mentioned Rachel.

'And you probably won't.'

'So how does she get a producing credit?' Lil asked, her last several days interacting with LPP having given her a crash course on the importance of getting your name into the closing credits.

'This.' He threw his arms wide. 'To get this kind of rapid resource, you have to give to get. I needed money and lots of camera crews. Apparently Patty's always had her heart set on a producing credit.'

'Got it, and speaking of . . . seeing as you're getting my girlfriend as your new star, any chance you could let Rose have a spot in your tent?'

'Not a problem. Come, meet the wife. Excuse me.' He listened to the bud in his ear. 'Whenever you're ready. How far away is she? Then I'd get started. Remember, more is more.'

Lil tried to figure out who Barry was talking to, while getting her first close-up look at Jeanine Stromstein. Yes, she'd seen her in the distance and had thought, *beautiful woman*. But from ten feet away, she found it hard not to stare. She glanced at Barry, not a bad-looking man with his full head of dark hair and his even features, but his wife could easily have graced the cover of any fashion magazine.

'Hi,' Jeanine said. 'Lil, is it?'

'And this is Ada's mother Rose.' She didn't know where to put her gaze, mesmerized by Jeanine's beauty. Even under the shade of the tent the woman's hair was an explosion of reds and golds. Her complexion was pure cream and the green of her eyes glowed like a cat's. Lil detected an accent, not strong, probably mid-west. She felt rude, but couldn't stop staring. Like studying some master-piece, searching for the flaw and finding none. She noted a few ungracious thoughts like, *how exactly did Barry wind up with this woman?*

'Pleased to meet you, Rose.' Jeanine selected a chair with arms and set it at the edge of the tent so the older woman could have an unobstructed view. 'Ashley,' she called to her daughter, who was playing on a blanket with a fashion doll and an improbable purple plastic pony. 'Say hello to Lil and Rose.'

The little girl looked up. 'Do you live here?' She looked first at Lil and then at Rose.

Lil smiled, unable to stop the thought that while little Ashley was adorable and would grow up to be pretty, she would pale in comparison to her mother. 'We do,' she said. 'I grew up here, not in this house but in Grenville.'

'I'm going to live here,' she announced. 'I want to ride horses like my mommy.'

Lil smiled. 'That sounds like fun.'

'We've been looking at houses,' Jeanine said. 'Could I get the two of you some coffee? Tea?'

'Some water, if you wouldn't mind,' Rose said.

'Not at all,' Jeanine said. She glanced back at the banquet tents. 'Something's happening.'

Lil saw movement by the electric gate across the drive. Two camera crews filmed as a pair of guards opened the gate to allow the first hundred shoppers into the estate sale. Lil recognized a few locals in the surging throng. Her camera was out, and she zoomed in on the action. There was a lot of pushing and shoving. People waved their cardboard numbers at the guards and once through the gate they sprinted the last fifty yards to the tents. Pocketbooks flapped from shoulders, and one woman fell to the ground, nearly setting off a domino effect among the eager shoppers.

With Rose settled, Lil sidled next to Barry, whose focus was riveted to the unfolding drama. She overheard him speak into the headset. 'It's not enough. We need more density . . . at least the next two . . . I don't care . . . if anyone says anything just say you lost count . . . just do it.'

She followed his gaze back to the gate. One of the guards had a hand to his ear. He nodded and the gate opened. Lil lost count as they let at least another two hundred into the estate. The guards had stopped checking numbers. Her anxiety surged as she looked back toward the tents and at Ada being filmed while the first shoppers descended on Lenore's earthly possessions. This was going to turn into a riot.

Her attention was suddenly pulled by a noise overhead, like a burner on a gas stove. She looked up. 'What?' She was startled to see a rapidly descending hot air balloon with the LPP logo, a line drawing of Lenore's lips.

Barry glanced at her. 'Yeah, Trump likes to come in with a helicopter. I thought this was a nice touch.'

Even before she zoomed in with her camera, she knew who'd be in that oversized wicker basket. She started to snap, pushing her telephoto lens as far as it would go, and angling to minimize the sun's glare. But there she was, and Lil had a gut-twisting moment of thinking it was Lenore – the auburn bob, the perfect make-up, even the posture, erect but with the signature head tilt that could convey anything from interest and concern to quiet amusement. 'You knew she was safe.'

'Not at first,' he admitted. 'It was Melanie's idea and, I might add, a brilliant one.'

'Did the police know?' she asked.

'No, and I'll leave that for the lawyers to sort. That's why Melanie didn't tell me. She knew they'd question me and that's all I need – to get arrested for obstruction, or some other bullshit charge. I seem to be the one they focus on, even though I haven't been alone long enough to take a piss – excuse me, that was crass.'

'It's got to have been stressful,' Lil said, as she followed the pink-and-white balloon's descent.

'Naah. It's just a day at the office.' He glanced from the balloon to the film crews in place at the landing pad, and along the path that would take Rachel from the balloon to the tents.

Lil tried to wrap her head around what was happening. In the midst of a murder investigation Melanie deliberately faked the abduction of a woman who might easily be the killer, or a possible victim. In disbelief she muttered, 'And the police didn't know.'

Barry exhaled with a sigh and pointed at Kevin Simpson in a Grenville Police blazer. Kevin was red-faced and sprinting across the lawn while speaking into his cell. 'They do now.'

TWENTY-NINE

Ada would always remember the moment when hell broke loose, like watching an accident in slow motion. The chaos started when two women grabbed an antique Turkish prayer rug. It was worth several hundred dollars, possibly more. Marked twenty bucks, it had been planted, along with several other fantastic bargains, for just this reason. Neither woman was going to give ground.

'I saw it first,' one screamed.

'The hell you did! It's mine . . . let go!' And the younger of the two gave a violent pull that sent the older woman tumbling forward, her momentum – and body – caught by a pair of men digging through a box of hand-wrought aluminum from the fifties.

'Watch it, lady,' one said, as he pushed her off.

She turned and saw her competition for the rug race off with the prize in hand. 'That's mine!' she shrieked, and gave chase.

To Ada, it was as though a spark had been lit on a pool of gas. *Why are there so many shoppers? There were only supposed to be a hundred*, but clearly there were many times that.

It reminded her of the annual bridal blowouts at Strauss's, an event that would have soon-to-be brides and their mothers grabbing racks of heavily discounted dresses. She'd always been careful not to exceed the store's lawful limit and they'd always had extra security. As she watched from her spot next to the checkout register in the center tent, she noted several things. The crowd, most of whom had waited for hours in the dark to get an early number, were like children at a birthday party who'd had too much cake and ice-cream. The actors, hired as security guards, were not intervening in the growing number of arguments and shoving matches. There were now twice as many camera crews as there'd been when they'd started that morning and something was happening that included multiple sirens.

She looked at Tolliver, who was to be her companion through the sale, their banter about the various items being sold to be worked into segments. He shook his head, his accent – even though he was born and bred in Grenville – pure BBC British. 'Quite the sale, wouldn't you say?'

'I'd say something,' and she caught the flashing blue of a police cruiser pulling past the tents. 'I'll be back,' and, not caring that her instructions had been to stay with Tolliver at the checkout line, she headed outside.

Her pulse raced; *this doesn't feel safe.* Her eyes blinked in the bright sun, and her attention was drawn to a giant pink-and-white balloon with the LPP logo that rose mushroom-like by the pool. She saw a second cruiser surge through the crowd, followed by Mattie's black SUV with a blue flasher in the front window.

The noise in the tents was deafening. A man screamed, 'That's not fair. I had it first!'

She glanced back to see the cameraman, boom operator and assistant director, who'd all been with her since the start of the week, a couple yards behind her. They were following Melanie's instructions: *Do not let her out of your sight.* She had a moment's pause; a week ago having a camera follow her would have seemed bizarre. Now – *me and my shadow.* She moved fast toward the deflating balloon and the flashing lights.

The assistant director – a girl who couldn't have been much older than Aaron – prompted her, 'Ada, tell us what you're seeing and what you're doing. Keep up a steady stream.'

As her heels sank into the lawn she thought of what she'd learned about FWC, and here she was. Fine; if this was the job, she could play along. If Tolliver was going to be BBC British she'd play the crazy fifties housewife shtick to the hilt. 'Quite the exciting day at the estate of Lenore Parks, and it looks like we have an unexpected visitor.' She stopped, faced the camera and made a game show hostess wave in the direction of the rapidly deflating balloon. She smiled for effect, feeling the heavy sapphire earrings brush against her neck.

The assistant director gave her a thumbs up, and then she gasped. Ada looked at her, and then at the cameraman, who for the first time that morning went against Melanie's instructions and shifted the focus off of her to something, or someone, behind her.

Ada turned. 'Oh my God. Lenore – Rachel.' Coming toward her, flanked by police – including Mattie and Jamie – was Rachel Parks, who from a distance looked just like her mother, from the carefully coiffed auburn locks to her tightly cinched waist and full figure artfully draped in a breezy pink-and-white striped A-line.

Ada stood transfixed as Rachel, shielding her eyes from the sun and ignoring her retinue of police, camera crew and a few autograph-seeking shoppers, waved.

For the briefest of moments Ada wondered if this was a dream. But no, dreams made sense. Rachel had gone missing; there'd been blood and a police search. Now, dressed and sounding like her mother, she'd dropped from the sky in a balloon.

'Ada!' Rachel shouted.

She wondered what would happen if she answered, *Lenore*. 'Rachel, you're safe.'

Rachel broke into an easy jog, as did her growing entourage. She seemed oblivious to the questions being fired at her by Mattie, who was clearly flustered by the cameras and this unpredictable girl ignoring her.

'Ada!' Rachel shouted, as though they were long separated lovers in a made-for-TV movie. 'Ada,' and she swept Ada into a tight embrace.

'You're OK,' Ada whispered. She tried not to stiffen, reminding herself of all this poor girl had been through. All she was going through, a murdered mother and brother, a pregnancy which, if the truth were known, could turn her into a societal pariah.

'I'm fine, silly,' Rachel said. She pulled back and looked at Ada, and then toward the tents, which were being entered by uniformed Grenville officers and state troopers attempting to control the shoppers. 'How wonderful.' She stared wistfully toward the estate. 'People showed up. Do you think we'll make a lot of money?'

Not missing a beat, Ada said, 'Without doubt. I just hope no one gets trampled to death.'

Rachel's eyes lit up. 'There is something so exciting about all of this! And just think of how many children this will help.'

'Absolutely.' She caught Mattie's eye; the detective looked pissed off. Her face was flushed, and not just from chasing this out-of-control heiress. Ada nodded in her direction, knowing what had to be done. Just say the mantra: *what would Lenore do?* The answer was obvious: anything, as long as it's on camera. 'Rachel,' she said, taking the girl's hand. 'You've got to tell me where you've been. We've been so worried.'

Rachel stopped and swept a hand across her brow. 'I just had to get out . . .' She sighed. 'So much sadness. I needed to be alone and do some thinking.'

Right, Ada thought, realizing that this stunt had been orchestrated. 'Completely understandable,' she said, playing along. 'You've had a lot of people worried.' Knowing she ran the risk of triggering one of Rachel's mood swings, she pressed. 'There was blood, and last night you called me sounding so frightened.'

'I was.' She put a hand to her mouth. She glanced toward one of the cameras and gave a signature Lenore shrug and head tilt. 'I cut myself shaving my legs.'

'No one saw you leave,' Ada pressed, anticipating the questions Mattie needed answered.

'I called someone to pick me up,' she said.

'Who?'

'Let's not talk about this. I want to go into the tents.'

'Let's do that,' Ada said, 'but I'm dying to know how you snuck out so successfully.' What she felt like saying was, *You crazy bitch, we were worried to death that someone had murdered you and dumped your body in the lake.*

'Well, if you must know, one of the producers helped.'

'Of course they did,' Ada chuckled, noting how Mattie's face was now bright red. She wondered why the detective didn't detain Rachel and close down this insanity. But Mattie was sharp and Ada realized that she knew that Rachel would be more likely to give up the goods if she were doing it for a television audience. She caught the detective's eye and thought, *the ball's in my court.* 'I'm guessing it was Melanie.'

'Right in one. Has anyone bought any of the big-ticket items?' she asked. 'I keep thinking of all the children this will help.' She smiled at the camera and winked. 'Let's go in.'

One of the officers pressed through. 'Ms Parks, I don't think that's a good idea.'

'Oh please,' Rachel said. 'It'll be fine,' and before anyone could stop her, she grabbed Ada's hand. 'Let's go.'

In the minutes Ada had been out of the tent, the sale had turned into a melee with the police attempting to maintain control.

Tolliver was backed against a tent pole, his British accent gone, trying to explain to an enraged dealer with a bow tie and a bad comb-over, who was clutching a pair of silver candlesticks and a box of bubble-wrapped porcelain, that there were no discounts for the trade. 'The prices are firm,' he said.

'This is bullshit!' the dealer spat back. 'This whole show is a sham. I can't believe it's legal. And you,' he jabbed a candlestick into Tolliver's chest. 'If you think this is going to help your over-priced store, you've got another think coming.'

Ada recognized the dealer and knew that he'd auditioned for *Final Reckoning* and been turned down. She'd seen several such wannabes shooting angry glances toward her and Tolliver.

'If you don't like the prices,' Tolliver said, 'then leave. No one's forcing you to buy anything.'

'This is rigged!' the dealer screamed. 'You think people are going to watch this shit?'

And that's when things went from bad to beyond bizarre.

'People!' Rachel shouted. 'PEOPLE!' She'd grabbed a chair and, using it as a step stool, climbed on to a table covered in pink Depression glass.

Ada turned as a hush spread through the tent.

'I wanted to thank each and every one of you for coming to my . . . I mean, my mother's estate sale. Lenore would be thrilled.'

Ada watched as people paused in mid grab and shove to get a look at the celebrity. Hundreds of cell phones were out and raised overhead as people filmed, clicked, tweeted and posted to Facebook. On the one hand, Rachel looked young and attractive in her pink-and-white get-up, her wrist scars concealed beneath chunky silver cuff bracelets. On the other, she was a ringer for Lenore *circa* 1980.

Ada looked around and, with the crowd in Rachel's thrall, she spotted Lil at the edge of the tent. Her camera was out, likely in video mode. Next to her was Barry Stromstein, who was starring at Rachel. At one point he turned to Melanie and pointed. She smiled. He shook his head.

Ada wondered if Barry knew about this stunt. How could he not? Although . . . as the crew had described the principles of FWT – sometimes FWC – a key element was the surprise, to throw people off balance and capture their reactions on camera.

Through the tent opening she spotted Rose in the distance chatting with Barry's little girl and his gorgeous wife. The trio seemed removed from the chaos of the tents and Rachel's dramatic entrance.

There was something idyllic in their little picnic with her white-haired mother, the titian-haired beauty and the little girl with her toys. An idea formed, fueled by Lil's *What would Lenore do?*

Her train of thought now shifted to Rachel's tabletop soliloquy.

'Every fifty dollars is a little boy or girl whose cleft palate will be repaired,' Rachel said with an impassioned throb. 'Two hundred dollars fixes an infant's life-threatening heart condition.' She paused and took a deep breath. Her voice cracked with emotion. 'And a thousand dollars is a prosthetic leg for a young victim of a landmine in Afghanistan.'

Ada watched and thought, *It's the second coming of Lenore.* But something about the girl had both calmed the crowd and ennobled their pawing through her mother's possessions.

She spotted Melanie looking on, a woman who'd had an affair with, or at least slept with, Lenore, whether by choice or career necessity Ada didn't know. So perhaps it wasn't just *What would Lenore do*, but *WHO would Lenore do?*

Finished with her spiel, Rachel gave the crowd one final exhortation. 'Now go out there and shop for the children!' Her smile was bright as she stepped down on to a chair and then to the ground. 'What do you think?' she asked Ada.

'I think you did good,' she replied, knowing that was what Rachel needed to hear.

'You think so?' Her every word and movement was captured by multiple cameras.

'I do,' and Ada moved in close, as she'd learned over the past few days of filming. With the fabric of their dresses touching, Ada and Rachel strolled through the packed tents, like a pair of generals surveying a battlefield. With two camera crews in front of them and one behind, Ada scanned the activities. Rachel signed autographs and reminisced over the merchandise.

'That was Richard's bike, I remember when he first got that. He taught me how to ride.'

Tolliver and his film crew had made their way through the crowd, and he interjected a few quick sentences on whatever object Rachel picked up. 'A lovely nineteenth-century Imari punch bowl made for the European trade.' He flipped up the tag. 'Priced to sell at three hundred dollars.'

At this a woman in the crowd shouted, 'I want it!'

Tolliver nodded as a camera framed the excited woman, who was already burdened with several bulging totes slung across her back and shoulders. He handed over the colorful porcelain. 'Enjoy, it's lovely.'

As they walked, Ada felt as though her mind had been split in two. She kept a smile on her face, aware of the cameras and how she needed to keep in tight frame with Rachel, while behind that facade her thoughts skittered over more dangerous realms. Something evil lurked below the surface, something that had led to two murders. Another of Lil's truisms, this one a hand-me-down from her physician husband, popped to mind: *pus under pressure must be lanced*. Lenore had kept secrets. She had used people in despicable ways and had ruled her empire through the manipulation of fear and desire. It was time to lance that boil. It was time for her own FWT.

'So Rachel,' she said, her expression pleasant, 'other than within the inner circle, why did Lenore never come out as being gay?'

Silence spread through the crowd, like ripples from a pebble dropped into a pool. The shift was eerie, as shoppers whispered and strained to hear.

Rachel's eyes widened as she looked from Ada to the camera.

'My mother wasn't gay.'

'Yes she was,' Ada said, her tone matter of fact. 'And more than that, she used her fame and her position to get young women to sleep with her.'

Amid the stunned silence Ada saw dozens of phones raised in the air and pointed in their direction; others were more subtly held, as though the operators were too embarrassed to admit they were filming such an awkward moment.

'Why are you saying this?'

Ada wondered if she'd miscalculated. Perhaps the things Peggy had told her were lies, but Peggy wasn't the only source. The rumors and jokes at LPP were rampant. If she'd been Lil writing a story she'd have had someone get confirmatory proof. 'Rachel,' she said, turning to the young woman, whose eyes were bugging out, 'it's OK . . . or maybe it's not. But for all of her supposed openness and honesty, your mother kept some big secrets.'

Rachel's Lenore-like mask crumbled. Tears welled in her eyes. 'It is true,' she said. She looked from Ada around at the crowd. Her gaze took in the cell phones, some of them already uploading this to the Internet. 'It is true,' she repeated. 'There were lots of women, young women.' She found her camera and spoke directly into it. 'I don't think they were all gay, and some of them didn't want to. She didn't think that Richard and I knew . . . that we saw . . . that we heard.'

'What did you hear?' Ada asked.

'The deal being struck,' Rachel said. 'Although I don't know if deal is the right word. With Lenore, there wasn't much negotiation.'

'Do you remember specifics?' Ada pressed, noting the silence.

Rachel looked past her camera. She pointed. 'There's one. Melanie, Melanie Taft.'

Ada looked as the field producer stared back. Her eyes were wide, her jaw hung open and she was shaking her head.

Ada watched as camera phones shifted to catch a glimpse of the attractive brunet.

Time hung suspended. Melanie looked at Rachel. She nodded. 'Yes.' She swallowed and seemed uncertain of what to do.

Ada had no such uncertainty – *pus under pressure must be lanced* – 'Was it your choice to sleep with her?' she asked.

'Talk about game changers,' Melanie said, and she stepped in close to Ada and Rachel. 'Yes, I slept with her. I'm not sure if it's what I wanted, but there wasn't much choice.'

'Can you explain that?' Ada asked. The on-screen proximity created an intimacy that forced the onlookers to stay deathly silent if they wanted to hear.

'She was going to pull the plug on our team. Wow, this really is reality TV, and I'm about to come off as a big whore.'

'You said you didn't have a choice,' Ada offered.

'We always have choices,' Melanie replied. 'She told me that if I did what she wanted, even if Barry's team was laid off, I'd still have a job, and I knew she wasn't lying.'

'Because?' Ada prompted.

'Because there were others, and they still had jobs.'

Rachel snorted. Her hands pressed her temples and she shook her head. 'You're not kidding.' She turned and bumped a table; several mugs crashed to the ground. 'This feels good,' Rachel said, as she stared at the broken crockery, then at a woman across the table whose cell phone was being held in a shaky hand. Rachel caught her eye. 'Use your other hand to steady it,' she said.

What came out of Rachel's mouth next sent chills through Ada. It wasn't just the words, but her pitch-perfect imitation of Lenore's going-to-commercial tag line, as she stared into the camera. 'And whatever you do, don't go away, because what's coming up next, you will not want to miss.'

THIRTY

I t was all Lil could do to keep from running to Ada. What held her back was Barry. 'She'll be fine,' he said, as they stood transfixed by the unfolding drama.

At least the shoppers had quieted, their lust for Lenore's worldly goods momentarily stemmed by Rachel's salacious revelations. Lil's stomach was in knots, but what could she do? She knew Ada wouldn't lose her head, and if Barry were telling the truth – a big if – the crowd would be gone before long, and they'd finish the day and be back in the security of their own home. But there was more; she knew that Ada wouldn't stop until she'd wrung the truth from Rachel, possibly dangerous truths at the heart of two murders. *Be careful, Ada.*

Nervously, she glanced back toward the mansion at Jeanine, who was sipping tea and chatting with Rose while her little girl played with the plastic pony. She had images of Marie Antoinette: *Let them eat cake.*

Barry's hand went to his ear bud. 'What?'

Lil inched closer, barely able to hear a woman's voice, possibly Melanie's.

'Of course we keep filming.' His eyes were fixed on Rachel, Ada and Melanie, who was saying something into her headset.

'What did Melanie just tell you?' Lil asked.

'Shh,' he said. 'Something's happening.' His hand was still to his ear. 'No. Damn it! I told you, keep filming. That's an order, Mel . . . I don't care. Film it!'

Lil watched as Ada put a hand on Rachel's shoulder and led her toward the edge of the tent.

Like a giant amoeba, the shoppers surged and followed, leaving just enough room for the three women in the center and the two camera crews.

Lil, with Barry at her side, raced around the back of the tent to keep them in view.

'See,' Barry said. 'Ada's fine. And this is fabulous TV.'

Rachel raised a hand to shield her eyes from the sun that was just over the mansion. With her other she tapped Ada on the shoulder and then pointed her forefinger in Lil's direction. For the briefest of instants Lil wondered if the FWT was outing her and Ada on national TV. But as she stared back she saw that Rachel's finger was pointing a bit to the left of her and Barry, toward Jeanine and Rose.

For Lil, that moment lengthened like time frozen, Rachel stock still in pink and white, her hand outstretched, surrounded by a red-faced mob.

Jeanine stared back and then sprang to her feet. Her tea dropped from her hand. She looked at her daughter playing on the ground. 'Get her out of here!' she shrieked to Rose, the crowd's continued hush letting her words carry across the distance. 'NOW!'

Barry looked up the hill at his wife. 'Jeanine, what's going on?' His right hand was cupped over his ear. 'What's she saying? . . . Hell no!' He stared at his wife, his mouth hanging open and his head shaking. 'No . . . that's not true!'

Rose was visibly startled by Jeanine's frantic change. She stared at the broken tea cup and then back to the distraught young woman. 'What's going on?'

'Please,' Jeanine said, her expression panicked. 'Get my daughter out of here. She can't see this. She can't hear this. Please. Help me.'

'OK.' She didn't understand what was happening, but Rose was aware that the little girl needed to be away from whatever situation was unfolding. 'Come on, Ashley,' she said, 'let's take your pony inside and pretend to give it a bath.'

'Mommy.' Ashley stared up wide-eyed at her distraught mother. 'Mommy?'

'Be a good girl and go with Rose, baby.' Jeanine looked at her little girl. 'Mommy loves you,' and then she sighted Barry, who was running ahead of the advancing crowds and cameras.

'Jeanine, what's happening?' he called out, and then spoke into his mouthpiece. 'Yes, stop the cameras. Shut them down! That's an order!' He ran toward his wife as she backed away.

'I'm sorry, Barry. I did it for you, for us. Always.'

The crowd, led by the backwards walking film crews and by Rachel, who'd linked her arm through Ada's, was less than thirty feet from the dainty picnic tent. Rachel's voice was clearly audible to Barry, Lil and Jeanine. 'Her,' Rachel said.

'No!' Jeanine shrieked.

'Yes, and you can't deny it, sweetheart,' Rachel said, as one of the cameras swung around to capture Jeanine Stromstein's anguish. 'It's all on tape.' As though having a normal conversation, Rachel explained to Ada, 'Lenore taped all of her assignations. It's quite naughty, but sometimes Richard and I would watch.' Her voice shifted, and it sounded like she'd gone from impersonating Lenore to being little older than Ashley. 'It was icky.'

'Barry.' Jeanine backed away from the tent. 'It's not true . . . I did it for us. For you. It was always for you. I love you.' And then she bolted. Her hair was like fire in the sun as she sprinted toward the pool, where Rachel's pink balloon, now mostly deflated, flopped in the breeze.

'Stop filming!' Barry screamed into his mouthpiece and at the camera operators. He glared at Melanie, who was shaking her head in the negative as she stood between the cameras that were trained on Ada and Rachel.

Lil realized that even if they followed his order, which seemed unlikely, there were hundreds of camera phones capturing the scene, which now included the fleeing Jeanine being pursued by uniformed officers. From the mansion's elevation she was able to follow their progress as they vanished into the woods.

The crowd split apart. Some followed the cameras, cops and Jeanine, others stayed to hear Rachel, while other determined shoppers scurried back to the tents. Lil had no such dilemma and moved in next to Melanie, who was transfixed by the scene between Ada and Rachel.

'Your mother was having an affair with the producer's wife, Jeanine Stromstein?' Ada asked.

'Oh yes,' Rachel said in a lisping little girl's voice. 'They did naked things together. Dirty things.'

'How do you know that?' Ada asked.

Lil started as she felt Mattie Perez's shoulder nudge hers. The detective put a finger to her lips, as though she didn't want anything to interrupt Ada's interview.

'The tapes.' Rachel's tone modulated back to that of an adult. 'It was important to know what . . . who . . . my mother was up to.'

'So both you and Richard would have known who her current girlfriend was?'

'Put an "s" on that. Lenore wasn't monogamous. And it's a shame. I think she could have been a decent human being if she'd just come out of the closet and been with one of the women who really liked her.'

'Like Peggy?' Ada said.

'She's cool . . . Jeanine's tapes are sad. What she said is true.' She looked across at Barry, who stood next to Lil, his gaze darting between the crowds pursuing his wife and Rachel's on-screen revelations. 'She did it for you. Lenore was going to pull the plug on your crew, said you "hadn't lived up to your potential". Your wife made a deal. She traded her body to buy you time.'

'No,' he stammered. 'You're lying.'

'I'm not, and I wish it weren't true,' Rachel said. 'It wasn't a one-time thing, either.' She stared at him. 'This is so sad. You really didn't know.'

He shook his head and stared down. 'This can't be true.' He turned toward the direction in which Jeanine had run. He looked as though he might vomit as he stared past Lenore's pool to the edge of the woods. 'Jeanine,' he whispered, as horrifying connections sank in. He went from total disbelief to knowing it was true. His beautiful Jeanine's words, *'It was always for you.'* He felt them looking at him. He raised his head and caught the detective's gaze.

'You'll need to come with me, Mr Stromstein. I have some questions to ask about your wife and her whereabouts.'

He nodded. 'I'm not saying a word without an attorney.'

'That would be wise.'

He realized that the cameras had never stopped running. He glanced back at the house, glad that Ashley hadn't seen or heard. Then he looked at Ada. His gaze narrowed. 'You did this.' His tone was harsh.

'She didn't,' Rachel said. 'But she did figure it out.' She looked at Ada and then Lil. 'And this is just the tip of things, isn't it?'

Ada nodded. 'I think so.'

'You think she killed my mother and my brother?'

'I do,' Ada said simply.

'Why?' Rachel gasped.

'For love,' Ada said, her eyes on Barry. 'When the truth comes out, I've no doubt that we'll find she did it all for love.'

THIRTY-ONE

B arry Stromstein's migraine, triggered by stress and the pine-scented cleaning fluid in the Grenville police station, was blinding. He had no medication on him and once the wavy lines and bright lights at the periphery of his vision had danced away the headache, like a sledgehammer, pounded with the beating of his heart. He sat in a hard-backed chair in the lobby. The detectives had told him not to leave and, while he wasn't under arrest, he had no doubt that the two uniformed officers behind the counter, and the two outside the door, would stop him should he try to leave. He thought of his daughter and knew that Rose, Ada and Lil would watch after her until . . . But it was Jeanine . . . how she'd looked sprinting toward the woods. He'd wanted her to escape, knowing it was unlikely. His world was falling apart, as the mystery of 'who shot Lenore and Richard Parks' came into focus. He replayed conversations with Jeanine. The day he'd been chewed out by Lenore and feared he was about to get the ax. Hours later and Lenore was dead, shot a single time by someone who knew their way around the studio, Lenore and a gun, like his raised-on-the-farm wife, who'd apparently slept with his boss. And earlier in the week, when Richard Parks had nearly pulled the plug on *Final Reckoning*, again he'd confided in Jeanine, bared his insecurities to the one person in this world he knew loved him unconditionally. Not twenty-four hours later Richard was dead.

'Mr Stromstein.' He looked up and saw the shorter of the two female detectives. With his migraine on the rampage, he couldn't remember her name.

'Yes,' he answered, remembering that it started with a P . . . Parlour, Parvez, Pomanade . . .

'Mr Stromstein, I know you're waiting for your attorney, but we think you should talk to your wife. She's refusing representation.'

'Yes, detective. Please, let me talk to her.'

He followed her behind the counter through a locked door and then through a second that led on to a hall with three cells. The pine smell was overwhelming. Even so, it didn't fully conceal other earthy scents – sweat, piss and microwave popcorn. 'She's in the one on the end,' the detective said.

'Are you taping this?' he asked.

'No,' she said. 'But she needs an attorney. She'll be charged with the murders of Lenore and Richard Parks.'

He wanted to ask what proof they had, but that would come. Usually so quick with words, it was all he could do just to nod. 'I'll talk to her.'

'Good. Last one on the right. It's unlocked.'

His footsteps landed loud in his ears as he walked the hall. He saw Jeanine on the edge of a bare cot through the wire-mesh window and pushed the door open. 'Baby,' he whispered.

She turned at the sound of his voice. Her full-lipped smile, the perfect teeth and green eyes. 'I'm so sorry.'

He was at her side. He wrapped her in his arms. He breathed in the smell of her. The pounding in his skull eased. 'We'll get you out of this. Marvin's sending the best criminal lawyer in the business. I'm going to get you out of this.'

'Oh sweetie.' Her hair tickled the side of his face and neck, her voice soft as a spring rain. 'I don't need a lawyer,' she said. 'I don't want one.'

'Jeanine.' He pulled back, surprised at the determination in her tone. 'This is serious. They're going to charge you with murder.'

'I know,' she said. 'It's not so serious. You are. You and Ashley. An attorney will just suck away everything we've worked for. Look at me.'

He found himself caught in the depths of her gaze, like seeing his wife for the first time. 'Yes?'

'What Rachel said is true . . . and there's more. Do you believe me when I say that everything I did was for us, for you?' Her upper teeth bit the lower corner of her lips. She waited for his answer.

'I do.' And he did. 'I'm so sorry, Jeanine. I would never have asked that of you.'

'I know, and I never wanted you to know. As long as I know you love me, this will be OK.'

'Of course I love you.'

'Good. I'll tell them everything, but I'll tell you first. It gets bad. Promise you won't hate me.'

'I could never hate you. And no matter what you tell me, I will love you till the day I die. I don't care if you killed them, or even that you slept with her. I get it. I get why. And all this time . . .'

'It's OK.' Her fingers stroked the side of his face. 'I knew you'd understand. I never cared about the Birkin bags or the clothes or the apartment. It's just you, it's always been you.'

'Oh my God! You threw the final competition in *Model Behavior*, didn't you?'

'Of course I did. The prize was a year's around-the-world modeling contract. I had no intention of leaving you. And I was worried that if I won people would say the competition was fixed because you wanted to get in my pants.'

'I did want to get in your pants.'

'I know.' She leaned in and they kissed. 'So sweetie,' she pulled back, 'no lawyer.' She looked down, and then toward the half-open door. 'Not for that anyway,' and she whispered in his ear.

Barry pulled back. 'No. That's a joke, right?'

Jeanine bit the corner of her mouth. 'It's not. She said if I did it . . .'

'Right.' Tears tracked down Barry's cheeks. He looked around the small cell, and then back at Jeanine. 'You did it for me.' His gaze landed on her still flat stomach. 'It's OK. I get it. But we will need lawyers . . . and a publicist.'

'Yes,' she said, knowing her husband and loving him with all her heart. 'A publicist would be best.'

THIRTY-TWO

The rest of that Sunday at Lenore's mansion passed in a blur for Ada. With the cameras still running and the crowds thinning, Rachel begged Lil and her to stay. 'I can't be alone. I don't trust myself.'

Ada heard both a plea and a threat. 'Of course we'll stay,' she said. 'Maybe Dr Ebert could come and see you for a bit.'

'Do you think he would?'

Ada held her tongue, knowing the Manhattan-based psychiatrist was well compensated for his twenty-four seven availability. 'I think he'll find the time.'

Melanie wrapped up the shoot. 'We've got more than enough. We could easily stretch this into three or four shows. Tomorrow we can film the *Final Reckoning* spiel, where we say just how much we raised for charity.'

Ada's heart sank at the thought of another day. 'The show goes on?'

'Absolutely!' Melanie's excitement was like that of a child who's found the golden Easter egg.

'Right,' Ada said.

'You were fabulous!' Melanie gushed. 'I cannot wait to work with you again. This show is going to be huge.'

Ada kept quiet.

Melanie's expression darkened as she stared at Ada. 'What?'

Ada glanced around. Barry had been taken away for questioning, and it seemed they had a strong murder suspect in Jeanine. The red lights had gone off the cameras, and the crowds had dissipated. A glance back at the tents showed a long line at the checkout registers where Tolliver Jacobs was soldiering on with a cast of extras, as people clutched Lenore's possessions and paid with plastic and wads of cash.

'Please don't judge,' Melanie said. 'You don't know what this industry is like.'

Lil stood at Ada's side. 'We don't,' Ada said. 'But aren't you concerned?' She looked at Rachel, who was quietly staring at the tents. 'If all Rachel said is true.'

'It's all true,' Rachel said, her voice dull. 'All of it, and more. My mom was a pioneer, in lots of ways. And she was a narcissist, probably a sociopath, who treated everyone around her like shit. She went through people like they were tissues, something you use once and throw away.' She shook her head. 'It feels good to clean out the secrets. She'd have hated it. Richard would have hated it. But they're both gone . . . just crazy Rachel and the baby I'm going to have.'

Melanie looked from Rachel to Ada. 'With the two of you in make-up, maybe we should try and film the last scenes after all. I know it's late, and weird. I'm just thinking . . .'

'It's fine,' Ada said, feeling anything but fine. She wondered if this were how Rachel operated, put on a happy face and don't let anyone see the turmoil beneath it. 'Let's just get this done.'

And they did. They tallied the sales. Ada's brow raised as she stared into the monitor. 'The Final Reckoning at today's estate sale . . . one hundred and five thousand four hundred and eighty-two dollars and fifty cents.' A representative from the charity, who'd been on site the entire day, gushed about how many Third World pediatric surgeries and artificial limbs that would finance.

Rachel, at times in tears, talked about her mother and her brother, and how this was exactly what Lenore would have wanted.

It was well after dark when Melanie finally said, 'It's a wrap.'

Ada took Rachel aside, away from the camera and prying eyes and ears, and asked, 'Rachel, are you going to be OK?'

The young woman looked Ada straight on. 'I don't know. I feel numb and beyond tired. And, knowing me, I can't be trusted like this.'

Ada shuddered.

'So instead of asking what Lenore would do,' Rachel continued, 'I tried to think about what Richard would want.'

'And?' Ada prompted.

'He'd want me to be safe, until I figured things out. So I called Ebert and I'm checking myself back into Silver Glen as soon as Clarence can drive me there. It can't be just about me any more. I've got a child to take care of, and I am not going to let anything bad happen to him.'

Ada felt a surge of relief. 'That sounds like a good plan.' And she spotted the groundskeeper/chauffeur with bag in hand.

'I know I must seem like a total nut job to you,' Rachel said, her fingers suddenly gripping Ada's, her eyes moist with tears. 'And I don't know what all of this must seem like to you . . . but . . . I'd like us to be friends. I don't have many . . .'

Ada interrupted her: 'Rachel, what the two of us have been through could make for the start of a friendship. You'll call me from Silver Glen to let me know you got there OK, and when you're ready for visitors, Lil and I will swing by. OK?'

'Thank you,' and with tears streaming she caught Ada in a frantic hug, kissed her on the cheek. 'Bye.' And she ran to Clarence, who wrapped her too-thin body in a black wool coat.

Relieved, Ada stared as the two vanished into the night.

She looked around and spotted Lil and Aaron, who'd taken Rose and Ashley home after Jeanine had been taken into custody. 'Thank you for staying,' she said. She mussed her grandson's hair and fell into Lil's embrace.

'What happens now?' Lil asked.

'Which part?' Ada said. 'The show? Jeanine Stromstein?'

Lil pulled back. 'I guess with the show.'

'According to Melanie and Rachel the show will definitely air. So what did you find out?'

'I did a bit of information horse trading with Mattie, so I think we can safely say that Jeanine shot Lenore and then Richard. The motives were love and her husband's career, which was about to tank. The tawdry details will follow. She's refusing a lawyer and, according to Mattie, is going to go straight for a guilty plea.'

'What about Barry?' Aaron asked. 'Did he know?'

'Doesn't look that way,' Lil said, 'or else he's letting the wife take the fall, but . . .'

'But what?' Ada asked. She gave Lil a searching look. 'You spoke to him, didn't you?'

'It's possible,' Lil admitted, her lips in a tight smile.

'And?' Ada pressed.

'And . . . of course he was heartbroken.'

'Hmm,' Ada pondered. 'I'm not certain he has that particular organ, but go on. Heartbroken and . . . ?'

'And thinking about his next big show.'

Ada's eyes widened. 'OMG,' she said, mimicking the endless abbreviations the *Final Reckoning* crew threw around. 'He's planning another reality show, isn't he?'

'How'd you know?' Lil asked.

'It's going to be set in prison, isn't it?'

'Now you're just scaring me.'

'A women's prison,' Ada continued. 'And it's going to focus on women murderers. Am I right?'

'Yes, you are,' Lil said. 'For bonus points, do you know what he's going to call it?'

'Give me a second,' she said.

'*Women Who Kill*?' Aaron offered.

'No.' Lil said.

'How about *Babes Behind Bars*?' he said, on his second try.

'Not even close,' Lil said.

'Wait,' Ada said, 'I think I have it, but please tell me I'm wrong.'

'I haven't heard it yet,' Lil said.

She looked at Lil and shook her head. She pictured Jeanine and Lenore, and reflected on how this whole *Final Reckoning* show was about packaging something sad and real as entertainment. 'He'll call it *A Woman's Touch*.'

'No,' Lil said, 'but it's not fair. I left out one small bit of information.'

Ada cocked her brow. 'Out with it.'

Lil shook her head. 'Jeanine Stromstein is pregnant . . . with twins . . . Lenore's twins.'

'Oh no,' Ada said. 'So she's the mystery surrogate. I suppose that makes even more sense.' She shook her head. 'And I know just what he'll call it – *Pregnant and in Prison*.'

Lil nodded. 'Yes, we have a winner.'